Advance Praise for
Disturbing the Peace
by P.D. LaFleur

"As good as Ludlum or Forsyth. You'll have a hard time putting this book aside."

—*Book Pleasures Reviews*

"A modern retelling of a knight's tale . . . the characters are finely drawn and clear of purpose. Begins with suspense and curiosity and bounds headlong to a dramatic finish."

—*North American Book Review*

"International intrigue meets the Suncoast. A well-woven tale."

—*Charlotte Sun*

"A true page-turner and hard-hitting thriller."

—*Susan Klaus*
Author and Host of Authors Connection Radio

D0111014

Disturbing the Peace

سَلَام

Also by **P.D. LaFleur**

In the Company of Strangers

Vengeance Betrayed

Mill Town

P.D. LaFleur

Disturbing the Peace

RGI
Press
Punta Gorda, Florida

Copyright © by P.D. LaFleur, 2009

RGI Press
A division of Ramsden Group, Inc.
Suite 1139, Box 261
1133 Bal Harbor Blvd
Punta Gorda, Florida 33950

This book is a work of fiction. Names, characters, businesses, organizations, places, events and incidents either are the product of the author's imagination or are used fictitiously. Any resemblance to persons, living or dead, events or locales is entirely coincidental.

ISBN 978-0-9792597-2-2

1   3   5   7   9   10   8   6   4   2

Cover design: Vivid Invention (vividinvention.com)
Author photo: John Zawacki (JZStudios.com)

Author website: www. pdlafleur.com
Publisher website: www.rgipress.com

PRINTED IN THE UNITED STATES OF AMERICA

RGI
Press

Author's Note

Dodge County is fictitious and a product solely of my imagination, but the Peace River does flow from central Florida to Charlotte Harbor and the Gulf of Mexico. I ask readers familiar with this part of the world to forgive me for taking the liberties I did with Florida's geography.

Acknowledgements

Writing this novel was not a solitary effort and I am grateful to many people who helped me. Greg Larrison, Jahn Zynda, Derek Woods and Sue Benidt played important roles in the process, and Sue's background in editing proved especially helpful. James Abraham and Steve Reilly used their extensive writing and editorial skills to raise several key questions in late versions of the manuscript, some of them devastating questions, that make this a better book. Suzanne Lancaster and Larry Join, who makes RGI Press one of the finest small press publishers in the country, were always there with patience and encouragement to see the project through. And my wife, Suzanne LaFleur, is the one who reads the beginning, middle and end of every draft and outline. Her criticisms are sharp and on point, but she tempers them with a degree of tenderness that keeps me going.

P.D.L.

For Suzanne

We miss more by not seeing than by not knowing.
—Sir William Osler

Blessed are the peace makers, for they shall be called children of God.
—Matthew 5:9

PART I

The best laid plans of mice and men go oft astray,
And leave us naught but grief and pain for promised joy.
—Robert Burns

Organizing is what you do before you do something, so
that when you do it, it is not all mixed up.
—Christopher Robin in *Winnie the Pooh*, A.A. Milne

ONE

The flight attendant brought the tall man in seat 3A a glass of Jim Beam neat and placed it on the small surface adjacent to his seat. "Here you are, Signore Zegna."

The man in seat 3A had one leg crossed over the other, his fingers holding the laces of his right shoe. He did not react and his eyes were fixed straight ahead into space as if in a trance. The flight attendant gave him a gentle tap on the shoulder that brought him back from his dream state. He shook his head in mild surprise, nodded, smiled at the attendant, and took a sip of his drink. Another brief bit of lost time he could not explain. He checked his watch. Only a minute or so, maybe less. Noticeable enough to cause mild embarrassment but short enough for him to dismiss the episode as just another sign of aging. People expect their elders to drift off now and then, he reasoned.

He took another sip, closed his eyes, and mused how, after fifty-six years of living on earth, many of them in modest circumstances, he was now reclining in perfect comfort in the first-class cabin of a wide-body jet coursing over the Atlantic. Life, he concluded, not for the first time, was full of surprises.

If the man known on this flight as Signore Gilberto Zegna ever imagined he'd be in this position, he never expected that the reason would be connected to a group of over-the-hill Chechen rebels who lived in London and who were intent on revenge against Mother Russia. He'd never been to Chechnya, nor did he ever intend to go. Cursory research showed it to be a fierce and unforgiving country in every way. Chechens were at war for much of recorded time, if not with the Turks, then with the Georgians or the Russians. As for Russia, his only visit there was to Moscow for another assignment many years earlier, and due to the bitter cold of its weather and its inhabitants he likewise had no desire to return. In the end, he cared little about the Russian-Chechen antagonisms; if pressed, he regretted only that one side would eventually have to win.

Nevertheless, the Chechen war horses in exile hired him because they needed his specialized skills and were willing to pay his considerable fee. He neither admired nor respected this crude cluster of relics, but he had been quietly hoping for an assignment, if only to end his career and enter full blown retirement on a high note. His last assignment ended in disaster and he came too close to spending his remaining years in a British prison. In his line of work, failure was not only unacceptable but could well prove fatal. He was lucky to be alive to face another sunrise.

Sunrise. Tomorrow, if this Al Italia flight from Caracas to Rome arrived on time, and with some good fortune and timely trains, he could be enjoying the next day's sunrise over the golden Italian hills of Camposanto near the ancient city of Modena. In Camposanto was his precious farm of olive trees.

He reflected that he owed, in a convoluted way, some debt of gratitude for this his precious farm to Russia in general and to one Russian in particular. He still carried a dimpled scar on his left buttock, the result of an errant shot from a Russian pistol. The headaches that began after that episode and persisted for years were gratefully gone now.

It was twenty years ago that he was mid air when a shot from that Russian pistol rang out, his feet barely clearing the cast iron rail on the edge of a parapet on a Prague roof. He crumpled and rolled when he landed, his skull colliding into a wide brick chimney. He managed to crawl to cover behind the chimney, the moonless night a silent ally. He knew his assailant well. He and Dmitri had enjoyed a glass of pilsner only a year before at a small café in Ghent after an assignment in which they were allies. But his was a profession built on skill and nerve. Old alliances can change, as evidenced that evening in Prague, and friendship had little to do with anything. He had no time to examine his wounds, but drew his pistol from its ankle holster and waited. He knew Dmitri could not leave the task unfinished. In moments, he saw Dmitri lean over the edge of the roof to seek his wounded quarry, his Russian-made Makarov held in both hands and panning the area. It was then that he raised his own pistol, a compact Beretta, from the chimney's shadow below and fired, the round finding Dmitri's right nostril and the orbit of his right eye.

Dmitri lived, horribly scarred and missing one eye, but the man in seat 3A and known for the moment as Gilberto Zegna went on from that Prague roof top to heal his cracked skull, his gluteus maximus and his pride at a hillside villa owned by a friend in Italy. It was during that period that he fell in love with the area and determined that when he amassed enough cash, he would own a similarly beautiful and serene piece of real estate. Fifteen years and dozens of assignments later, he did just that.

It was to this estate, his own hundred acres of rolling hills he would repair tomorrow and spend his remaining days as a gentleman farmer. His assets in land and bank accounts were substantial, and he could and would reject any and all offers for future assignments. He would drive his ancient tractors across his property, pedal his battered bicycle into the village and enjoy espresso and a sweet roll at the café. All the while he would know at his core that his last exploit was a success.

To be sure, this assignment did have its negatives, including some fatalities. Death was part of the job, though, and he tempered his regrets with a combination of professional acceptance and the selfish pleasure of his own survival. Survival was never guaranteed, and he came perilously close in the past weeks to missing that objective. He would wonder for the rest of his days how he managed that. For all his skill, planning and cunning, he should be dead and cold on a slab in a Florida morgue. It was more than mere good fortune that kept him alive.

At his feet in a brown leather valise was a small package, a gift he bought in a rude roadside market stall near a bus stop in a Mexican village three days ago. He reached down and removed the gift, still wrapped in tissue paper. He held the silver frame in his hands and looked at it. How appropriate, he thought. Inside the frame in flowing Spanish script and on heavy ivory parchment were the words of Christ from his Sermon on the Mount: *"Bienaventurados los pacificadores: porque ellos serán llamados hijos de Dios."* He held it close and thought of the man to whom he would send it, anonymously of course. He hoped the recipient would appreciate the sentiment, and felt certain he would.

When the flight attendant walked by seat 3A a few minutes later and picked up his empty glass, the man known as Gilberto Zegna shook his head at the offer of another beverage, and she continued down the aisle. He sighed, and if he'd been somewhere else unencumbered by the white noise and steady whoosh of the jet engines, he was certain it would be audible. He looked around; the other passengers in the area were either asleep, reading or watching movies.

Outside the porthole of the jet he saw only the reflected light on the tops of the clouds from the nearly full moon above. The bourbon warmed his insides and he felt sleep coming on. He removed the tissue covering the small silver frame and again read its inscription, reminding himself as he started to doze of how this whole episode began.

TWO

When Grigori Malko graduated from the University of Moscow, he had several offers from firms in the new capitalist haven that was Russia. It was an uncertain new world, though, and Grigori Malko had studied too many examples of Russian business enterprises that flared like rockets towards the sky, only to flame out, explode, or get shot down. He could make a fine living in the untamed private sector, but risk-taking was not part of his make up. Instead, he looked at opportunities that were safer, more controlled, less feral.

A job at the Ministry of Finance was his eventual choice. The position provided modest prestige and a reasonable income in a country where there were no guarantees. A humble apartment in a better section of the city was part of the appeal. In retrospect, on almost every count, his decision was a fortuitous one. Sixteen years and several promotions later, Grigori Malko became a special liaison to the Ministry of Foreign Affairs. The economy of the Russian Federation was growing more comfortable in its capitalist garb but remained uneasy with its self-image on the global stage. There was a native Russian sense of inferiority that military muscle had overcome in the cold war days. Now, unable to sustain a formidable military, it had to compete on other stages.

In this position, Grigori Malko was almost a fixture at important state events and he caught the appropriate attention. Most recently, he'd been tapped to be a Special Advisor on Finance to Nikolai Mironev, the current President of the Russian Federation. Grigori Malko, the young accountant from Volgograd, was on a first-name basis with one of the most powerful men on the planet. With his wife and two young daughters, he now lived in a large apartment in a lovely section of the city and even had a vacation home on the river fifty miles from Moscow.

His parents were both dead now, but his mother never approved of his taking the job for the government. "After what the Russians did to our family! You want to join them?"

She had her personal reasons for detesting the government of the Russian Federation. As a product of Grozny, the capital city of Chechnya, she lost many relatives in the successive failed wars of rebellion with Mother Russia. The few relatives still alive in Chechnya were financially destroyed and destitute.

Grigori met only a few of his Chechen relatives and never shared his mother's zealotry, but her ardent hatred of Moscow was ever in the back of his mind. He'd hoped, when he first took his government job, that somehow there would be some conciliation between Moscow and Grozny and that some amity might develop into what could be a flourishing relationship. After all, oil was the new Russian currency, and Chechnya had both oil fields and proximity to the European marketplace. Maybe then, his thinking went, his mother would have been more pleased with her son's choice of employer.

"Bah," she told him once when he described his hopes, "you think you can make heaven on earth, and you will end up only with hell."

Over time, Grigori Malko saw that concession and conciliation were unlikely. Chechnya was considered by the Moscow elite to be a stronghold of ignorance and backwardness. It was hopeless, he heard many times, for these one million barbarian Chechens, most of them Sunni Muslims, to believe that they could ever get close to the twenty-first century. Malko never raised a protest, never objected to these descriptions. Better to go along, he thought, and perhaps make changes from the inside.

Meanwhile, Moscow sent many of its own, true ethnic Russians, to take the best jobs in Grozny, and the region settled into an uneasy period of relative peace. The oil-rich fields of Chechnya and its enormous refineries were managed by Moscow; native Chechens had only their terrible jobs, their terrible homes, and terrible shortages of almost every basic need. This was Russia's plan: When younger Chechens see how well life can be apart from their stubborn parents who wish to continue the fight, they will drift away from their nationalism and become entirely Russian. In time, the Russian leadership calculated, Chechen resistance will simply disappear.

In his position, Malko saw that changing things from the inside was the hollow wish of a coward. Moscow would never consider the Chechens as anything more than a collaboration of vulgar brutes.

When he was first contacted by a distant cousin eight months ago, Malko had already acknowledged the futility of his hopes for his mother's homeland. He never had that roaring fire in the belly about Chechnya in the first place, but whatever optimism he harbored was barely a tongue of flame when the call from his cousin first came.

"Please," his cousin pleaded, "you are in such a wonderful

position. You can help us without really helping us. You can remain safe and protect yourself and your family, but we need your help."

The "help" turned out to be minimal, practically nothing at all. Pass some information along from time to time; report on any comments about Chechnya he might overhear on occasion. It required little of him, but any help he did give was graciously accepted and he felt some ancestral bond. Doing these little jobs also helped him redeem himself, however artificially, in his memories of his mother. What he did not do in her life, he would do for her in her death.

Nine weeks after his cousin's call, as he prepared for a diplomatic trip with President Mironev to London, Grigori was asked to relay a message to a Chechen sympathizer there. This was the biggest risk he'd taken since his weak alliance with his cousin was formed, but it was a sufficiently easy task to accomplish. Simply drop off a coded piece of paper at a hotel front desk in London during the president's visit. He'd done what he was asked.

That Grigori Malko had access to the highest levels of Russia's government made him a man of extraordinary value to a number of constituencies. Among them were the shreds of the gutted Chechen resistance, a collection of tired warriors that regrouped in London and continued to work for Chechen independence. It was a daunting uphill battle. Chechnya was a chokepoint in the flow of Russian oil and the power in Moscow would not tolerate a move towards independence, especially from these fossils whose fanaticism exceeded their capabilities.

Negotiating with Russia was out of the question. A few back-door mentions of that possibility through diplomatic channels were immediately shot down in Moscow. Direct action, like the frequent apartment bombings that Chechen rebels planted in many Russian cities, killed more innocents than guilties and rarely led to positive results. No, there had to be leverage, skillfully applied and at the proper points. The question was how?

Could the leverage be international? Could there be such a public outcry that Moscow would finally pay attention? The Russian Army and the FSB, Russia's Federal Security Police, conducted wide-scale torture of Chechens and clear photographs and eyewitness confirmations made their way into significant news journals, inside and outside of Russia. The Russian government had a long tradition of heavy handedness and brutality. What about the United Nations or some other forum?

Russia, in spite of its diplomatic clumsiness and difficulty in practicing qualities like honesty and candor, was seen as an ally to many nations of the world, and Russia's unwavering insistence on retaining Chechnya as part of the Federation was generally respected. Further, Chechnya was an important cog in Russia's petro-economy; any country that incurred the wrath of Russia would need to be sufficiently significant in size and might, and would have to have little need for Russia's oil for any leverage to prove effective.

The one prominent non-Chechen advocate was the British actress Vanessa Redgrave. How much mileage on the international stage could the Chechen resistance get out of the endorsement of an aging activist? Chechens were grateful but understandably not flush with excitement at her support.

Other sorts of pressure began to be considered. Chechen rebels in London met regularly to consider their options. Everything was on the table. Most were dismissed as wild-eyed schemes that would generate only more hostility against those Chechens still inside the republic. One plan entailed systematic assassinations of diplomats from the Russian Federation until the nation's leadership capitulated. Even with a shortage of arms, finances and personnel that faced the Chechen rebels, that plan was nearly approved.

That's when one member of the London group suggested a new approach. "We bring to this table our collective commitment, but if our objective is to change the behavior of Russian leadership, we have little of value on our side. We have access to no one with the talent or the capacity to conduct a sophisticated operation. We need to speak with someone else who brings us other assets. Otherwise, we will be like the primitive terrorists hiding in the hills and sending only our money to build bombs and our best wishes for success."

The suggestion was greeted with nods from a few, puzzlement from others. One was vocal in his sarcasm? "Where do you suggest we find this talent? Do we just Google for 'covert operative?'"

The oldest man at the table, a former member of the Grozny secret police, he with the leathery skin, wrinkled brow and the long crooked scar etched in his cheek, leaned forward in his seat and said in a low voice, "I know of a man."

THREE

The initial call was made from London to a small automobile repair shop near Milan. The message was relayed from there to the owner of a villa in Camposanto, a small town near Modena in Emilia Romagna, Italy. Emilio Fortino was not the real name of the villa's owner. In his most recently completed assignment, he went by the name of Patrick Keough. As Keough, he was hired to conduct a two-phase task. Phase one, in the US, worked well enough, but phase two was planned for England, and it failed in spectacular fashion. The man known then as Patrick Keough was badly injured and nearly put away for the balance of his days in a British prison; his escape from a heavily guarded hospital and subsequent disappearance continued to baffle the security forces in the UK.

In previous assignments, he'd been Massimiliano Bruno when he arranged the demise of a meddlesome Serbian political figure, Marcel Proulx in another scheme involving a Parisian detective-turned-informer, and Ernesto Peña on another project in Barcelona linked to an Asian importer who took too many shortcuts in quality control. His missions were generally performed well; it was only the collapse of his most recent job that gnawed at him. His venture as Patrick Keough was not his proudest.

He returned to Italy after his escape to heal and enjoy the life he'd chosen as an olive farmer. He was not anxious to return to the physically and psychologically tiring lifestyle that had provided him with the ability to acquire his rolling acres in central Italy. Of late, he'd experienced the troublesome spells where he was certain he had missed a moment, perhaps several moments of lucidity. They were rare and fleeting, and he sought no remedy. He just hoped they were not obvious to others. They might even be figments of his imagination. He had little way of knowing and less urgency to find out.

When the London call from the exiled Chechens was relayed to him, he almost dismissed the opportunity. He would, he conceded, give it some thought but promise nothing. He would respond within seventy-two hours, but warned that if he chose to accept, the price would be high.

Two days later, the London call was returned and meetings arranged. Those meetings, held in Amsterdam, were often contentious. Patience and planning, Emilio Fortino insisted, was absolutely crucial. No, we must strike hard and fast, came the retort. Then find somebody else, he said, and he rose to leave. No, we will listen, but we cannot wait forever.

Not forever, he said. A surgical approach: Quietly capture a single human being of great importance, a spouse, a parent, a child of a Russian leader, and exert influence upon Russia to make the concession you seek. If the right individual is selected the scheme would work. The requirements cannot be so great in the mind of the Russians that they would never concede. The concessions must be substantial but incremental. The captive would be released unharmed and in absolute silence. Russia would have the ability to announce its concessions to the Chechens in the spirit of doing the right thing. No one outside of a small group would have to know what brought Russia to such a conciliatory mood. In the end, Russia would actually gain some prestige on the world stage, while it grudgingly caved in to Chechen demands on a hidden back stage.

But target selection was crucial and not just any wife or daughter or grandson would do. Then, after selecting the *who*, then *where*? And *when*? Strategy, tactics, planning.

The discussions turned into haggling, but the agreement was struck: Patience and planning won out. The rebels would gather intelligence and Fortino would develop a strategy. They would meet again in ten days.

It was at this second meeting that the name of Grigori Malko surfaced for the first time in Emilio Fortino's presence. The fact that Malko had access to the senior levels of Russian government intrigued Emilio. "What is the President's schedule? Where will he be in the next three to six months?"

"Six months! We cannot wait so long. Our people in our homeland are being tortured as we sit here and speak."

The discussions turned again to haggling but the arguments were short-lived. Emilio insisted that he have access to Grigori Malko and he wanted to select his target.

He already had two good ideas, but wanted to settle on just one very soon. When the Chechens heard the suggestions, they were aghast. It will never work. Too daring, they said. Emilio was tired of the give and take ritual. Either he be given free rein to manage the process or he was out. No hard feelings.

Besides, he told them, if you cannot agree on basic strategy and tactics, you will never be able to agree on the expenses involved, nor my fee. The expenses would depend on the ultimate target and the method of extracting that target, but they should expect to be prepared to bear at least one million pounds in expenses; his fee for professional services was fixed at another million pounds.

Emilio was right. Expecting to come up with two million pounds was next to impossible. At most, they insisted, they could squeeze their treasuries for one million, maybe a bit more. How, they asked, can we come up with so much?

Emilio's need for compensation was limited. He was a wealthy man. His need was psychological; rather than drift softly into the good night, his most recent assignment a failed expedition, he wanted to spend his days capable of recalling a successful venture. He still had some good years left and his skill levels remained high. He would put himself to the test once more before he retired forever to his hills, his trees and his wine cellar. He would adjust his fee, he said. With that, the agreement was made and Emilio returned to his olive groves to study and make plans.

His trees were ancient and gnarled and toughened against the warm dry winds that blew across the rolling fields and the blazing sun that blessed them with fruit. The olives were beautiful this season and he enjoyed the din that surrounded the farm. Tractors and workers and baskets and trucks. The aroma of the fruit and dust filled his senses and he wondered why he would ever want to become involved in the Chechens' concerns.

His plan would work, he was certain, and he went to work selecting a target. He would prefer his target to be at once well-known and accessible. He also wanted to find someone who had strong connections to an important figure. The daughter of someone in power would be ideal but a son would do. Finally, he would like the target to be relatively easy to mimic.

The Russian president, Nikolai Mironev, was the husband of Raisa, a lovely brunette who gave up a career in publishing upon their move to the Kremlin. They were parents of two children: the elder, Alek, was twenty-five, a playboy of sorts and a frequent source of tabloid gossip, and Ksana, just fourteen and kept well protected by her family and security personnel.

Young Alek Mironev appeared to Emilio to present the ideal target. He was out in public frequently and therefore accessible, and certainly less well-protected by security personnel than his younger sister. In fact, Alek Mironev made it known publicly that he resented the intrusiveness of his assigned security team, and he was known to have slipped their coverage on several occasions. If Emilio could arrange to capture Alek Mironev, pressure could be brought to bear on his father to accomplish the Chechens' objective. That done, Alek would be released, Emilio would have his fee, and he could retire from his profession and become the full-time olive producing farmer that he'd planned on.

He would need to check on the young Mironev's travel plans and put some traces on his activities. Where does he like to go? Who are his friends? Is he straight or gay? Does he have a steady girlfriend? His contacts were good and the information was relatively easy and cheap to obtain. Photos came in that showed expressions and clothing and hair styles. Audio recordings of his voice from radio and television interviews were assembled.

Alek spent a good deal of his time in London, was seeing a lovely young brunette, a venture capital intern there, but it wasn't particularly serious right now, and besides, he was known to favor blondes. Since he graduated from the University of Moscow but spent one year at Cambridge and another at the University of Bologna, he spoke unaccented English and rapid-fire Italian. That led to his decision to study international law, at least occasionally, while he occupied himself by attending sports events and film openings, and dodging paparazzi. If his parents had some concerns with their elder child's profligacy and high-flying lifestyle, they kept those to themselves.

Emilio studied the photographs and looked at the films. A switch, preferably away from Moscow, would afford Emilio some time for the Chechens to apply their pressure on the Russian President. A body double was ideal, a substitute for Alek Mironev who could be seen in public on occasion, just long enough to keep his face in the news. With such an appropriate temporary replacement, few would have to know about a capture and the ransom that could be paid in concessions to Emilio's Chechen employers. Everything would stay, as the Americans say, 'below the radar'.

Little struck Emilio as difficult to imitate except for the curious front teeth of Alek Mironev. The young man's front teeth were slightly crooked and noticeable even from some distance, and any candidate would likely undergo some form of dental work to mimic the young man's trademark smile. Otherwise, he did have somewhat of a jutting and dimpled chin and a prominent brow. If Emilio could come reasonably close to finding someone who bore a passing resemblance to Alek Mironev, he could arrange some minor cosmetic surgery along with dental caps or implants.

With a phone call to a private number, Emilio next made arrangements to access files that were available to few individuals beyond those in law enforcement. He listened to four rings before his call was picked up. There was no sound but that of raspy breathing, no greeting, no announcement. Emilio broke the silence and spoke in fluent French.

"You will recall, I am certain, a late acquaintance, Detective Dominique Jalbert of the Paris police?" It was expressed as a question, and Emilio could almost hear the electric hum and clicks of his listener's brain synapses processing and considering a response. He counted three beats and continued.

"It was not Interpol's finest moment, you will agree."

"Marcel Proulx." The first words in response were spoken in a resonant basso-profundo that flowed through the phone line like warm syrup.

"Among other names, yes. I need access to some files."

"You were paid." The deep voice took on a gruff tone that suggested that no such access would be granted, but Emilio pressed quickly.

"And I have a record, on tape, of our conversation when you and your colleagues gave me specific instructions about my assignment as Monsieur Marcel Proulx. The recording is remarkably clear, by the way."

This evidently caught the man by surprise for there was another pause and an almost imperceptible intake of breath.

"Insurance," Emilio added.

"What do you want?"

"Very little. I wish to look through your files of those arrested, including their photographs, what I believe our American friends call 'mug shots'. I should think this would be a simple request."

Emilio waited for the man to consider this and the answer was given: "When? Where?"

"I can do this from a distance if you give me an access code. Don't you love the Internet?"

This time the response was quick. "That can be too easily traced."

"Then let us meet. You will gain access to the files and I will look over your shoulder."

This idea seemed to gain some traction and Emilio waited, patient and assured, for the answer. He knew the man travelled frequently throughout Europe; a meeting place and time would be uncomplicated.

"I will be in the south of France, in Perpignan, in two days. At the Kyriad Windsor. Meet me there and bring this 'tape' you speak of."

"Certainly." Emilio's answer was nimble, too agreeable for the man, and given in a way that made clear that other copies of any tape delivered would exist and could surface elsewhere and at some other embarrassing moment.

The owner of the deep voice understood and Emilio could feel the sense of resignation coming over the line.

Emilio pored over thousands of screen images in Perpignan and noted some potential candidates. All the while, his deep-voiced Interpol friend remained seated, glum, and anxious for this meeting to be over. So far, the search through Interpol's photo files had taken nearly three hours.

He made seven screen prints, noted their physical characteristics, such as height and weight, and the actual crimes involved. Alek Mironev cooperated in the effort by being of relatively average height and build. These seven, Emilio considered, were sufficient to provide him with potential candidates, and with a nod he left the room to the great relief of his Interpol acquaintance.

Emilio went back to his own hotel in Perpignan, the Mercure, and pored over the photos and the data he collected. He poured himself a glass of wine and sat on the balcony of his room enjoying the drink and a lovely Cuban cigar. Every candidate met the initial screening for appearance; they were approximately the same size and age as his target. Hair color and eye color were easy to modify with dye and contact lenses. The young Mr. Mironev's slightly crooked front teeth would take some artful dental work, but replicating Alek's trademark smile was essential.

One candidate fit Emilio's requirements almost perfectly. The young man had the right build and his facial characteristics would require only minor modification. He was no stranger to law enforcement and was recently released from prison. Emilio studied the man's background and criminal history; he knew the type, and this fellow was destined to spend a lifetime in and out of jails. He made plans to visit the young man right away.

Four days later, Emilio took a call from London. The funds for the project would be wired to an account of his choosing, although there was some haggling about a twenty-five percent holdback until every phase of the scheme was completed. Emilio relented. They understood that there were no guarantees, but they made clear to Emilio that failure was not a desirable option for someone who wished to return to the quiet life of a gentleman olive grower. The warning struck Emilio hard. He did not know how they found out where he lived and what he did there, and he considered for more than a moment calling the whole plan off. Why did he need these threats? He'd think about it.

That night, as the sun set over the hills and silence replaced the day's music of the harvest, Emilio considered his options. Stay or go? Enjoy the fruits of his labors at his extensive olive groves, or enjoy the fruit of what another one million pounds would buy. Did he need the money? Not really. The grove was producing well and he had cash assets stashed in several overseas banks. Did he need the challenge? Ah, there's the rub.

After careful consideration and two glasses of wine, his decision was reached. His was a viable plan. It would have numerous small details to make sure everything worked on schedule and precisely as planned. He already knew most of the right people and in the right places. He relished working out the little pieces and how they fit together. The money was just a bonus.

The threat from the rebel relics in exile? They were self-righteous and ham-fisted, but he'd call tomorrow and accept the proposition.

* * *

With the target selected and a suitable candidate arranged as a body double, Emilio pressed the Chechens to meet with Grigori Malko. This lunch in Paris was organized for three reasons. First, he needed to track young Mironev's travels, and Grigori Malko had access to the young man's itinerary. Second, he wanted to meet face to face with Malko; the risks entailed by this plan were enormous and Emilio wanted to make certain that his contact appreciated the dangers. Failure could mean a long prison term if they were captured, or death if they were not.

Malko showed up at the table at precisely one o'clock. Emilio was already swirling a garnet-colored Cote de Rhone in a stemmed glass when Malko arrived. Emilio nodded at the open chair and Malko took a seat. No hands were extended in greeting as civility was not part of the arrangement.

"I am told you have a plan and that the initial payment was wired to your account. I do not wish to participate any further; I am in enough peril already."

Emilio smiled a smile of amusement. Malko had a career that entailed extensive international travel and frequent meetings with his counterparts in other nations. He should be fluent in at least French, among other languages. Instead, they would conduct their discussion in English, Emilio in his English public school accent, and Grigori Malko in a crudely chopped Russian-accented version of English. It seemed to Emilio like he was finding himself cast in a bad American cold war film.

"I ordered a small plate of cheese and vegetables. Are you hungry, Grigori?"

"Just beer for me."

"Beer? Here? This isn't Belgium, you know."

"Wine, then." Malko's manner was tense and worried. "Whatever you have."

Emilio signaled the waiter and ordered the wine and a plate of bread.

"You'll want something to eat, Grigori? You look like such a mess."

"It is dangerous, no?" He glanced around, his voice low.

"It is dangerous, yes." Emilio appeared natural and relaxed. You have the information I asked for?"

"Here." Grigori handed an envelope to Emilio. "You will find information on Alek Mironev is complete."

Emilio removed a slip of paper from the envelope and looked it over. It was a schedule for young Mironev with dates, places and times. One bit of information snapped him to attention. In late January, Alek Mironev would be in the US for several days, in Florida, the guest of a financial services firm at the American Super Bowl.

"Florida?"

"Planet Capital has office in London and Alek Mironev is popular figure."

"According to the tabloids, Alek Mironev is among the top twenty-five bachelors in the world."

"He will be at Super Bowl as celebrity guest. Mingle with clients, have good time. Alek is very good at that."

"How very convenient." Emilio was intrigued at this twist. He was already running some possible scenarios through his mind when Malko interrupted his thoughts.

"If you think to maybe make plans for Florida, then you should take this." Malko removed another envelope from the breast pocket of his jacket.

Emilio was unprepared. What is this? A bonus?

"I have someone who may help you. She lives now in US, in Florida."

Emilio opened the envelope and removed a piece of paper. On it was a name, Vanya Zakayev, and an address of a circus troupe in Sarasota, Florida.

"A performer?"

"Acrobat. Also trapeze. Born in Russia and now living in Florida. Her mother is my cousin, also Chechen."

"A zealot?"

"Very much zealot."

"Do you have pictures of this Vanya?"

"Also in envelope."

"'Also in envelope.' You should study your languages, Grigori. A verb here or there would help. I swear, you Russians are as insular as the Americans."

He studied the photographs, a publicity still in full color and two grainy black and white shots that looked like surveillance photos. Emilio suspected with great certainty that these were taken by Russian police authorities. The woman named Vanya Zakayev was petite, lithe, blonde, and a classic Russian beauty. In her eyes, even in the grainy photos, Emilio saw sparks."

Malko leaned forward. "She is OK?"

"I will meet with her. I will let you know."

"No. I must contact you. My calls are . . ."

"They are monitoring your calls?"

"Possible. For security, they monitor many people."

"But you are still in the same position? You travel with the president?"

"Yes. This is not changed."

"And they know you are here?"

"They know I am in Paris. Holiday. My wife is at hotel."

Their plates and wine arrived and they remained silent while the waiter was in the immediate area.

"So, this Vanya. What can you tell me about her?"

"Lived in Moscow most of life but has relatives in Chechnya. Many killed during wars there."

Emilio understood the potential value. Vanya Zakayev would have valuable personal reasons to want his scheme to succeed. He slid the photographs and paper into the envelope, placed it on the table and sat back, a portrait of serenity and self-assuredness. Grigori Malko, he saw, was anxious, eyes darting at passers-by, a single bead of sweat traveling down from his brow to his cheek, even on this mild Parisian day. "Grigori, tell me, you said your wife was in Paris with you?"

"Yes. At hotel. Why?"

"And your daughters? Katerina and Anastasia?"

The mention of his children's names caused Grigori Malko's eyebrows to rise. The question could only mean that Emilio Fortino, a person he knew to have links to many assassinations for hire, had done some investigating on his own.

"Yes." Grigori Malko tried to remain calm. "First time in Paris."

"You love your wife and daughters, Grigori?"

"Of course."

"Then you will want to protect them. You will want to make sure that you keep your end of our bargain. Otherwise . . ." Emilio shrugged his shoulders.

"I will uphold bargain."

"Otherwise, you could never rest knowing that your family may be visited at your vacation home on the river. It is a lovely place, by the way. And your younger one ? Anastasia ? she just loves the water, doesn't she? You are very lucky."

FOUR

Boca Grande, Gasparilla Island, Florida

His luncheon appointment in Paris with Grigori Malko was months in the past now, and Emilio sat at his desk at the Gulf Breeze Inn on the barrier island of Gasparilla on Florida's west coast. He flipped through a short stack of files until he found the one he was looking for. "Vanya Zakayev". He opened it and looked at the collection of his photos and notes. Here was a force in life. This woman, all ninety-nine pounds of her, was on fire. Strong, capable, focused, committed. Her astonishing good looks added to the package and met with precision his requirements. He was taken at once by her appearance and her ability to turn on the charm. That was her business, turning on the charm in extraordinarily difficult situations. Alek Mironev wouldn't have a chance.

As an acrobat and trapeze artist, Vanya Zakayev was familiar with hard work, and accustomed to endless hours of demanding practice sessions. Since her early teens, when she joined the Great Lights Circus in Moscow, she spent part of every day bending, twisting and stretching. It was a ritual that consumed two hours every morning. Afternoons, if she was not performing, she swung from the bar and practiced her moves. The equipment she used in Russia was old and rusting, so she learned to check, double-check and triple-check every rope, every bar and every weld. There were few second chances in her line of work.

Moving to Sarasota last year was not part of a long-term plan but born of necessity. Vanya was only twenty-three, but she needed to leave Moscow before she did something stupid; she'd taken part in several pro-Chechen demonstrations and her photograph was in every security agency's file. The KGB was gone, but paranoia politics and power were alive and well in the Russian Federation. In the new Russia, Vanya Zakayev saw some promise of liberty and tolerance, but even in her youth she recognized that the old ways die hard. If Vanya Zakayev wanted to continue voicing her opinions and stay healthy, she understood that she may need to relocate at some time in the future. She had a few vague plans, idle hopes really, to leave her country, but nothing concrete. Then came the catalyst for turning those plans into a firm resolve.

Vanya Zakayev was familiar with Anna Politkovskaya, the Novaya Gazeta journalist whose reporting exposed the torture by Russian troops in Chechnya. Still in her teens but even then a noted performer, she met with the controversial reporter many times to talk about Vanya's three cousins in Grozny. All three, Aadil, Durrah and Majdy, were found dead after they'd been interrogated by Russian Federal Security Police, the FSB, about arms trafficking in Chechnya. Her cousins were automatically suspects whenever the FSB needed suspects. In their case, the three were dragged from Aadil's home during a birthday celebration for their mother, taken to an empty warehouse outside of Grozny and subjected to horrific torture until they died.

Anna had the nerve to put the story into print in a series of articles in the Novaya Gazeta about atrocities in Chechnya, much to the dismay of some important politicians in the Russian Federation. Days after a particularly scathing report on the Russian government's policies in Chechnya, Anna Politkovskaya was met with four rounds, three in the chest and one to the head, when she walked into her Moscow apartment building at the end of a work day. Anna never revealed Vanya's role in the preparation of the story, but her violent death was a clear signal to Vanya that she could never walk down the streets of Moscow without wondering who had her in their crosshairs. Vanya Zakayev had an Aeroflot ticket to London in her hands four days after Anna's funeral.

Vanya understood that if she did leave Russia and her job at the circus, she still needed to earn a living. Sarasota is the center in the US for the circus industry and Vanya used her connections in London to make the necessary arrangements. When she landed in Sarasota two months later, she hit the ground running. After five weeks of practice and rehearsals, she was in one of the top touring troupes in the business. Now she was getting recruited, so far unsuccessfully, to be the star of a new Cirque du Soleile show in Las Vegas. Too soon, she thought to herself. She'd already been recruited, successfully, by the tall gentleman who went by the name of Emilio Fortino for another job, and success in this endeavor meant success for her Chechen kin. Revenge is a powerful motive.

Emilio flipped open a second file folder, this one labeled "Jay Finney". Young Jay Finney was as perfect a body double for Alek Mironev as Emilio could expect to find in the extensive Interpol files of criminals. Finney was British but had worked for a year in Moscow as a technician for a television company. He was far from fluent in Russian, but knew enough to fool a few wealthy Americans who would be attending the Super Bowl as guests of Planet Capital. Besides, Emilio had seen enough film footage of Alek Mironev to know that he spoke the clipped English of a typical British university product, which he was. Finney's working class accent was crude by upper crust standards, but with a little coaching would be polished enough for the American guests. Emilio mused on the US phrase, "Close enough for government work."

James Philip Finney had an extensive record with British law enforcement and welcomed the opportunity to leave the UK and perhaps reinvent himself elsewhere. Going to "the States" sounded wonderful to Jay Finney, and the promise of significant money made the young man eager to please. Jay met most of the required physical characteristics and needed only a bit of alteration. A small, rather straightforward surgical chin implant was put in place by a physician acquaintance of Emilio in Amsterdam. The same doctor used a few additional stitches to give Jay Finney the right cleft chin and the slightly protuberant brow.

Alek Mironev's trademark smile, the smile that made women swoon, featured curious crooked upper front teeth. Jay Finney's teeth, in spite of a diet of fish and chips and sweet puddings, were perfectly straight. A dentist friend of the Amsterdam physician fashioned and installed crowns for Jay Finney, and now, at least to those whose exposure to Alek Mironev was limited to celebrity magazine photos, Jay Finney could pass easily for the playboy son of the Russian president.

Emilio Fortino smiled every time he looked at the *before* and *after* photographs of Jay Finney and placed them adjacent to the photos of the real Alek Mironev. This will work, he thought, and it will work beautifully.

PART II

It takes two to make a murder. There are born victims, born to have their throats cut, as the cut-throats are born to be hanged.
—Aldous Huxley

Murder is always a mistake. One should never do anything that one cannot talk about after dinner.
—Oscar Wilde

FIVE

Monday afternoon in early February

The Super Bowl was finally over, and the team in dark jerseys and black helmets barely beat the team in light jerseys and silver helmets. Emilio Fortino didn't care who won or lost, but he joined the entire Tampa-St. Petersburg area in exhaling today in one enormous and almost audible sigh of relief. The crowds and noise and general revelry that clogged the streets and filled the hotels, bars and restaurants for the prior week were over, and the party-goers were jetting across the sky on their way home to New York and Seattle and London and Dallas. Contrails cross-hatched the skies over the three nearby airports, jets both public and private loaded with fans, sponsors, executives and politicians, most of them hung over and in considerable need of some quiet time back home.

Emilio Fortino drove his yellow Jeep Wrangler, canvas top up under a clear sky, along the interstate heading south. In moments, he'd cross the steep Sunshine Skyway Bridge that spanned the calm azure waters of Tampa Bay. The contrails caught his attention and he smiled, silent and smug, reflecting on the success of the task accomplished over the past several days. Every-thing went rather well, considering the complications that could have run the scheme off the rails at any time. But plan-ning . . . Emilio was all about planning . . . was essential, and this plan was well-conceived, thoroughly considered, and with a few minor exceptions, brilliantly executed. He moved the dial on the radio, found the classical station in Sarasota, and eased up the volume a notch, his spirits soaring with the trumpets of Beethoven's Seventh Symphony.

He checked his watch, an inexpensive Timex Expedition, and calculated his arrival at his hotel in Boca Grande, eighty miles away. He should be there at about two-thirty, or "half-two" as the Brits, including his passenger, would say. Before he reached his destination, he would drop off his passenger at the small motel in Venice where he arranged a room, and by three, Emilio hoped for a bit of solitude on the veranda at his hotel, sipping lovely single malt. He wanted some respite, however brief it might prove, some sanctuary while he awaited the re-sults of the next phase of the plan. The news would arrive by way of a phone call. Glenlivet Scotch, he thought. Fifteen years old. He'd seen a bottle of it on the shelf of the small bar at his hotel. Just the one. Peaty, smoky and sweet. He deserved that much. Even seasoned professionals like me, he thought, need a break now and then from the physical strain and the mental stress that came with his occupation.

He'd noticed of late that the tension was taking its toll. He was not the young man he once was, and therefore more likely to encounter disturbing side effects, like nagging aches in his back or the unsettling tendency to lose time, his thoughts drift-ing into some unknown space.

His passenger liked to chatter, and that made the last several minutes of silence both unusual and welcomed. Jay Finney was otherwise preoccupied as he applied spirit gum in small, careful daubs to his jaw and upper lip, affixed the layer of beard, a small mirror wedged between his knees, and brushed the result with precision to achieve just the right look. With the addition of the spectacles and baseball cap, both of which rested now at his feet, and a quick change to a faded tee shirt and scruffy jeans, Jay Finney would be just another visitor to southwest Florida. No longer would he be the copy, the exact carbon copy of Alek Mironev, the young fellow who would be at the center of this week's anticipated trans-Atlantic conversations.

Alek Mironev, at this moment, was confined elsewhere by heavy ankle chains to an enormous animal cage designed for beasts like mature Siberian tigers or silverback gorillas, large enough for an adult human male to stretch and even walk about a bit in a standing position and sufficiently stout as to defy escape. The cage was inside a faded, abandoned, whitewashed fishing cottage on a secluded island, surrounded (or so Emilio Fortino communicated to the young Mr. Mironev) by a multitude of the most fierce, easily provoked and highly poisonous snakes known to man.

In truth, Emilio considered, there were snakes, and many of them, in the area surrounding the cottage. The few he'd seen were quite long, four feet or more. Whether they were poisonous, that was a question to which Emilio didn't know the answer, but snakes did in fact live among the scrubby palmettos and the few tall palms that dotted the otherwise barren landscape of the island, so the frightening story he'd told to Mr. Mironev was not downright fabrication, and it had the desired effect.

"There." Jay Finney spoke for the first time in nearly thirty precious silent minutes. "How do I look, mate?"

Emilio loathed the familiarity; he was no one's 'mate' and resented Jay Finney's use of the term. He looked straight ahead, fingers tight on the wheel.

"I said how do I look?"

In spite of himself, he glanced over and the physical transformation was indeed remarkable. He did a double take and blinked his eyes to better absorb the sight, for Finney was no longer the clean-cut, effete, rather callow young man he'd pretended to be for the prior five days. Now he was the scruffy, somewhat tattered, rather callow young man he really was. There was little resemblance now to Alek Mironev, no hint that Jay Finney just accomplished a rather astonishing act of switcheroo on an unsuspecting public. No suggestion that the young man had achieved, through meticulous preparation, exhaustive training, and native guile, a feat of chicanery that could alter the course of nations half the world away. Emilio would know better in a few hours or perhaps a few days if the ruse was as successful as he expected it was, even though the bulk of his fee was already paid and deposited in a numbered account at a discrete bank six hundred miles to the south on Grand Cayman.

Meanwhile, Alek Mironev still looked precisely like Alek Mironev, dark hair clipped short, button nose like his mother, and with that trademark grin. The smile was part of the Alek Mironev franchise. It gave him, as one celeb magazine wrote, "a look of vulnerability, a slightly off-center look that women find irresistible."

His was a face the British tabloids featured regularly and prominently for the prior two years, and that the international celebrity press around the world joined in describing as belonging to one of the twenty-five most eligible bachelors on the planet.

Jay Finney had portrayed Alek Mironev for the past five days, had lived his life, attended the pre-Super Bowl parties to which Alek had been invited, sat in his luxury sky box seats at Raymond James stadium to witness the world's most watched sporting event, sipped the finest wines that were meant for the discerning palate of Alek Mironev, luxuriated in the penthouse suite at the Don Cesar in St. Petersburg reserved for Alek

Mironev, had had his photograph taken perhaps three hundred times standing with celebrity hounds, executives, their fawning wives, daughters, sons, girlfriends ... without a single snag.

Just before Jay Finney's unannounced departure from the Don Cesar, which he achieved by making his way through the service hallways and meeting Emilio at a prearranged parking spot in the side lot of the hotel, Jay placed a handwritten note on the desk in his suite. The note was prepared by Emilio based on the few handwriting samples of Alek Mironev he'd been able to trace, and was written in the sort of tone Alek would use: "I'll be delaying my journey back to London for at least a few days ... so much to see here in the states!! New Orleans beckons and I hope to spend a few enjoyable days in the Big Easy before returning to drab wet England. I'll make contact when I get there. God Bless America!! Ciao! A."

This was just the sort of thing a young, carefree celebrity might pull, with all its arrogant disregard for the host, Planet Capital, which had a plane fueled and fully crewed for the transatlantic journey back to Heathrow, and for his family, which was getting unfortunately accustomed to the young man's impetuosity. And the sign-off ... since his university time in Great Britain and Bologna, Alek considered himself to be quite continental in his ways. The flourish of a single letter 'A' was right in character.

Emilio looked over to his companion and saw a young man with a beard and mustache, and not at all like the ever-groomed, every-hair-moussed-to-precisely-the-right-spiked-peak Alek Mironev.

"Just great, Jay. Just wonderful." Emilio meant it. The physical alteration was remarkable.

"And we'll go fishing tomorrow, right?" Jay was keen on the sport of angling, a pastime that, to Emilio, presented all the thrills of watching paint dry. "There's a storm headed this way, but I saw on the telly that it won't get here until Wednesday. Could be a bit choppy tomorrow. Are you sure you want to go?"

"A promise is a promise, Jay." He watched a smile spread across Jay's face, the dental implants that mimicked the Alek Mironev smile just barely visible beneath the false mustache fringe. "I rented a fishing boat on the Peace River, so we shouldn't have any weather worries. It's far enough from the Gulf of Mexico to avoid any rough water. By the way, I rented it in the name of Peter Billings, so bring the driver's license you have with that name. You have a rental car reserved in your name next to the motel as well."

"I have it right here in my wallet, mate. I don't know who makes your false documents, but the license is perfect. You think of everything."

The lad was right. He did think of everything, or of most things. "Planning is everything," he said to the young man.

"I understand, I really do. It's just such a change for me. I've always been one to do some planning, but then you have to go with your instincts sometimes, know what I mean?"

He knew enough about Jay Finney to understand that his instincts were unreliable and therefore dangerous. Otherwise, young Mr. Finney would not have spent thirty-one of the most recent thirty-seven months of his young life behind bars in a British prison.

"The Peace River," Jay went on, "that's beyond Charlotte Harbor isn't it?"

"The marina is a few miles past the northern edge of the harbor. The boat is reserved and I'm told it's a remarkable fishing location. I have a map in the door panel; take a look."

Jay removed the map and fiddled with it until he saw what he was looking for. "It branches off into several creeks. It looks like it has some islands as well. Should be good places for fish to hide out. We'll just have to go and find them."

Emilio had studied the river with some thoroughness, but his investigations had little to do with the fish that inhabited it. Instead, the Peace River served his purpose for different reasons. The slow moving water wound through some remote scrub land on their way from central Florida to Charlotte Harbor and the Gulf of Mexico. The river was dotted with low islands, islets really, and teeming with voracious alligators. When his work on the river tomorrow was done, Emilio only had to guide the fishing boat further up the Peace River to an overpass where he would abandon it in the thick brush along the river banks. Vanya would pick him up and drive him back to the comfort of the Gulf Breeze Inn.

"Do you mind if we stop at the next exit? I'd like to get a pack of crisps and maybe a Pepsi."

Emilio did not verbally reply, but did flip his turn signal and make his way for the exit ramp. A small shopping area had a gas station with grocery and he pulled in to a spot right in front. "I know this place, Jay, and it has a little bit of everything."

Finney opened the car door and asked, "Can I get you anything?"

Emilio didn't smoke, but for an occasional cigar, and didn't eat candy or snacks, but he did enjoy mints and chewing gum. "I'll go in with you."

Finney walked up and down every aisle while Emilio waited at the register, a packet of Dentine, a container of Altoids and a cylinder of Tums in his hand. When Finney's purchase . . . two bottles of soda, two candy bars and a large bag of potato chips . . . were rung in, Finney reached for his wallet, but Emilio waved him off. He put his own small items next to Finney's and reached for the money in his pocket.

US money always caused Emilio some level of confusion. Raised with lira in Italy, he'd grown up trading in French francs, Swiss francs and German marks, with their multiple sizes and colors. With the conversion to Euros, the custom of varying bill sizes and colors was preserved. He understood the logic: small bills for small denominations, larger bills for the larger, with distinctive colors and designs assigned to each. Here in the US, every bill was of identical size and there were only subtle color differences for the various dollar amounts. Add the coinage, and he always wondered how such a country, proud of its heritage as innovators, could be so parochial when it came to its currency. Even with practice, he struggled to establish a suitable level of comfort with the differences.

The total charge was $13.67, and Emilio flipped through his folding money to find a ten and a five . . . no that was a single . . . and settled on a twenty dollar bill. Then he tried to assemble sixty-seven cents from his pocketful of coins. He fumbled with the nickels, the quarters, the one-cent coins, until in frustration he put the handful on the counter and picked out the correct coins to satisfy the charge. Emilio had seen the clerk before when he bought gas. Tall, gaunt, tattooed and pierced in multiple locations. He put his change of seven dollars into his pocket and they returned to the Jeep and the Interstate.

Emilio watched his passenger gobble up a chocolate bar and a bottle of soda and wondered how Jay Finney avoided a face full of pimples. He was such a child.

Emilio concealed his angst at the thought that today was to be the smiling Jay Finney's last full day on this earth, the young man's purpose now spent. He anticipated the gruesome details of tomorrow's planned events, all the while holding a fixed grin for the benefit of his oblivious companion. Everything was planned, and dispatching Jay Finney would take place by about mid-day. Planning.

Jay's smile remained. So trusting, Emilio thought, like a naïf whose father promised a trip to the carnival. So willing to please. Unfortunate that Jay Finney's early years were spent on the grim, seedy streets of Manchester's toughest neighborhood, unfortunate as well that he'd associated with the worst elements of its gangs, unfortunate that Jay had a predilection for young boys and had been caught, twice, in the act of sodomizing lads half his age. Life was a series of misfortunes for Jay, with a worthless drunk for a mother and a father with his own dodgy past. Jay had exacerbated those ills with some spectacularly bad choices. Some of his pathology was destined the day of his birth; the rest he brought on himself. That made tomorrow's task a bit more palatable for Emilio than it otherwise might have been, but he didn't relish the thought of ending Jay's horrid life. He recognized his rationalizing for what it was: The world will be better off without Jay Finney, and unsuspecting young lads would never again be victimized by this creature.

Emilio also appreciated that his life would be more secure without Jay, for as long as he remained among the living, Jay Finney would be a loose end, someone who, if caught, would identify Emilio as the lead character in this dangerous international fraud. For all his bravado, Jay Finney would fold like a cheap suit under pressure from law enforcement. He considered that American metaphor: 'Fold like a cheap suit.' It had some meaning, some concrete basis that lent some visual support to the words. If Jay were able to get out of the area safely, he was the type to brag in order to boost his self-image, and such personality deficiencies were reason enough to bring Jay Finney's miserable existence to an end. Emilio resolved to complete tomorrow's task and almost sighed when Jay said, "Then I'll be there, Emilio, with bells on."

Bells? No bells. No alarms, no drawing attention. Emilio was a student of idioms in several languages, and he never stopped marveling at the world's predilection for them. 'With bells on?' In his native Italian, there were other idioms, many just as inane. Like 'Buona notte al secchio', or literally, 'good night to the bucket.' Its English counterpart was 'we're screwed,' and Emilio never figured out why a bucket was involved. But how did the English ever translate the simple thought 'there you have it' into 'Bob's your uncle and Fanny's your aunt'? That made even less sense than his Italian bucket.

He drove on, looking forward to dropping Jay off at a motel and having some solitary time with his Jeep and his music. A selection of Verdi arias was scheduled for the next hour, and he almost ached with homesickness at the thought. Then, after the Scotch he promised himself, he'd assemble his fishing tackle and the other implements he'd require for tomorrow. He'd given Alek Mironev a look-see early this morning, boating to the secluded island and providing his captive with nourishment. He would watch the evening news for signs that some successful conclusion might result from this past week's scheme and then Alek Mironev, too, could be part of Emilio's past. He didn't expect a quick response; in his experience, governments tended to move slowly in the best of times, even when there was a kidnapping involved. His own birth country, Italy, was notorious for the inefficiency of its official government agencies, so perhaps that colored his perception, but no, he still did not expect any announcement tonight, or tomorrow, or even the next night. He would have to be patient.

For now, the disappearance of Alek Mironev was just being learned, for the private flight back home to London was scheduled for a four o'clock departure from the Sarasota-Bradenton International Airport. Just about now people at the Don Cesar on St. Petersburg Beach would be looking for Alek, and unable to locate him, begin to panic. Emilio imagined the frantic scene at the grand beach hotel as it might unfold, all according to script. The stateside participants were unaware that the real Alek Mironev had been taken days ago, that the man they got to know over the past few days as Alek Mironev was in truth a pathological liar, a pedophile ('paedophile' on the Interpol crime file Emilio looked into) named James Philip Finney who was now posing as Peter Billings, just another Florida visitor on holiday.

Emilio did hope for a telephone call later giving him some sense of the progress, but any expectation beyond a status report was a pipe dream. Alek Mironev was the son of the illustrious Nikolai Mironev, the current President of the Russian Federation, and President Mironev ought to be getting his own telephone call from someone on the Planet Capital security team at about this very moment informing him that his son should not be expected to arrive back at his London apartment early tomorrow morning as planned. Something about wishing to visit New Orleans on the spur of the moment. Nikolai Mironev would likely become frustrated at this bit of news, but he had long ago become accustomed to his son's rash decisions and would chalk this up as one more example of Alek's free spirit.

Some hours later, the Russian President would receive a second call providing the elder Mironev with a variation of the 'non-returning son' theme: Alek was unharmed but in captivity. The President would be instructed on those specific conditions that must be met to effect his son's timely and safe release. No Russian police. No publicity. Any involvement by the Russian police, Interpol, the FBI or any other law enforcement agency would spell certain death for the young Alek. The caller would be clear on this.

When Nikolai Mironev responded appropriately, Emilio would be notified. He would then take yet one more boat trip through the scattered small islands that dot Florida's west coast Intercoastal waterway, secure Alek Mironev, and deposit him, alive and well as promised, at a location where he'd be found and returned to the loving arms of his parents, family and friends.

Emilio grinned almost as broadly as Jay at the thought. Jay glanced over and thought that Emilio was smiling about the thought of tomorrow's day of fishing, presuming that Emilio shared his enthusiasm for hooks, rods, reels and monofilament.

Emilio caught Jay's glance and kept up the appearance. Nothing was left to chance. With all of the careful planning, all of the continued success the scheme enjoyed, the job all but complete, the cash safely stowed in the offshore bank, nothing at all could possibly go wrong.

SIX

Emilio Fortino watched the falling sun from the veranda of the Gulf Breeze Inn on Gasparilla Island and sipped his scotch, enjoying the warm sensation of the amber liquid. He was never fond of Scotland, the damp chill of its climate or the frosty manner of the people he'd met there, but he was keen on the Scots' talent at creating some of the finest liquor ever conceived by man. From ice cold streams, fields of peat and some barley grains, grand dreams were marshaled, aged and bottled. He raised his glass in a solitary toast to their remarkable achievement.

When he finished his drink, he walked through the lobby to his guest room, slid the key card through the lock and listened for the soft click. Years of being careful taught him to open the door slowly and slide his hand along the wall to flip the light switch. Old habits, he acknowledged, were hard to break.

There was no likelihood here in the quiet seclusion of Boca Grande, where he was seen as just another well-heeled guest enjoying a spot of sunshine and relative isolation, that he'd be surprised by an intruder out to do him mortal harm. The days of trading karate blows in Budapest, or creeping across steep tile rooftops in Paris, dressed in black like a cat burglar on a deadly mission, had passed, replaced by the more cerebral methods of one whose flexibility and daring were on the down slope. The habits were just that, and he found that reliance on rote memory comforting.

He expected nothing out of the ordinary and got what he expected. He retrieved his tackle box from the floor of the closet and placed it on the desk next to the newspaper he received at his door this morning. He spread several thicknesses of newspaper on the desk and opened the tackle box. The nest of the top folding trays held an assortment of hooks, weights, flies and lures. Fishing may not be his favorite pastime, but he knew that props were important. When he first met Jay Finney at a Leeds pub and learned that the young man had a passion for fishing, he filed that small bit of data away for later retrieval. Tomorrow Emilio would feign some degree of pleasure at the sport, if only for some short time until Jay was sent to another dimension.

From the lower compartment of the tackle box, he reached for a gray cloth, neatly folded and concealing a cleaned and oiled Ruger MK II .22 caliber target pistol that sat on another gray cloth that he'd sprinkled earlier with gun oil. The pistol was much longer than he liked, fitted as it was with an eight-inch suppressor tube so that it sounded no louder than an air pistol when fired. Nearly soundless. Not in any way a defensive weapon, this Ruger was a dependable workhorse and, so configured, an ideal offensive tool in close quarters.

The Ruger was one of two pistols he acquired for this assignment; his other pistol was a Sig P250 that he kept at hand for his personal protection. He also acquired two rifles, although his plans, if they went well, would not require their use. If he had any further requirements, he recognized that he was in Florida, where firearms are almost as easy to obtain as a used car. All one had to do was ask. The Ruger had only one function to perform, and it would then find its way into oblivion. His Sig was a personal favorite, and he hoped it would survive and manage to find its way back with him to his homeland, but he appreciated weapons as the tools they were, and attached little emotion to them.

The final item in the tackle box was a box of fifty Fiocchi twenty-two caliber long rimfire cartridges. He removed ten rounds from the box, nine more than he expected he'd need tomorrow, and loaded them with practiced ease into the Ruger's magazine. With the safety moved up to the "on" position, he wrapped the pistol in the oiled gray cloth and placed it on the newspaper.

He made some mental calculations, brow creased, the tip of his tongue peeking between pursed lips, a habit his mother used to describe as his "concentration face". He repeatedly placed the loaded pistol in the compartment and removed it, trying to achieve absolute silence as he did so. When he was satisfied, he placed the oil-dampened gray cloth on top of the Ruger, closed the trays, lowered the lid of the box, and secured the two snap latches.

He turned on the television and tuned in to The Weather Channel, looking for the latest information on the approaching storm. This was the major weather story for the moment, especially since this area was so prone to severe weather. The official hurricane season ended eight weeks ago, but the weather here obeyed few rules. He didn't understand the difference between an El Nino and an El Nina, but he appreciated that the Gulf of Mexico was warmer than normal, and a low pressure system will seek out warm water for fuel. Such storms, even if they never reached hurricane status, could cause severe damage here. The highest land elevation within fifty miles was perhaps fifteen feet above mean high tide, so storms and heavy rains deserved due respect.

The storm was on a meandering track and its ill-defined center was expected to arrive in three days. Downpours were expected to accompany the winds, and a storm surge could occur, possibly extending several miles upriver. He'd heard of storm surges but never experienced one close up. The threat didn't seem to bother the Boca Grande population, though, and he suspected that the people here had the same fatalist approach to their meteorological environment as the Kansans who experienced tornadoes, or the Californians who learned to expect lightning-ignited wildfires and the shiver and shudder of earthquakes as merely a price people pay to live where they wish.

Emilio calculated that his schedule tomorrow would put him back at Boca Grande by sundown tomorrow. That meant the storm's center would still be a day away, with some advance rough seas beginning tomorrow night. He would be far enough up river to avoid the worst of it.

He switched channels to the local news. Nothing remarkable beyond the usual pap. One report showed clean up crews working in the areas surrounding Raymond James Stadium in Tampa in the aftermath of the Super Bowl; "A world record in the annals of trash," the reporter said. Another news item told of the upcoming storm. "Unusual, for this time of year," the forecaster said, "but nothing close to hurricane strength."

One news item did catch his attention. A video of Alek Mironev stepping out of a limousine and entering the stadium was a backdrop for the report that the son of the Russian President was enjoying his visit to the United States longer than anyone expected. There were rumors that Alek and a companion (no mention of the gender, but the viewers could imagine a pert maiden) were spending a few quiet and private extra days, perhaps in New Orleans. "Channel Two will keep you informed," ended the smiling reporter with a wink, herself apparently of barely legal age and sporting a scooped neckline with more than a teasing splash of cleavage. How could she know,

Emilio mused with a curled grin, that it was the pedophile Mr. Finney whose image was being replayed, and that the real Mr. Mironev was actually caged like an animal not thirty miles from the station's broadcasting headquarters?

Alek Mironev, not for the first time, wondered what evil he could have done in his short life to deserve this treatment. Chained at the ankle to steel bars, bottles of water and a cooler of food stowed in one corner, a lidded pail for his urine and feces stowed in the other. The only air movement coming from a slowly spinning ceiling fan suspended above the cage; the only light from the edges of the window shades and two bare light bulbs in the ceiling fixtures.

In truth, the food was passable. The sandwiches were fresh and varied, and even he could appreciate that they were planned and prepared with some care. He had plenty of water and enough fresh apples, oranges and bananas to feed an entire circus. He was not certain how he arrived here, but he did recall the events with great clarity the days before his arrival at the Sarasota airport. He closed his eyes and leaned back against the bars of his cage as he recounted the series of episodes that landed him here.

Even for Alek Mironev who was accustomed to the special treatment that attends those on society's A-list, a trip across the Atlantic on Planet Capital's Gulfstream 200 was a thrill. He had come to expect first class accommodations, to be sure, and limo service from his flat in Mayfair to Heathrow was part of that package. But now, he was soaring nearly seven miles above the western Atlantic with a glass of 15-year-old Balvenie at his right, and the only other passenger, a lovely young lass from Penrith who served as the flight attendant, at his left. In another ninety minutes, they'd reach Sarasota International Airport where another limo would whisk him to his hotel, the opulent Don Cesar at St. Petersburg Beach, where he'd be ushered into his suite. Later this evening, a private reception would be held by Planet Capital at the Salvador Dali Museum on the St. Petersburg Pier where he'd have the opportunity to shake hands with movie stars, corporate moguls, and some current and former superstar athletes. The wine would be the finest and the hors d'oeuvres would be delectable. This was the Thursday before the Super Bowl and the parties promised to be lavish and plentiful.

Alek finished his drink and began to nod off. In his reverie, he was a youngster leaping across the stones of a brook near the dacha where his parents arranged a secluded home for summer holiday. His father was a rising star in Russian politics, one of those rare individuals who could engage both sides of acrimonious debate and reach consensus. It was that talent that led to his ascension to Foreign Minister, and later to President of the Russian Federation.

Alek's mother disdained the attention of the press and the public requirements of her husband's office, and even in this dream she worked diligently to preserve her privacy and that of her family. She much preferred her life before her husband's political career when her holidays were spent on the streets of Sorrento or a hillside in Provence, ignored by the press and left alone to read, to take family snapshots and to bathe in the Med. Alek, though, reveled in the attention of those who perched on rooftops waiting for that one photogenic moment that would end up on the front pages of the tabloids. His younger sister, like his mother, avoided the limelight. Well, he thought, good enough for them, but I'll enjoy these grand moments while I can.

He felt a nudge at his elbow and heard the flight attendant (was her name Candice? Caitlin?) suggest that he fasten his seat belt. "We'll be on the ground shortly, Mr. Mironev," she told him in a seductive voice. Pure fantasy material, he thought as he sat upright, snapped the clasp, and watched her rump sway as she made her way forward to her jump seat. Too bad she was headed to New York immediately after refueling, he'd enjoy a bit of a romp with her.

Keira Wilkins slipped the harness over her shoulders and snapped the buckle to the waist belt, fully prepared for landing. She glanced out the porthole window absently, purposefully avoiding eye contact with Alek Mironev. She could feel his eyes on her, had in fact become accustomed to feeling the eyes of men rove over her face and form. She knew she was attractive and knew how to play the game.

Alek Mironev, she knew by reputation, was living life in the fast lane, enjoying this period of fame, however reflected from his father it was, for however long it lasted. He wasn't the most attractive man she'd run into since taking this position with Planet Capital, but he did have a fun way about him, a sense of humor, a reasonable degree of intelligence, and the certain cachet of being the bachelor son of a world leader. But Keira also sensed that Alek Mironev would be lost in a few years when his father became tired of the leadership responsibility, or the nation grew tired of him. Alek was, after all, more than a bit shallow with no shred of introspection she could discern in the conversations they shared in the past few hours. For Alek Mironev, life was good right now, and the way he spoke of the Super Bowl this coming weekend and the special invitation he'd received from Planet Capital, he appeared to believe that people presented such invitations because of his charm, wit and importance. Once his father was just another formerly important person, unless there was a sea change in his attitude Alek would only then begin to wonder why the special treatment ceased, that his desirability derived from something he did not merit. The world was full of old politicians whose titles and relative importance outlived their utility.

Keira was born to a family of shopkeepers, and she could not remember any extended period in her childhood where the lack of money did not intrude upon the household. There was no royal blood, no fancy political connections, no significant wealth that rubbed up against the Wilkins clan. Whatever modest pleasures were derived by her family were earned by diligence and constant worry about the rent, the taxes and the increasing costs of doing business. Alek Mironev had no idea.

She smiled to herself at the thought of young Alek Mironev ending up in the labor pool. She knew in her soul that the privilege he enjoyed would not vanish entirely after his father's service to the country ended; he'd likely land on his feet and cleanly in a job he didn't deserve, in some position better suited to someone without the name and connections Alek had. But she stoked the thought of his depleted worth to the world of available women and lush accommodations. Having to stay in a three-star hotel one day would be such a fall for the boy, she just might hear the thud no matter where she happened to be in the world.

Now, alone, confined and reeking of stale sweat, Alek Mironev stood and gazed at the ceiling fan as it spun slowly and blew puffs of air across the space. He contemplated the minutes after his plane landed and rolled to a stop near the general aviation terminal. He recalled that a mobile stairway was placed against the door of his plane, and he walked down the steps to the tarmac and through the open doorway where someone, a uniformed woman, awaited his arrival. She turned out to be a US Customs Agent who greeted Mironev with a warm smile, a portable fingerprint reader, a scanner, and the words, "Just a formality sir. I need to take a fingerprint with this and may I see your passport?"

The approval was instant and he replaced his passport in his jacket pocket. There was no checking through his luggage, no prying questions from Customs officials; Alek fairly inhaled the VIP treatment. The Customs Agent directed him to a doorway to the terminal building where a gentleman built like a tall concrete pillar and dressed in gray slacks, white shirt, silver tie and navy blazer welcomed him with a firm handshake. "This way, Mr. Mironev." On the jacket of his blazer, Alek read the three lines on his name badge: R. Henderson—Planet Capital—Security.

When the Mironev family travelled to foreign countries as a group, the security arrangements were heavy on armed personnel and armored vehicles. Today, travelling alone, Alek Mironev had only scant security, and R. Henderson turned out to be part of a three-member team providing private duty protection and hired by Planet Capital. He was hustled down a private hallway and told something about a waiting vehicle at curbside. That's when the young blonde woman appeared, walking across the end of the hallway, in somewhat of a rush, and spilling the contents of her purse, lipstick, credit cards and coins scattering in every direction. His automatic response was to offer assistance, but his escort grabbed him stiffly by the elbow and tried to steer Alek around the commotion. He shook the much larger man off with a brisk move and was kneeling at the feet of the lovely young waif and gathering her things. Chivalry, he said under his breath, was very much alive. Besides, he thought, she's lovely and flustered and needs help right now. Tiny as a bird, "Tinkerbell" to his "Peter Pan."

"I'm so sorry . . ."

Alek remembered her first words and recalled the tears streaming down her cheeks, porcelain cheeks needing little make-up and eyes whose irises were splattered with silver flecks that called out to him with gratitude. He continued picking up her things and paused to note her name on a credit card. It was rude, impetuous, prying. A perfectly wonderful way to find out her name.

"Please, let me help you, Miss Zakayev." He smiled the smile that appeared on magazine covers, the one with the curi-

ous, endearing wrinkle, accompanied by the almost imperceptible squint. A young Cary Grant, it had been said. And just as
gallant.

Miss Zakayev, Miss Vanya Zakayev, was sobbing, short of
hysteria, trying with some clumsiness and limited success to
stuff everything back into her purse as fast as he handed it to
her. His security escort was impatient, scanning the few people
who traversed the terminal's main hall, the identity of the new
arrival not yet registering on the faces of the passers-by. Most
of them were either businessmen hustling to some important
engagement, or private pilots, more concerned with their pre-
flight checklists than some stumbling young woman and the
young man who was helping her.

Alek stood up and touched the young woman's arm to
steady her. "Please, take a moment to relax. Everything's all
right now."

"I am so grateful," she said, this time in her native Russian.
"Thank you. I just need to sit down for a moment."

"I understand," he said, responding as well in his native
tongue, looking in the vicinity for a convenient seat and finding
none. His security man was plainly irked by this delay and
made his displeasure known with a smirk. Alek was accustomed to privilege and disregarded the look.

"Over here," she said, "there's a powder room." She took
his hand and motioned to a ladies' room a short distance away.
Alek started to blush but followed, turning back only to motion to the security guard. It was a curt wave of the hand, a
small chop that meant, "Wait for me here." The guard shrugged
his shoulders, took a step back, leaned against the wall and removed a walkie-talkie from his back pocket. Among the last
clear memories of Alek Mironev was of the guard speaking into
the microphone, probably telling his colleagues in the limousine that there would be a moment's delay.

Alek remembered the young woman opening the door to

the ladies' room and motioning with a girlish smile for Alek to follow. Her expression was half plea, half mischief, and he fell for it like a stone off a cliff. He stepped in. The ladies' room was brightly lit and she turned to him in a grateful embrace. He met her lips with his and she tasted of ambrosia. Welcome to the USA, he thought. A small pin prick on the side of his neck . . . he couldn't be sure . . . and everything began to go to deep shadow and move at a slow pace. He knew he was fading, unsure if this was death or some temporary state, and all went black. No pain. No memory.

Alek Mironev considered the sequence repeatedly in the past few days. He knew he was the subject of a kidnapping but unsure of the reasons why. A captor visited him, whoever he was, from time to time. There would be plenty of food, some refreshments, and some fruit. His bucket would be emptied and washed out. There were always fresh towels, a wash basin and a pitcher of water. The man appeared clad in a ski mask, but he was taller than average and moved with grace. Alek heard the man's voice only in small bursts. Nothing to identify, nothing he could use to help capture the man when he was eventually released.

Eventual release, he felt certain, was assured. He was unharmed, well fed, and supplied with a few magazines to help him pass the time. He was not in pain and never felt threatened by his captor.

A political kidnapping, that was Alek's conclusion, and he should have expected this at some point. Somewhere, his father was being targeted and Alek was the bait. At least he hoped this was true.

Wherever he was, the weather was mild. He'd heard no rain on the roof of the house, saw blades of sunshine at the edge of the shaded windows. He guessed he was still in Florida, but had no idea where. His captor referred to the poisonous snakes in the area, most likely a cautionary tale to make Alek think twice before plotting an escape. Not that the thick bars of his cage would bend or break. Escape was not an option.

He could hear the occasional sound of a passing boat motor from his place of captivity, and the loudest always signaled the arrival of his captor. He might be confined to an island. He heard nothing else beyond a few bird sounds, the flapping of wings, the chirping.

Alek never considered himself a patient human being, and his friends even described him as impetuous. He was, in truth, annoyed by delays and detested just hanging around and waiting. For at least four days, perhaps more, he'd been confined here. He couldn't be sure of the exact timing; he recognized he was drugged and groggy for some period before he fully awoke and realized his predicament. But this solitude did afford him a wealth of time for introspection. He didn't take to it quickly or well, and only after the first forty-eight hours did he feel he must resign himself to isolation and idleness.

He wondered about the young woman. An actress of some sort, a lure whose purpose was clear to him now. She spoke perfect Russian. Whoever plotted this had done their homework. Pretty, young, blonde, small . . . these were all designed to fit the profile and Alek bit on the attractive bait. Putting her in some sort of trouble . . . the dropped purse was a clever idea . . . was just perfect.

She had a Russian name. He tried to remember but things became a bit clouded. Sasha? Svetlana? He wasn't sure. She could not have weighed seven stone soaking wet. A tight body, lithe, muscled. Light eyes with flashes of silver, smallish breasts, a scant bum. *That* he could remember.

Then blackness.

SEVEN

Emilio received no telephone call this evening. That fact was not welcomed, but neither did it surprise him. Even if the appropriate contact was made with Nikolai Mironev by the Chechen rebels, an instant response would be unlikely. Emilio just did not want this scheme prolonged more than necessary. Alek Mironev might be safe and secure, and his location could be kept secret, but Emilio recognized that time was his enemy. Brevity was good; delay was bad. No good could come from keeping Alek Mironev locked up beyond a minimum amount of time. He would speak with Vanya tomorrow to reinforce this point. Because she would be working in concert with the same exiled Chechens who hired him, she would have little direct influence on moving the plan along, but she could make contact and enforce the same sense of urgency on them that he felt here.

He prepared for bed and resolved to speak with Vanya early in the day tomorrow as she drove him to the marina on the Peace River to meet Jay Finney. His head rested on the pillow, he closed his eyes, and then recalled the initial meeting that he arranged between Vanya Zakayev and Jay Finney. Was it just two weeks ago?

In truth it was thirteen days ago that Vanya Zakayev was at her Sarasota apartment twisted up like a pretzel when her cell phone rang. She straightened out in an instant, grabbed the phone and checked caller ID. It was Emilio, and she was pleased that he finally called and punched the 'talk' button at once. Time was running short and she wanted to spend some time with her new and as yet unseen colleague, Jay Finney. Emilio promised he'd be introducing him to her soon.

"Yes?"

"Emilio. I'm coming over in twenty minutes with Jay Finney. We'll do a walk through, OK? Are you ready?"

This was what she was waiting for and waiting was not her strength. "Bring him over. I am ready. My question: Is he?"

Vanya knew her role and had practiced her lines and her movements; she felt supreme confidence in her ability to accomplish her objectives. Now would come the matter of coordinating her movements with someone else.

Coordinating movements. That is what being a trapeze artist is all about, she thought. In her circus act, every move was timed so that her release from the bar would occur at a precise moment. She would hear the silence of the crowd beneath her, their breath held tight as she soared and tumbled through the air. Her catcher would time his movements to be in the exact location to grab her wrists and swing in unison. Planning, preparation and timing. That was her life.

But this new man, this partner, had not seen the location where Emilio's scheme would play out. He had not been twisted up for as long as several hours, suddenly having to move with speed and agility. If the plan was to succeed, every move had to be choreographed, and she was wary of such an unproven companion's ability to perform under pressure.

She went about her small apartment and picked up some stray glassware and saucers. She'd been living alone since she left home at seventeen and understood that the first impression ought to be the best impression. Once, after she invited someone, a fellow acrobat from the same circus, to come with her back to her tiny apartment in Moscow, she was horrified when she opened the door and found the dirty breakfast dishes she neglected to clean and put away hours earlier. She could not forget the bad impression she made on her new friend, even though no mention was ever made. It was enough that Vanya was ashamed; it was enough that Vanya was unprepared; it was enough that Vanya never let a lack of preparation ever infect her again.

When she answered the door and saw Emilio, she did not at once see 'Mr. Mironev' who was standing behind him in the hallway. When Emilio smiled at her and then walked inside, she lost her breath when she saw her new colleague for the very first time. "My God," she said into her hands which she'd raised to her lips. "He's incredible."

"On the contrary, Vanya, he is extremely credible. That's the point, isn't it?"

Jay Finney, aka Alek Mironev walked up to her and took her hand, gently, gentlemanly, and put her fingers to his lips.

"Enchantée," he said as held her hand. "A pleasure to meet you, Miss Zakayev."

It was Vanya who was enchanted, not in a hedonistic way, not that she wanted to bed the young man, but she could hardly have expected such a twin of the man she'd been studying on video. The similarities were astonishing. He was perfect. Slim, a charming off-center smile. If there was some flaw in his appearance, she could not see it.

Emilio had slipped his jacket off and draped it over the back of the sofa. "I trust, Vanya, that you approve of our new Mr. Mironev, if your gasp was any indication."

"Beautiful. Just perfect." She shook her head as if to clear it. "Can I get either of you a beverage? Tea? Coffee? Diet soda?"

"Let's just sit down and review the plans for a bit, shall we? We can take a break in fifteen minutes, if that's OK."

He waited for an objection and hearing none said, "OK. Jay, take a seat over there. Let's look at the book and we'll get oriented." Emilio opened a three-ring binder inside which was a set of tabs separating four sections. The first was 'Physical Layout' and Emilio opened to the first page.

"This is a photograph of the ladies' room entrance at Sarasota-Bradenton International Airport. Vanya, you are familiar with this airport, but Jay, you are not. The word 'International' may be part of its name, but it is a small airport that serves medium duty planes for the most part. The gate reserved for international travel is B-8." He pointed to the airport map. "In most instances, passengers would exit the plane onto the terminal's upper level and walk down this hallway. But the Planet Capital jet carrying Mr. Mironev will arrive on the opposite end of the terminal building over here." He used a pencil to indicate a point on the opposite side of the terminal building. "This area is used for VIP arrivals, and our target certainly qualifies. He will exit the plane and be greeted by someone from US Customs, a formality to be sure, and then through this entry door. Right here in this entryway is where our young Mr. Mironev will meet the young lady in distress. A few feet away is the restroom." Emilio watched Vanya Zakayev and Jay Finney follow his pencil. They were nodding.

"Vanya, you have seen this area before and are familiar with it. Jay, I will be bringing you into the restroom in advance. Just be aware of the surroundings."

He turned the page of his notebook. "This next one shows three views of the same room. As you can see, there are three stalls and three wash basins. The acoustic ceiling panels are in two-by-four-foot removable sections. The single solid door on the side is a closet for janitorial use and it is kept locked at all times. I have a master key for it. Approximately two and one half hours before the Planet Capital jet arrives, I will deliver a blue barrel labeled 'janitorial cleaning solution' and leave it inside the closet. Jay, you will be inside the barrel."

"Is the Planet Capital jet still scheduled for early afternoon?" Vanya wanted to know.

Emilio nodded. "The entire episode has to be completed in ninety seconds. When Vanya leads Mr. Mironev into the restroom and injects him with the sedative, the effects will be instantaneous. He will fade quickly and lose consciousness entirely within fifteen seconds."

Jay interjected, "What if there is someone else using the restroom at the time? How will that be handled?"

"Good question, Jay, but this is a low traffic area of the terminal and that is unlikely. If there is someone else, though, Vanya will know because she will be in the area before the plane arrives."

Vanya picked up the explanation. "I can stall Mr. Mironev for a few moments if necessary, but I will still lead him into the restroom. I will have to engage him for a few moments, which I can certainly accomplish. That is where acting comes in."

Jay gave a knowing nod. He understood that Vanya could engage any man. He continued, "When Vanya knocks on the barrel twice, then once, I'll be out of the barrel and open the door. Is that right?"

Emilio shook his head. "She will knock on the door, not the barrel. The barrel will be inside the closet. You will hear her knock twice on the door, then once. You will climb out of the barrel and open the door. Meanwhile, Vanya will bring the unconscious Alek Mironev into this stall." He pointed to indicate the stall at the far wall and nearest the closet door. You will enter the stall, remove the clothing from Mr. Mironev and work quickly to get dressed in them. Vanya will stay outside the stall in case another woman happens to step inside. You will tap once on the door, lightly, when you are fully clothed. Vanya will place Mironev in a sling and hoist him into the ceiling space."

Vanya interrupted to say, "Don't forget to replace the lid on the barrel, Mr. Finney. And I hope you're doing plenty of stretching exercises," Vanya added, "for you will be called upon to move quickly and smoothly on a moment's notice. Being twisted inside a barrel for hours doesn't lend itself to this."

"Every day, four times a day. I do the regimen that Emilio gave me."

She responded quickly. "The same regimen I gave him to give to you. We can't afford untimely cramping."

Emilio cut in. "You've got only seconds to get reassembled in cramped quarters. Vanya will take care of getting Mr. Mironev positioned and then hoisted into position."

"By herself?"

"I work on the trapeze, Mr. Finney, and when I catch my 120-pound partner, flying through the air at speed, it's like lifting 250 pounds. By comparison, Mr. Mironev will be easy. Besides, I will be using a pulley system that reduces the required exertion by 75 percent. It is already in place."

Emilio added, "I placed the pulley system in the ceiling cavity three days ago. It is ready to go."

Jay turned to Emilio and asked, "So you've opted against placing Mironev in the same barrel I will be vacating?"

"Mironev will be unconscious, but his limbs will be stiff for several minutes after the injection. People respond differently to fast-acting sedation. I'm afraid he cannot be forced into the barrel without risking a broken bone or two. One hour after you leave the restroom and are on your way with the Planet

Capital security team to your hotel, I will retrieve Mr. Mironev from the ceiling. By then, he will still be unconscious, but his limbs will be sufficiently flexible to get him inside the barrel without harming him."

Vanya added in Jay's direction, "Emilio will leave a ceiling panel askew so I can reach up and retrieve the ropes and pulleys. I can raise him and place the ceiling panel in less than 35 seconds."

Jay had another question for Emilio. "How will you have access to the ladies' room to drop the barrel off and then pick up Mr. Mironev?"

Emilio smiled. "Another good question, I will be just another janitorial supply contractor dropping off cleaning materials. In disguise, of course. A simple plastic cone in front of the doorway will keep the room free for me to gain access and complete my task."

Emilio turned the page. "Now, let's just go over the likely personalities, shall we? Planet Capital has a private luxury suite for the Super Bowl, one of one hundred sixty-five suites that will be filled with VIP fans at the Super Bowl. The view to the field from each suite is enclosed in glass, but the windows are retractable. Unless the weather is horrid, they will be wide open for the Super Bowl. Each suite has a private bar and restrooms. The suites are accessible only by special elevators." He pointed to a series of photographs. "These are shots of the interior of the suite that will be used by Planet Capital, the company that invited Alek Mironev as its special guest."

In silence, Vanya Zakayev and Jay Finney studied the array. "How many people will there be in the suite?" Vanya was looking at the photographs that showed plush sofas and chairs.

"Normally twelve to fifteen, but for this event, probably twenty five. This larger furniture you see in the photograph will be replaced by smaller furniture to accommodate the number of people. Of course, you will not be anywhere to be seen,

Vanya. Once your episode is concluded at the airport, you will not be seen by anyone associated with Planet Capital."

Vanya hoped that Jay was as good an actor as she in this regard. Over a period of several days, Jay Finney would be Alek Mironev. He would mingle at the advance cocktail parties and rub shoulders with Planet Capital's special guests in the luxury suite.

Emilio turned the page to the next section. It was marked "Attendees" and the first page had wallet sized photos of the executives of Planet Capital. "I took these from the firm's latest annual report. I can't be certain that everyone here will be at the game, but most of them will, some with their wives. Or perhaps their mistresses."

The next page had four more photos. "These are some of Planet's most important clients. These are people who will definitely attend. The first two are pension fund managers for two enormous labor unions. The bottom two are individual clients. Big investors. The fat man on the left is Robert Lee Kennert, 'Bobby-Lee' to his friends. He owns a trucking company in Arkansas and has two hundred million dollars invested with Planet."

Said Jay, "Look at all the rolls of fat on that man. Two hundred million ought to buy him a good lipo."

"Actually, he also controls a family trust and the trust has another one hundred million invested with Planet. Hence his importance to our friends at Planet Capital and the primo seats."

Emilio pointed to the second photo. "This ferret-faced fellow here is Domenic Palatino, who inherited his mother's cold cut company and made a deal with the mob about twenty years ago."

"Cold cut?" Vanya had not heard the term before.

"Salami, pastrami, meats you'll find in delicatessens. He has a decent product and a clever advertising mind. The mob gives him the necessary distribution channels, along with a strong sense of market control. Stores that don't do business with Palatino's company usually find themselves in various states of distress, all of which comes to an end when they sign a contract with his firm. He has a tidy three hundred million stashed with Planet plus, I'm sure, many more millions in some offshore banks."

Vanya asked, "Is he here because of his invested capital or because his associates twisted some arms?"

"I suspect both. I don't know and I don't really care. Look at the next page."

Jay interrupted. "I am assuming that all of these clients and all the Planet Capital executives have been scrutinized by all security."

It was another good question and showed some surprising depth. Emilio said, "They have all been through a fairly rigorous process of background checks, and they will all undergo a thorough screening for weapons and the like when they enter the stadium."

"No special consideration then for the ultra wealthy."

"None. There are too many important people at this event. Secret Service and FBI will be out in force. At this stadium, they will also use facial recognition software on every person that enters the event. Cameras are located at every entry point and every face will be scanned, digitized, and matched against an enormous database of criminals, terrorists and other unsavory types. They can do instant checks on every single person without anyone really knowing." He turned the page.

"Do I have anything to worry about?"

Vanya scoffed, "I can't imagine that you won't be recognized as Alek Mironev. I still can't get over the likeness."

Emilio continued. "You'll be attending two pre-game parties and these same people will be there, along with various celebrities. You'll be expected to have your picture taken with many people, even the rotund Mr. Bobby-Lee Kennert. Make your appearances, smile. A little British charm will do wonders. Your security detail from Planet Capital will be at your elbow and watching everyone around you, and if you exhibit any discomfort, a quick nod will get you moved away to someone else and a different conversation. Now, let's take a break."

When they were standing on the deck of the apartment and sipping their ice waters, Emilio said, "Until the switch, I'll want both of you to stay close to home. Vanya, you will stay inside your apartment. Jay, you'll be staying indoors for the next few days at your rental. I'll pick you up in the van the morning Alek Mironev is scheduled to arrive." Emilio left them on the balcony and went to use the restroom.

Jay waited until Emilio was out of earshot. "He's a strange man."

"He is that. But he's very good at his work. Very thorough."

"The little gaps. He seems to go into a trance on occasion. Do you notice that?"

Vanya didn't enjoy discussing the personal affairs of others, but she responded, "I call them his 'shoe lace moments'. He'll be lacing a shoe and just drop out. For a moment. Ten seconds, maybe twelve. He always comes back. It is nothing."

"Strange. He has me on a short string, I'll say that. I like to go fishing on my odd hours, but he's got me studying videos of Alek Mironev, watching tapes, reading celebrity mags. Sometimes, I feel like I actually *am* Alek Mironev."

Vanya was studying Jay Finney's face, looking for any weaknesses and finding none. "You had to undergo some surgery for this job."

"Minor, really, and it's reversible. The dental work, however, that's rather permanent."

"I am on vacation from the circus for the next five weeks,

but I have to stay in good physical condition at all times, so this preparation was not really so bad."

"So, you swing from a trapeze. That's what you do for a living?"

She took a sip and looked at Jay Finney, holding his attention with her eyes. "No, I make people hold their breath." She saw a haze of puzzlement cross Jay's brow. "Anyone can swing on a trapeze. But when I let go of the bar and do a double flip ... in those few moments when I'm tumbling in the air, high above the audience, and before I grab the other bar ... that's when people hold their breath, That's what I do for a living."

Jay started to go back into the living room to continue their preparations when he said, "I hope this scheme works the way it's supposed to."

She put her hand on his arm and held him back for just a moment. He turned back to face her. "Do not doubt, Mr. Finney. There are many people counting on us. It will be flawless."

She held him in her stare for three extra beats before she released his arm and they walked back in for the balance of their review of Emilio's plan. For Jay Finney, whose only contact with the plan so far was with Emilio, her seriousness of purpose was not unexpected. Emilio had described Vanya as Chechen by birth, patriot by upbringing, resister by nature and Russian émigré by necessity. To Emilio and Jay, this was a job for which they'd be compensated. For Vanya, Jay could see this was personal.

EIGHT

"Teach me about guns."

Vanya was ever able to shock. If she had a subtle bone in her body, Emilio had yet to find it. Beautiful, intelligent, athletic, committed. But never subtle. He found often that the best response to Vanya's outbursts was to challenge her and divert her attention. She was usually instantly reactive and he hoped he could do this again.

"You are prepared?" Emilio knew the answer before he asked it. Of course she was prepared. Emilio had secured the rope and pulley system above the dropped ceiling of the ladies' room at the Sarasota International Airport and Vanya had been training with an identical system of ropes and pulleys. She'd conducted trial runs with Jay until she was satisfied that he could do what was needed when the moment arrived: Secure the limp form of Alek Mironev in the pulleys, hoist him into the ceiling space, and replace the ceiling panels to conceal their work. Everything was set and ready to go as soon as the wheels of the Planet Capital jet touched ground.

The stare that Vanya gave Emilio let him know that she was

not pleased with the question, and he could see in the depth of her silver-blue eyes a ferocity that he hadn't yet recognized to such an extent. This young woman, waif-like in size, was a powerful force, all sinew and muscle, who could do enormous physical harm to any foe; she was also fierce in her loyalties to her Chechen brethren and their plight. The combination was intense.

"I am bored. Waiting does nothing for my personality."

"I can see that. You think learning about firearms would help?"

"I want you to show me how to handle a weapon. Teach me."

He tried once again to shift her focus. Give her something else to fight about.

"How will you capture the attention of Mr. Mironev?"

"We've been over this a hundred times. You're stalling and we have several days to keep practicing. I will do so, but I will not practice sixteen hours every day. Mr. Mironev does not arrive for another eight days. Jay is doing fine work in practice. Besides, when he wants to take a break, he goes fishing. For me, fishing is like . . . like watching one of those four hour Swedish films in black and white where nothing happens. Teach me about guns,"

And he did. Starting with a small rifle.

Finding a place to practice was not difficult in south Florida, especially in a Jeep equipped for off-road use. Emilio chose a location well inland and northwest of Lake Okeechobee. He left the main road and they lurched and bounced three miles until Emilio stopped the Jeep and turned it off. Every afternoon for two hours, Emilio worked on developing Vanya's skills with weapons. He had two rifles at his disposal and took only one with him for Vanya's initial training. The .22 was light weight, easy to break down into components, and fairly simple for a novice to manage.

As Vanya treated every challenge in her life, she approached the .22 with attentiveness and tenacity. She was a wonderful student, and she mastered the safety issues at once. Emilio appreciated the lethal nature of even small arms and practiced weapons safety at every step. He'd seen too many cowboys shoot a toe off, or take their skills for granted with fatal results.

Sighting the .22 was straightforward and the Thompson/Center system was a good introduction for a novice: line up the rifle on the target using the front and rear sights and fire. Emilio marveled at Vanya's breathing, the methodical way she controlled her respiration to maintain laser focus and perfect calm. She wanted to see the weapon taken apart and reassembled, memorizing the name of each part as the process continued. After her first rounds, when she hit her target with remarkable accuracy, Emilio noted no joy on Vanya's face, no lightening of mood. Only a cool mechanical authority, for to Vanya, shooting was not sport; firing a weapon was business. Even as he resolved to bring his more complex, more powerful Blaser Professional .30 caliber on their next outing, he wondered if he was looking at his successor, a lovely, cruel legacy to a world where contract crime was simply part of the complicated arrangement of gears and springs that kept the planet spinning on its axis. If in one fashion, he looked on Vanya as his potential heir, in another, he took no pleasure at the thought.

He did bring his Blaser the next time; she mastered it with a calm and concentrated effort. As she fired, reloaded, and fired again, Emilio gained not just a greater respect for Vanya's weapons skills, but a deeper appreciation of the frightful serenity, the absolute chill that travelled from the base of his spine to the top of his neck as he watched her perform. She had impressed him from the start with her ability to accomplish a change from icy princess, resolute in her intentions to secure some measure of justice for Chechnya and vengeance upon the Russian Federation, to coy ingénue and fresh-faced lovely whose charge was to seduce Alek Mironev into a position with her clean good looks and shy smile.

There was some level of pride for Emilio in observing the achievements of Vanya Zakayev as sharpshooter, his own Annie Oakley. There was also a cold shiver at watching this young woman's passion nourished by the steel, copper and lead she held in her hands.

He himself had never shared that same enthusiasm. To him, weapons were tools, worthy of respect but not the devotion that Vanya seemed to impart to them. He wondered if her quest for justice for her Chechen kin was the driving force behind her ardor, but concluded that there was much more to her infatuation with firearms. Hers was a fury unbound by simple reasons like anger or vengeance. In Vanya's eyes of crystal blue, he saw the aperture to a beast inside, a ferocity that raged in pain and sought expression.

The Blaser was to her like a musical instrument, and she the impresario. She was raised a child of the circus and relished the applause of an adoring, awestruck crowd at her spectacular leaps and flips. Perhaps, Emilio mused, she is growing indifferent to their tribute, numb to the clapping and expressions of amazement. With rifle poised, breathing measured, round fired, Emilio could witness the wonderment and fearlessness that celebrated loudly in her soul. Vanya's delight at smacking bullets into bull's eyes and smelling the wisps of cordite was as satisfying as a standing ovation.

On the return trip to Vanya's apartment in Sarasota, weapons stowed and locked in the rear of the Jeep, they were silent until Emilio turned into the parking lot. She did not exit right away but turned in her seat to face him.

"How do people contact you?"

A simple question.

"The people who wish to hire me know how to reach me."

The answer did not satisfy. "Is it by reputation alone that you are sought?"

"My reputation and their needs meet somewhere in the middle. The road to their needs is complex and built on reasons I do not try to understand. My reputation was built on small experiences and those grew into larger tasks. I did well enough, apparently, to receive a sufficient number of assignments over the years."

Vanya seemed to digest that. He saw puzzlement and added, "Eventually, the arcs of my clients' needs and my abilities cross somewhere and they find me."

She considered that and said, "This kind of work, this contract work that you do, I think it becomes me."

"Why do you say that?"

"It provides one with freedom, with excitement. I can only imagine the amount of your fee. I enjoy all of those things."

"Enjoyment? Such an odd word to describe the killing of human beings."

"But you have done that, and you are very good at it."

"I do it, yes. But I do not ever enjoy it. There is a big difference, Vanya."

She was silent for some time and Emilio could see that Vanya was ruminating. She turned back to face him when she was ready.

"Is it not a job? I have a job now. It takes hours of practice every day until my muscles ache. I have fallen many times, sometimes from great heights. Every job has its unpleasant aspects, no?"

Emilio did not answer right away. When he did, he did so with a question. "What drives you to think that killing another human being is an 'unpleasant aspect'?"

"Ah, you are a man with regrets. A man who likes to think he has a soul. I have met men like you. So brutal one moment, so tender the next." She put her hand on his. "Emilio, have you ever seen what another human being looks like when they are tortured? Have you ever seen that?"

He looked down at her hand, not appreciating the closeness with the young woman. She was stunning to the senses and Emilio would forgive himself the passing fantasy, but her fingers were like ice.

He answered her. "I have seen my share of pain and death, but the process is generally not prolonged. No, Vanya, I cannot say that I have seen real torture. I am guessing that you, on the other hand, have seen the results. Your cousins?"

"My cousin Majdy was my age. As children, when we visited Grozny, Majdy and I would leave the others and go exploring on our own. We would hike to the hills outside the city and climb trees. Believe me when I tell you that I was very, very good at climbing trees, but Majdy was just as good, and even more daring. From our perches, we could see for many miles in every direction and Majdy would tell me of his dreams.

"Majdy wanted to become a doctor. He'd read one time about Les Medicins sans Frontieres, Doctors without Borders, and he wanted to complete his training and join that group.

"Then, when my older cousins were brought in for interrogation . . . I believe they were seen in the same café as a Chechen rebel, and that was enough to bring him in . . . the Russians beat them with leather straps, then used electric wires to burn them in their privates. Perhaps they had some information about the rebels, but that is doubtful. Aadil was a teacher of languages in a grammar school, and Durrah was a cabinet maker. But they eventually died. Drowned in their own vomit. That's when the Russians searched for Majdy as well. It was Majdy's body that I saw. His eyes were gone, Emilio. They were removed with a knife and left on a table. The skin from his knees down was burned off, and I learned later that they made him stand in a tub of water while they added acid.

"So yes, to me, there could be unpleasant aspects of a job,

and yes I could deal with them. Would I derive pleasure from killing a person? I don't know." Vanya's eyes traveled somewhere else for a moment and she shook her head. "No, that is not true, for there are a few people, a very few, whose deaths I would thoroughly enjoy presiding over. But genuine pleasure when completing such an assignment? No, and I believe I am being truthful here, by the way. I understand that careers such as yours are being filled, and often by people who are as dumb as a sack full of hammers. I love that American expression, don't you? But it is true. They make a mess of the job, they are caught, and they implicate their employers. This will be your last assignment, or so you have said. If that is true, there will be room in the world for someone capable, confident and careful, and I am such a person. I ask you these questions for that reason."

Emilio absorbed her words and gained a greater understanding of the depth of this young woman, and the dangers that her zealotry could bring her way if she did in fact follow the same career path as he. He wondered what advice he could give and recalled the words of an old and dear friend, though not in the same profession by any means. The man was a member of the Carbanieri in his home town, a man whose job put him in proximity with the violently dead and those who killed them. He shared his words with Vanya. "Those who fight monsters must work diligently to be sure they do not become one."

She faced forward, hand poised on the door handle and considered his words in silence. She turned the latch, cracked the door open and turned back to Emilio. "Thank you." In a moment, she was gone and Emilio watched her bounce along the sidewalk like a carefree sprite towards her apartment door.

In the ensuing days, Vanya studied the Blaser and everything about it. The weapon was heavier and its recoil stronger than the .22 she trained on, and she learned to relax her shoulder to absorb the pressure. With the Leupold scope, she reveled in the astonishing accuracy from ever greater distances. Emilio marveled at her facility, her absolute oneness with the weapon.

Vanya wanted more practice with the Blaser than Emilio could provide. With some reluctance, Emilio let Vanya keep the Blaser in the trunk of her small sedan, along with two full boxes of shells. He also gave her a supply of paper bull's eye targets. "Out here, in the wild. Just targets, no animals, no tin cans." She nodded agreement, her face solemn. Inside, she was bursting with delight.

She folded the paper targets and slipped them in Blaser's gun case. As she zipped up the case she said, "I have given some more thought to our last conversation."

"About?"

"Killing. Enjoyment. I do not have a great education, but I do know how to pay attention. I watch you and how you conduct yourself. This business we are doing now, that is not who you are, Emilio, or whatever your real name is. You play the classics, like Beethoven and Bach while you drive, and you disappear into the music. You talk to me about opera, and your eyes tell me how emotional you are on that subject. You have seen the great ballets. You appreciate good wine and good food. Those are the things you treasure, and they tell me who you are. This work, this *assignment*, is only a way for you to afford to do the things you enjoy."

Emilio had his head cocked, listening to Vanya's words.

"Mr. Finney is a pedophile, and you surely took that into consideration when you made your plans. Please trust me, Emilio, when I tell you that such lessons are not lost on me."

Emilio smiled, as expansive a smile as Vanya had seen on the man. He put his hand on her shoulder and gave it a squeeze, then bussed her forehead with a kiss. "Piccolo angelo," he said with unusual tenderness.

NINE

*O*n the shores of the Peace River
Jay Finney wore a fishing vest and a broad grin. In spite of the thickening clouds and threats of a storm, he was anxious to go fishing. He was leaning against the fender of his rented sedan when the yellow Jeep pulled onto the shell driveway of Peace River Anglers. He waved to the driver, the lovely Vanya, who returned the gesture, but her face carried no smile this morning. Emilio Fortino stepped out of the passenger side and retrieved his fishing gear from the back seat.

Vanya whispered a good luck to Emilio before she drove off. They carried their rods, reels and tackle boxes down the road toward the boat rental office. Emilio was the first to speak. He nodded to a small red sedan parked near the marina building. "Is that the vehicle you rented in the name of Peter Billings?"

"I have to say, mate, with the quality of your documents, the ID never raised an eyebrow."

Emilio stiffened at the word, "mate", but Finney was correct. Emilio did have access to the finest document forger in the business. The man, who worked his trade in the basement of his home in Amsterdam, had served him well for years.

A crude painted sign announced the entrance to the marina office. Finney leaned his pole against the wall of the building and set his tackle box on the ground. "Are you coming into the office with me?"

"I'll bring the gear to the boat. I'm sure the marina owner is expecting you."

While Jay Finney, aka Peter Billings, filled out the rental paperwork and made the payment arrangements, Emilio carried the gear along the dock to a white flats boat that was tied off, about fifty feet along the walkway. Not precisely "flat", the boat was a shallow draft craft that could maneuver in so-called "skinny" water of just eight or ten inches in depth. Taped to the windshield was a plain piece of paper with "Billings" printed by hand in black marker. It was the only boat in the water, all the dozen or so others having been pulled out and stowed along the broad terrain in front of the office. They were all securely tied with heavy ropes and thick chain to a trio of heavy posts. Yellow kayaks were stacked like cordwood and lashed to stakes pounded into the ground. Clearly, the owner of Peace River Anglers was preparing for the coming storm. The Billings rental would be the last of the day, and no rentals were expected the next day.

Emilio stepped on board and placed the rods in the aft-most rod holding tubes. It was a center console arrangement with a fiberglass platform erected over the outboard engine. He placed the tackle boxes on the deck against the transom and looked back at the rental office. There was no sign of Finney, and Emilio opened his tackle box and took another look at the Ruger, nestled in the bottom compartment. It was ready for duty.

Emilio understood water, in spite of his aversion to sport

fishing. He spent the earliest years of his life in Portofino on the Ligurian coast. There, he learned about boats, the sea, and the raw beauty of deep water. This shallow water of the Peace River had its own stark beauty, but it was slow moving and meandering and it lacked the salty aroma of the Mediterranean that he recognized as home. In Portofino, there were no flats boats or light weight fishing gear. To Emilio, today's expedition in this setting was alien and he was only present to perform a single task.

Yesterday, when Emilio suggested a day of fishing, Finney used the opportunity to deliver a quick lesson in the art of angling, especially in Florida's shallow water. The instruction was pure boredom to Emilio but he did pay a bit of attention. "A silver spoon with a treble hook, Emilio," Finney advised. "That's what you want to use here."

"Whatever," Emilio muttered to himself. He thought he had one of those lures in his kit and he fumbled around to find it. It was hiding under a small yellow lure with some sort of white feather fastened to its tail. Emilio wondered: Did fish actually mistake these things for food? Are they so blind? The chrome spoon was still in its cellophane package. He removed it, careful not to stab himself with the three razor-sharp hooks and held it in his left hand, pinching the spoon. With his right hand, he took the end of the line on his fishing rod and held the clip of the leader open.

He slipped the clip on to the hole of the spoon and missed. This is worse than threading a sewing needle, he considered, cursing under his breath, "Vaffanculo". He knew that he had to continue the ruse of pleasure angling for an hour or so before he accomplished what he set out to do. He looked over his shoulder and saw Jay walking out of the rental office with the marina owner. Finney looked absolutely buoyant. Emilio pulled the bill of his cap down a bit more and made one more effort to slip the fastening clip on the spoon.

On his fifth attempt, he was close to success and needed to wiggle the lure just one fraction of a millimeter to pass the filament through the aperture. Jay stepped on board and the boat rocked back and forth. The spoon went one way and the line another. To keep himself from falling overboard, Emilio grabbed for the low rail of the boat. The spoon landed . . . where? Emilio went to his knees and looked in every direction as he simultaneously bellowed, "Merda!"

Finney turned red in the face and the marina owner's was turning white. Finney understood his error but was unprepared for Emilio's angry reaction.

The owner of Peace River Anglers, a small wiry man with leathered skin, tried his hand at cooling off Emilio. "Sir, it was a simple mistake. He said he was sorry."

"I'll give you another one," Finney said in an effort to mollify Emilio. "They're cheap!"

Emilio grit his teeth and continued to grumble, struggling to maintain composure. Relax, be methodical, he told himself. Look for the lure later on.

"Really, it's no problem."

Emilio let the tension flow down his arms and out his fingertips. He counted silently to ten.

The marina owner went through the rental drill as he did with every customer. "Your boat is due back here at five-thirty. It's extra if you stay out longer than that. Watch the weather. You've got a radio in the console preset to channel sixteen, but there are other weather channels marked on the dial. If you see lightning, don't wait for things to get worse; just get back here right away. In any case, make sure the boat is back by five-thirty. I want to get this boat out of the water and tied up before dark."

The owner put the keys in the ignition. The engine cranked and came to life.

The marina owner raised his voice over the rumble of the

motor. "You've got a full tank of fuel and there's plenty of oil in the reservoir. There's ice in the live well and there's a laminated chart in the console. Remember, you're drawing about ten inches of water with both of you on board and a full tank of fuel. That's important to know out here."

Peace River Anglers was six miles up Florida's Peace River. To the south, the river widened until it spilled into Charlotte Harbor and the Gulf of Mexico. To the north, it wandered across low-lying terrain into central Florida. The river was sandy-bottomed and dotted with small islands, a haven for shallow water fish. When the boat reached the middle of the river, Finney looked at the depth finder and saw three feet of water. He moved the wheel to the right pointed the nose of the boat down river. Emilio barked, "Turn upstream, Jay."

"But there's more water to the south, and the fishing's sure to be better."

"I checked with a fishing guide last night, and he tells me there are loads of bass and snook up river. That's what I'd like to look for. So please, let's head in the other direction. If we find nothing, then we can head back down."

Finney began to reverse direction, not wishing to incite another outburst from Emilio. He pointed the bow of the flats boat to the northeast, against his better judgment as a fisherman, and they motored slowly up river, keeping the motor at just above idle. The vegetation at the shoreline was rich and thick with leaves from the drooping mangroves and the stooping bald cypress that waded up to their gnarled knees in the stream bed. Vines climbed the limbs of taller trees, the pines and oaks, and draped with some grace over the river's surface. The sunlight that made its way through the leaves splashed the surface with flecks of silver and gold. It seemed a sacred place and both Emilio and Jay Finney maintained their silence as they slid past and made their way along.

Ahead and off the starboard bow, a solitary great blue heron stood at the water's edge and watched the boat approach, keeping the craft in steady view as it slid past. Coral beans provided streaks of bright red along the banks and hickories stood further back, stark and not yet in bud for their next season's leaves. A large turtle, oblivious to the boat's arrival, slid into the water and a cormorant sat on a weathered snag and ignored the travelers. A swarm of bees could be seen high in a hollow tree overhead.

"Keep the island to your left, but watch your depth."

"Have you been here before?"

"The fishing guide I met was simply loaded with information. Just stay this course. I'll tell you when to stop."

The spot Emilio had chosen was only three quarters of a mile ahead and he tapped Jay on the shoulder when they approached it. Jay returned the throttle to idle and surveyed the surroundings. "It doesn't look like a bass haven to me, but who knows? I've been wrong before."

"Trout. That's what the man said." To Emilio, "fish" was a pair of cold water filets dusted in flour and sautéed in butter; he had no real interest in the business of locating, capturing, or cleaning the creatures, and he would not know a snook if it walked up and introduced itself.

Jay was precisely the opposite and talk of lures and casting techniques evoked enthusiasm. "Now, snook I can understand. Great eating, too." Jay cut the engine. "We can stop here and drift, if you'd like. If we drift too quickly, I'll drop anchor. Emilio nodded, a forced smile on his lips. They removed their rods from the holders and Emilio watched Jay cast effortlessly into the shallows, whispering that perhaps the best fishing may be up close against the shoreline beneath the twisted branches of the mangroves that lined the shore. There were no houses near the shore, no other boats in the area. Out of sight, several hundred yards from the water's edge, cattle grazed and the occasional low bellow reached out and announced their presence.

Otherwise, the sounds were limited to the flurry of wings from a cluster of snowy egrets passing overhead and the intermittent wind coursing through the branches.

The silence was interrupted by the lonely splash of a leaping fish and a low, distant grunt.

"Hear that, Emilio? That's an alligator. They're all over the place up here."

Emilio already considered that fact when he made plans for this expedition. Planning and scheduling, after all, were Emilio's strengths. There were an estimated one million alligators in the state of Florida, and the upper Peace River was a known native habitat.

"Over there, look." Jay pointed to a stream of bubbles that broke the surface twenty yards away. "That's probably from an alligator that just slipped under the surface."

Emilio nodded and swatted at some unidentified flying insect that brushed his collar. To his dismay, he didn't plan on losing the spoon lure any more than he planned on the sudden onslaught of gnats and mosquitoes that swarmed around them. The spoon might remain missing, but Emilio was gratified that Jay came prepared with bug spray.

"Important part of every angler's kit," he told Emilio as he passed the canister to him. "Don't leave home without it."

Jay saw that Emilio was still fooling with his gear and took a treble hook from his own tackle box. He reached for Emilio's rod and slipped it onto the line with a practiced hand. Emilio was impressed.

Jay returned to casting in the shallows and Emilio let his line sit in the water with no inclination to catch a thing. He was on the alert for other boaters and anglers and saw and heard nothing to indicate that anyone was near. Up river to the northeast, a low island split the meandering Peace. It was dotted with trees and had a small sandy shore edged with mangroves. After a few minutes of silence during which neither felt the slightest nibble, Emilio pointed to the island and said, "There's a spot just like the guide described, Jay."

Jay looked at the island and nodded the knowing nod of an experienced angler. "Looks good, mate. Why don't you raise the outboard a bit and I'll use the trolling motor."

Jay stepped to the front of the boat, swung the narrow shaft of the trolling motor over the rail and tilted the prop into the water. He flipped a switch and the low hum was barely audible. In moments, they were easing slowly towards the island. Emilio pressed a button on the side of the Yamaha to raise the outboard's prop to within a few inches of the water's surface. When they were about twelve feet from shore, Jay asked in almost a whisper, "How's this?"

Emilio responded in the same hushed tone. "Wonderful, Jay. Just wonderful."

Jay smiled, at ease now that Emilio appeared to be over his earlier fit of anger about the lost lure. "I'm going to keep the nose upstream. The breeze is coming from the south and it will push us a bit towards those shallows." He gestured to a spot along the edge of the island where the sea grass broke the surface and mangroves draped over the water, their tangle of roots affording refuge for fish.

Silence took over and they cast their lines. After some moments, Jay said, "So beautiful and quiet on the water. It gives one time to think and relax. Don't you love this?"

Oh yes, Emilio thought. This is just my cup of tea.

Jay had rigged a lure at the end of his line and placed a small cork device with some red beads attached to the sides several inches behind it. "This is a popper. Watch this."

He cast his line gently over the bow with a light flick of his wrist and the lure landed with barely a sound. He began to reel the line back slowly, giving it a light tug occasionally.

"Listen."

Indeed, the device made delicate popping and rattle sounds when he tugged.

"That little noise will attract fish without scaring them off. They'll think there's a shrimp in distress."

Jay repeated the process, focused entirely on the task of trying to hook a trout.

Emilio watched Jay and marveled at the young man's absolute absorption in the act of tossing his line in search of fish. He could not share Jay's excitement but appreciated it nonetheless. Jay was about to meet his maker, and he would do so in a state of near rapture.

Emilio looked at his watch. Approaching noon. It was time. He opened his tackle box and reached into the lower compartment. Without a sound, he slid the modified Ruger from its place and turned towards Jay, keeping the weapon at his right hip and out of sight. He slid the safety off.

"Jay, perhaps you can put one of those poppers on my line." He held his rod out and Jay set his rod into a holder on the starboard bow.

"Certainly, mate." He removed a popper from his tackle box and moved sternward to fasten it onto Emilio's line. Still facing forward, he was four feet away from Emilio and with his back toward him.

Emilio rose slowly from his seat and leaned forward, bringing the Ruger into alignment. No more than five inches behind Jay's left ear, he squeezed the trigger.

The episode was over quickly. Jay sagged, then fell forward. The bullet tumbled within two and a half inches of the penetration point, tearing indiscriminately through tissue, nerves and blood vessels as it scrambled the soft insides of Finney's skull. Finney twitched only once and the wound barely bled. His heart stopped beating almost immediately after the round was fired. The gunshot was barely audible and did not even cause some nearby birds to ruffle their wings. The puff of smoke drifted and dissipated.

Emilio paused and placed the weapon, safety on, inside his belt. He switched on the trolling motor and brought the bow directly onto a length of sand at the island's edge. He felt and heard the hull slide onto the sandy surface of the river bottom. He gripped a dock line and went forward, fixed the line to a cleat on the port bow and stepped out of the flats boat and onto the island. He attached the other end of the line to a branch of a tree and secured it with a half hitch. He might not like fishing, but growing up on the Ligurian coast, he had plenty of experience with boats.

His movements were quick and practiced. Tugging once on the line to make sure it held fast, he reached into the bow and slid his arms under the lifeless body of Jay Finney. He slid Finney's corpse from the boat and dragged it to a spot nearer the small island's midpoint. There, he placed it near a clump of brush and looked around. He wanted the body found by the largest and most efficient predators in the area, the alligators that called this shallow river and these low islands home. He also wanted to make sure there were no such creatures lurking in the immediate vicinity at this moment, and put his hand on his pistol just in case.

Finney's eyes were closed and his mouth open. The facial muscles were relaxed. There was no sign of rictus, no evidence of tension, no indication of pain. He checked Jay's pockets and removed the false driver's license, credit cards and a few bills and coins. Those he stuffed into the pockets of his trousers. Then he used his pocket knife to slice away the clothing from the corpse. He wanted to be certain that the alligators would do their job unencumbered by cotton and polyester. He placed the clothing in the boat and went back to Jay Finney's final resting place. Perfect, he thought. He'd read of the marvelous competence and power of the Alligator mississippiensis as it ripped prey to shreds. One full ton or more of bite strength for a full grown specimen. Finney would be consumed soon, down to every last fingernail. The corpse would never be found and Jay Finney would never be missed.

For the next several minutes, Emilio searched every possible spot on the small boat for his missing lure, coming up empty. If it was on the boat, he thought, it was probably in the bilge. Otherwise, it was somewhere in the shallow waters near the marina. To most people, it was a missing lure of little value; to Emilio, it was evidence.

He scanned the area in every direction and released the lines, shoving off the small beach and climbing in. The water was extremely shallow, no more that a foot, and he untied the Stiffy pole and used it to reach deeper water. With the trolling motor, he eased away from the island and made his way to the midpoint of the channel. He also checked his charts.

Emilio knew that the path of the river, created as it was in some prior age, shifted from time to time, and especially from storm to storm. This was soft, sandy terrain and subject to the regular movement of the tides and the enormous power of the rare hurricane. A channel close to the eastern edge would take him further up the Peace River in the direction of the low overpass where he planned to leave the boat.

He passed to the north side of an island that would keep him out of view of the marina and continued for several minutes before he shut the trolling motor down and turned the gasoline engine on. It came to life on the first turn of the key. He tilted the motor, keeping it trimmed to avoid sand bars and snaring sea grass, and motored along slowly.

He turned on the VHF radio and turned to the weather station. Severe storm warnings were issued for areas one hundred miles south of his current position. Emilio was headed inland, away from the coast, but he expected winds here could reach forty miles per hour or more. Still no hurricane watches or warnings, but this could develop into a significant weather event, especially for this time of year. He took another look at his watch; even at his slow speed, he had plenty of time to meet Vanya for the ride back to Boca Grande.

Fifteen minutes passed before he spotted the low overpass of the county road ahead. He cut the engine to idle and drifted close to shore. The hull glided along the sandy bottom and the boat came to a stop near a tangle of mangroves and low vines. He reached for a stout limb and pulled the craft deeper into the growth. He turned the engine off and with a length of line, secured the boat to the mangroves. His movements were quick and practiced. Some of the heavier vines would be draped over the hull to keep it hidden from view. When he finished, he checked the shallow waters for signs of creatures. He would have to make two trips back and forth from the boat to the shore in the shallows to remove the fishing gear and Finney's clothing, and did not want to end this stage of his plan with a painful bite from a venomous snake or the vicious snap of a hungry gator.

When he finished, Emilio crouched low in the brush near the roadside and waited. His watch told him that Vanya Zakayev would arrive in eight minutes.

The escalating whirr of the whistling wind did nothing to disturb his state. He inhaled deeply and closed his eyes.

Today he fulfilled the repulsive task of slaying another human being. Even acknowledging the personal failings of Jay Finney, the young man's predilections for evil and the certainty that Jay Finney would never again inflict his sick self on another human being, Emilio could only describe the episode as murder. Someone's child, Emilio admitted, was now food for alligators, and there was no way to avoid some stab of regret that he was the cause of another human being's demise. Such was Emilio's internal mystery. Today's was not his first such killing nor his first sting of remorse. It did, however, provide him some sense that this final killing had removed an onerous weight from his shoulders.

Emilio knew some of the famed assassins of the modern era, like Carlos the Jackal (a bungler, he thought, and unworthy of the fame that came his way), and crossed paths with some noted Mafia hit men, like Joseph Barboza (a heartless butcher, he concluded). He shared nothing in common with these monsters. Emilio was never the braggart, never the rogue. If he acknowledged that he did possess the slippery conscience of a pirate, that trait was not yet forgiven.

He once crossed paths with a close friend of Joseph Martorano, a hit man for a Boston mob who confessed to killing twenty people, all for hire, and was later released after serving his prison term; Emilio met the friend of Martorano's at a Boston pub. Martorano's jobs were businesslike, the man claimed, and he did not enjoy a single one. Now, the friend said, that part of his life was over and Martorano wanted only to live out his days in quiet enjoyment. "Joe just wants to keep his head down and get on with his life," this friend said over beers, not realizing that Emilio shared many of Martorano's professional credentials. "He just minds his own business."

Emilio was looking forward to the same thing. No more dangerous schemes, no more convoluted plots, no more finding himself in a position of having to kill another human being. He wanted to spend his time raising plump olives, enjoying fine wines. The thought was calming and entrancing. He was resolute; Jay Finney's was the last death for which he would be directly responsible.

At precisely the appointed time, the yellow Jeep with Vanya at the wheel did appear, and she maneuvered the vehicle onto the shoulder of the road. In seconds, Emilio had the gear stowed in the rear and climbed into the passenger seat. They would be in Boca Grande within ninety minutes.

"Everything is done?"

"As planned."

PART III

Though force can protect in emergency, only justice, fairness, consideration and cooperation can finally lead men to the dawn of eternal peace.
—Dwight D. Eisenhower

Moral excellence comes about as a result of habit. We become just by doing just acts, temperate by doing temperate acts, brave by doing brave acts.
—Aristotle

TEN

Sheriff Lawrence Earl Garrison's turf is that flat swath of south Florida that lay miles beyond the shadows cast by the condominiums that rise like citadels along both coasts, and safely distant from the manicured plots of the gated communities and the artifice of the theme parks. This is old Florida, the flat crusty Florida of limestone scrub and slow moving waters, the Florida that carries cattle and spawns citrus.

For those who command that land, life affords some bounty. A few even live here, but most of those barons live elsewhere and well, enjoying the finer things of life that places like Sarasota or Miami offer.

The area did attract some members of the American middle class, and they could usually be found in the scattered single-family developments and well-tended mobile home parks on the edges of the county.

The single largest portion of Dodge County is that part of the American dream that envelops the lives of the two principle classes that dwell here: the poor and the very poor. Most of the people Sheriff Garrison swore to protect and to serve struggle mightily to pay their meager rents and their modest mortgages and to simply keep their disagreeable jobs. They strive daily with no days off for good behavior to fend off the lurking nightmares of alcoholism, financial ruin, domestic abuse, and untreated illness. They buy lottery tickets and they always lose.

Capitalism, with its reliance on the presumed logic of market forces does not galvanize this segment of Dodge County's population with dreams of wealth or even modest comfort. "The people of Dodge County," in the words of one deputy on Garrison's staff, "are taught from the cradle that capitalism is exactly what they want, and they get it good and hard."

Garrison was elected Sheriff after the previous Sheriff retired unexpectedly eight years ago. The ensuing campaign attracted four candidates. Three of them were local products who'd run unsuccessfully before. Garrison was the only one in the race not born and raised in the area. He did the usual campaigning and made some speeches, but he did so without enthusiasm. When asked at one such affair why he chose to run if he was so disinclined to campaign, he mumbled with a shrug, "Look at the alternatives."

To his one-time lover and to a very few who worked closely with Garrison, he was more expansive in his reasoning. "Most people here don't believe that things will get better. They expect little, and they think their low expectations are deserved and inevitable. Maybe I can do something to change that."

As election day approached, Garrison wondered if his decision to run for office was a wise one. His only prior experience in politics was as an observer. You either liked the candidate or did not. Nevertheless, he did visit most of the homes in the county and asked for votes. It was tiresome, repetitive and enlightening. The poverty he witnessed up close was worse and more pervasive than he encountered daily as a deputy. The racism was insidious, the whites in denial and the blacks in tightly demarcated neighborhoods. A few people, on both sides, were vocal in their resentments, certain that "those people" were criminal in their intentions, ignorant in their behavior, and intransigent in their unwillingness to see the error of their ways. Like a miasma that hovered and obscured the light, it poisoned the air. Trust did not exist nor was it encouraged.

The Hispanics, who were moving into Dodge County quickly and in great numbers, were enigmatic. They worked at jobs that most people rejected for the low pay and long hours. They pooled their money and bought small stores and gas stations, and their ambition was almost alien. They were true entrepreneurs who injected a sense of movement and change in Dodge County. To Larry Garrison, this was welcomed.

With the vote split four ways, Garrison won with thirty-nine percent of the ballots cast, an achievement for which he'd taken considerable criticism in the local press. "Garrison Winner by Default" the paper's headlines read. Its endorsed candidate came in third. So it was not on some overwhelmingly popular wave that Lawrence Garrison rode into office. He, more than anyone, understood what that meant.

Nevertheless, he was bold in the first changes he made upon his swearing in. Some senior people in the office were placed on traffic duty, for example. At first, the general sense was that he was retaliating, and the newspapers said just that. If the reporter had the sense to review the entire duty roster, he would have noted that every schedule included the name of L.E. Garrison doing routine traffic duty at least one shift every two weeks. No one could remember the last time a sitting sheriff had on a regular basis taken a cruiser and patrolled alone for speeders and drunk drivers.

He also posted every opportunity for promotion on the bulletin board and conducted interviews with every one that applied. Gone were the bag jobs where favorites were silently and swiftly advanced through the ranks.

There were other changes when he took over, and they were

generally popular with everyone except the old guard who craved the favoritism and chicanery of the old days. The old guard included several outside the department, those to whom debts were owed, financial and otherwise, or to whom deference was paid, whether earned or not. A few members of the county's small but self-important moneyed class, for example, tried repeatedly to gain special favors with Garrison. When he declined their initial requests and ultimate demands, he was called "not a team player" and labeled a "communist". These people came to learn that Garrison didn't treat them any differently than he treated anyone else; that grated on their beings.

He won reelection with ease, but he still generated a level of discontent among some in the community that went beyond the usual distrust of law officers. Among those who harbored some resentment was Virgil Swett.

Garrison pulled into a gas station and started to gas up his vehicle when he noticed a silver and purple Harley-Davidson Soft Tail parked on the side of the mini-mart. Next to it was a black-on-black Harley Low Rider. If he remembered properly, the silver and purple model was owned by Virgil Swett of the Dodge County Swett clan that owned eight percent of the county's land. Virgil returned to Dodge County only six months ago after a series of supposedly failed ventures in other parts of the county, but his behavior since his return suggested he had inalienable rights to the other 92 percent. Virgil was the youngest male Swett and the heir-apparent to the family's land fortunes. The Swetts were deemed to be land-rich and cash poor, but in Dodge County their name held sway, or at least Virgil acted that way.

Garrison preferred to ignore unsettling thoughts about Virgil Swett. The sun was low in the eastern sky, and thick swirls of gray clouds streaked across the west, the arc of its tail a reminder of the previous evening's storm. The month was February, not the usual season for storms in Florida, but extreme weather always loomed large in the state. For nine months a year, excessive heat and humidity was a way of life, interrupted occasionally by threats, often frighteningly real, of severe storms and hurricanes. In another few weeks, the heat would begin to reappear and rivulets of perspiration would run down his neck, back and chest, staining his khaki uniform in patches. For now, the relatively cool air was a welcome relief and Garrison enjoyed the winter respite.

He had no inclination to wander into Virgil Swett's path this morning and no desire to have Virgil wander into his. Nevertheless, as he held his hand on the gas pump and filled his tank, the door to the mini-mart opened and Garrison heard a flutter of racial remarks flutter across the thick air. The owners were immigrants from Guatemala, a small, dark-skinned cluster of ambition, hope and diligence. Virgil had difficulty achieving any level of common human decency and his voice, distinctive for its high pitch and cracker twang, reached Garrison's ears like an irritating swirl of dust and dirt.

Garrison finished gassing up, replaced the nozzle in the pump and walked to Virgil who was straddling his cycle and adjusting his groin with one hand, a sweating open bottle of Budweiser in the other. If Virgil saw Garrison approach, he gave no indication. He was engaged in conversation with his riding buddy, a bearded and tattooed behemoth whose smile suggested a lack of customary dental hygiene. Whatever remarks Virgil made to his companion, they were apparently a cause of some mirth.

Garrison stopped ten feet away from Virgil and said, "You're not thinking about operating this vehicle while you're holding an open container of alcohol are you, Virgil?"

Virgil Swett was wearing a black bandana over his shaved head, a leather vest over a faded H-D tee, and a pair of torn jeans. He looked up slowly, took a long swallow of beer, and pretended to study Garrison through reflective sunglasses. A toothy smile appeared slowly and Garrison thought of a hyena on the veldt, patient, hunched, ready to pounce on a weaker, perhaps injured victim.

"Well, good morning sheriff. How are you doing this fine morning?"

"Does your mama know that you use language like you just did with the fine people in there?"

"Now, sheriff, I'd suggest you leave my mama out of any conversation with me, but I do believe you are referring to the Mexicanos? Are you sure that new stock boy in there is even legal?"

Garrison could feel his molars grinding against each other and thought red thoughts. In another time, he would not have abided such ill will in another human being, and he would have made it his intention to inflict considerable physical harm. When the spiders reached his head, he knew there would be no avenue on which to return. He was careful to keep his fingers from clenching into fists and resolved at once to rid himself of the burden of Virgil Swett's presence in the dark part of his brain.

"You're not worth it, Virgil," he heard himself say in barely a whisper.

"What? What was that?"

Garrison turned around and walked back to his red Impala. Virgil remained on the cycle, finished his beer and tossed the empty on the ground. He started his Harley, revving the engine to make enough vibration to visibly rattle the windows of the store, nodded politely to Garrison and rode off. Garrison inhaled deeply, cleared his brain of its shadowy notions, and drove in the other direction. He was determined not to allow Virgil Swett to consume what was a beautiful day in Dodge County.

Garrison's vehicle today was not his official, marked SUV but a temporary replacement. His usual Ford Explorer was in the shop, its suspension undergoing extensive repair after eighteen months of tough use on bad roads. So the candy-apple red Chevy Impala SuperSport, confiscated from a drug crime two years ago and used since by his department as an "unmarked" was taking him on a pleasant, leather-wrapped ride to the firing range. He had no idea how much raw horsepower lay under the hood, but the exhaust produced a throaty rumble that predicted enormous strength. On the way to the range, he goosed it more than once, just to feel the force and hear the roar, something he hadn't done in a car since high school.

Walter sat in the passenger seat, his nose at the window, smearing saliva and shedding stiff brindle hairs as he struggled to maintain his balance on the smooth seat and his view of the outside world. Walter was a blend of setter, retriever, shepherd and something else that no one could accurately identify. The result was a shortish, shaggy, flop-eared friend that complained rarely and followed Garrison with a combination of blind loyalty and faith, certain that his bowls would be filled with food and water, prepared to grasp and shake the pants leg of anyone who gave the appearance of a threat against his master. During Garrison's brief encounter with Virgil Swett, he'd been sitting erect on the passenger seat, ears cocked, poised to scramble through the gap of the half-rolled-down window if he felt the need. Walter had as little regard for Virgil Swett as his master did. The threat now past, Walter was ready for whatever came next, his nose sucking the outside air.

Garrison signaled for a left turn onto an unmarked straight shell road. When he turned, he shifted into low gear and kept his speed under ten miles per hour. The rain washed the road into a series of deep ruts and rills and the car's springs complained more than once at the treatment. Ahead and parked on the side was a white sheriff's department sedan, marked with the standard green side stripe and county seal and with a row of red and blue lights across the roof. Three uniformed deputies stood outside, each of them holding clear plastic bottles of water. Garrison pulled up behind them and stepped out. Walter bounded from his seat and greeted the three men, his tail wagging and his tongue lolling. One of them leaned down and scratched Walter behind the ears.

"Mornin' gentlemen. We ready?"

The three nodded and they all walked along a path that had a chain blocking the entry of any vehicles, a crude wooden sign reading: "Caution: Weapons Range". Two of the deputies walked ahead and one, Rupert Zell, lagged behind to walk with Garrison and Walter.

"One of the rookies asked if we could take our shooting practice indoors during the summer. Seems his cousin is a deputy in Miami-Dade and they have an indoor range."

"What did you tell him, Rupert?"

"That when we could stop people from committing crimes in hot weather, we'll take our practice indoors."

"Good answer."

"That red Chevy is something else, isn't she?"

"Beautiful." Garrison watched a hawk swooping low over the adjacent field. "Me and Walter, we're liking it a lot."

"It'll reach a hundred twenty five without breakin' a sweat."

"I wouldn't know, Rupert. Would you?" Garrison squinted, following the hawk, the sun strong through his dark glasses.

"I read it on the Internet."

"Uh huh."

Rupert Zell was a local product, barely graduated from high school, who applied for a job as a deputy shortly after Garrison won election as Sheriff. Rupert was married to Betsy Zell, nee Cluff, who never made it past sophomore year in high school. Betsy was bright and good-hearted, but together they were resigned to living a life just above the poverty line. They had two children, and the four of them lived in a rented shotgun house near the end of a dirt road. No one in the house or in the group's extended family had much in the way of expectations.

Something in Rupert's behavior and work ethic caught Garrison's attention and after six months on the job, he was called into Garrison's office. When he sat down, Garrison asked, "Rupert, what do you want to be doing in ten years?"

The question took Rupert by surprise.

"I guess I'd like to be a deputy here, Sheriff."

"Not interested in anything else?"

"I like my job, I guess." He fidgeted in his seat and his skin felt flushed.

Garrison studied the young deputy with a mixture of pathos and pride. Here was an ingénue with perhaps seven teeth and as many tattoos, smarter than he believed he was, and without a single air of machismo that was such a bothersome trait in so many individuals who wore a badge and carried a sidearm.

"Ever think about taking a law enforcement course? Maybe at night? Or even on line?"

"For what? I went through a training program already."

"That was the basic program for recruits. I'm looking at a course here on forensics over at USF in Tampa. You know, things like fingerprinting, crime scene security, basic DNA. What do you think?"

Rupert shifted in his seat. "I've never been to college, Sheriff. I don't know. Besides, we already have a detective here."

"You're right. And he does a good job. But we have to look at the future, Rupert, and I think you might make a fine detective one day. Even if you didn't get that job, you'd be a better deputy after taking the course. And as for college, I'm thinking you could do that someday, too."

"Sheriff, I barely got through high school."

The high school principal mentioned as much to Garrison when he responded to the Sheriff's request for a recommendation.

"That was years ago when you were young and stupid and irresponsible. Am I right?"

"On all counts, Sheriff." Rupert smiled at his own youthful failings.

"Well, you think about this and we'll talk about this again soon. The course starts at the end of next month. Here, take the outline and think it over."

That years-old conversation replayed in Garrison's mind from time to time, and for some reason stayed with him this morning at the weapons range. The Sheriff and the group of deputies finished at the range in thirty minutes, all four paper reports in Garrison's shirt pocket. When he started the engine of his temporary ride and the resonant rumble of the exhaust captured the attention and envy of the deputies when he drove off, Garrison studied the clouds in the sky and mused at their shapes as he did as a child. Was that the trunk of a trumpeting elephant? The spouting of a massive whale? Fourteen minutes later, including time for a quick stop at the Dunkin Donuts drive through, he and Walter arrived at the department's head-quarters and walked through the door.

"Look, I can take a preliminary report, but I still need to send a deputy out to your place."

Tawanda Bradford's fingers flew over the keyboard as she spoke to the caller, the telephone cradled in the crook of her neck. This was a stolen boat call from the Peace River Anglers and the caller was more than just a bit upset. He wanted some-one to find his boat now! The storm had passed by the previous evening. The air was calm, but the water was still rising and there was a threat of a storm surge. He was so busy getting his marina property secure that he didn't have time to rattle on about all the minor details. His boat was stolen; find it, bring it back, and shoot the bastards who took it! Case closed.

"I'm sorry, sir. It doesn't work that way. I'm going to send out a bulletin to our officers and we're going to notify all the other jurisdictions that border Charlotte Harbor, but we can't just send a patrol boat out now to look for your boat."

Garrison was walking across the hallway with two cups of coffee on the way to his office when he overheard Tawanda's half of the conversation. Walter stayed close to his heels. Garrison walked behind Tawanda and looked at the computer screen to see what the call was about. He jotted a note and handed it to her. She read it without taking the phone from her ear.

"Why, sir, here's what I'm going to do. I'm going to contact Sheriff Garrison himself at his private number and tell him to get out to your place right away. Yes, I know there was a storm . . . No sir . . . I'm going to make sure of it . . . and if he doesn't get there by . . ." she glanced over to Garrison who signaled to her . . . "ten o'clock sharp, then you just call me back and let me know. Yes sir. No problem, sir. Tawanda Bradford, sir. Happy to be of service, sir. Good bye."

Garrison handed her a take-out cup of Dunkin's coffee.

"Black and hot?"

"Just like you, Tawanda."

"That kind of talk is going to cost you big time in my upcoming sexual harassment suit."

"Wait until I tell the judge the raunchy joke you told me yesterday. My ears are still blistered. Lord."

"How come you're so interested in a missing boat? You've got Rupert Zell in that area today and he can stop by." She held her arms out in the direction of the dog that walked over and proceeded to lick first her hands and then her face. "Walter, Walter, it's so good to see you. Just don't slip me the tongue."

"Scratch his ears and he'll follow you anywhere."

"I'll go check out this missing boat report and maybe stop by the repair garage and see how they're making out on my Explorer while I'm out there. They've had it for four days and I'd kind of like it back before I retire. Contact Rupert and ask him to meet me at the marina in forty-five minutes."

Tawanda made a note to do so and asked, "By the way, is my record still intact?"

Tawanda was a crack shot and established a department pistol shooting record when she was an active deputy. She won several inter-department pistol competitions and her record had not been approached since she left active duty.

"It's still safe, Tawanda. In fact, there are some barn doors in this county that are just as safe because most of us can't hit the broad side of one."

Tawanda knew this wasn't true, that the deputies in general were excellent marksmen, especially Rupert Zell, but she enjoyed holding on to the record anyway. If Garrison had concerns about anyone in the department, it was about his own deteriorating accuracy. Never the most reliable at the range, he at least could be relied upon to hold his own. Lately and with increasing frequency, he found his bullet holes falling wide of the mark. Age, he thought, was relentless and taking its toll.

Garrison turned and started walking to his office when he stopped and turned around. "Tawanda, what do you know about Virgil Swett that I don't already know?"

"That depends. I'm guessing you know he's a surly bastard and takes some perverse pleasure in engaging in bar fights." Garrison nodded at that assessment. "Odd thing is," Tawanda continued, "he wasn't really a bad kid growing up. There were plenty of trouble makers around here, but he wasn't one of them."

"What happened?"

"Good question. He went off to college somewhere and I never saw him until he came back here a few months ago. He joined the Marines and maybe he got screwed up there. Who knows what happens to people whose lives get twisted somewhere along the way? I'll run a background check if you want."

"I was just wondering." Garrison went to his office and sat behind his desk, flipping through a small stack of pink phone messages. He stretched and restretched his fingers a few times as he read the notes, trying to get rid of the numbness in his joints that he woke up with. Walter followed and turned in a circle three times before he found a spot to lie down. Nothing urgent in Garrison's messages this morning except for one call from a county commissioner, the new one on the board who wanted to cut every expense, real and imagined, in a county that was among the poorest in the entire state. He set that call aside for now.

Another message was from the Emergency Operations Director. The subject line on the message said "Storm." This call he'd return right away.

The conversation was brief and to the point. The threatened storm skirted the coast and winds in Dodge County peaked at only thirty-seven miles per hour. Reports of fallen limbs and maybe some downed wires were likely to come in during the day. "The biggest problem might come from the river. The storm surge was expected to be anywhere from three to seven feet. Seven is too high, but three or four seems likely. I know you keep your emergency boats high and dry and ready to go in case we have some problems along the basin, but a lot of people don't. You'll probably get some calls about some street flooding and a few boats that left their trailers because they weren't tied down. I'm sure that'll happen."

Garrison took note of the advice and made sure Tawanda alerted everyone on the road to watch for storm damage, especially tree limbs bringing down power lines and localized road flooding. Then he headed for the door.

"C'mon, Walter. Let's you and me go do something, even if it's wrong."

ELEVEN

The Peace River flows southwest through the middle of Dodge County and into Charlotte Harbor. Originally called the "Black-eyed Peas River" by natives because of their abundance along its banks, the name evolved first into the "Pease" before it morphed into its more tranquil and marketable form sometime in the past century. History showed the river to be anything but peaceful, especially in the cowboy days of the nineteenth and early twentieth centuries. Dodge County sat in the path of the cattle drives from central Florida to the southwest coast where the animals would be shipped on barges from Punta Rassa or Punta Gorda. During the Civil War, the cattle supplied Confederate soldiers with food. If you wanted the excitement of a gun fight, or wished to witness the lynching of a passel of cattle rustlers, sometimes three at a time, you'd come to the rugged and violent communities of Dodge County that lined the Peace River. After the cowboy days were gone and cattle made their way to the feedlots on trains, the lynchings didn't stop immediately. Most of the victims were poor blacks, accused of anything from looking at a white woman the wrong way to refusing to move off a sidewalk to let some white folk pass. It was rough, tough and altogether an unpleasant place to live and raise children.

Time had its effect on the area, and the rustlers and the lynchings were just a faint memory in the fading minds of a few old timers and a source of amnesia in the minds of others. Today, Dodge County is citrus country and cattle raising country, and Mexican food country, wild hog country and fishing country. It is still poor, increasingly Hispanic, possesses a high drop-out rate, and holds a fair-sized annual rodeo that draws an abundance of tourists for a few days every spring.

Garrison and others note the monochromatic aspect of Dodge County during the rodeo days. To those who come here for the rodeo or just drive through on their way to someplace else, Dodge County gives the appearance of being populated largely by long-booted, tall-hatted redneck cowboys, all of them white, all of them drinking cold beers from long-neck bottles. They and their cowgirls dress in pastel shirts with pearlized buttons for the duration. Even the motorcycle riders stayed away, although they return in the hours following the last rodeo event to reassert their claim as the roughest element in the county.

Garrison was in his third term as sheriff and wondered often at the wisdom of his decision to settle here and seek the office. He enjoyed most of the people he worked with and saw through some major positive changes in the way the office operated. His deputies were now better paid and better trained, and most of them were engaged in some form of continuing education. Rupert Zell was a good example. Three years ago, he finished work on an associate degree at the community college and was taking courses at night and on-line for his Bachelor's degree.

There were remnants of the old days, to be sure, but Garrison contented himself with the hope that they were the last of their breed and that their deaths would bring about changes that education and good example could not.

As Garrison pulled into the yard of the Peace River Anglers, he saw Rupert's vehicle already present and pulled off to the side. Rupert exited his sedan and greeted Garrison with a nod. Garrison told Walter to stay in his vehicle and relax.

"Twice in the same day, Sheriff. Tawanda tells me a boat was stolen from here."

"Rented and never returned. Let's check it out."

The owner of the boat yard was in his office. All of the boats and kayaks were already stowed on dry land and secured by ropes to trees. He had copies of everything related to the rented boat in front of him and handed the papers to Garrison.

"It's not a brand new boat but I just rebuilt the engine and it's in great shape."

"It says here the renter was Peter Billings. Can you give us a description?"

"Medium height, maybe five-foot-ten, about a hundred sixty pounds, maybe a little more. Dark hair and a light beard. Wore a fishing vest."

"Nothing unusual?"

"He didn't say much, but I'd guess he was from England. He said a few things that just sounded like he was English or maybe Australian. I can't be sure. And the other guy with him, I'd say he was American, but he spoke a bunch of languages."

"There were two of them?"

"The other one was older, maybe in his fifties but in pretty good shape. Tall guy. He stayed outside and put their gear on board. When this Billings guy and I came out to the boat and Billings stepped on board, this fellow dropped something, a lure of some kind, and he let loose with a cuss word in Eye-talian."

"How could you tell? Do you speak the language?"

"I was in the Navy for twenty-two years and I heard just about every cuss word there is, and in just about every language. I'll tell you this guy had the accent on the right syllable."

Rupert asked a question: "He dropped a lure and he got that upset?"

"He must have been threading his lure onto the line. The boat rocked a little and he dropped it. That set him off."

"Must have been an expensive lure." Rupert knew about all things fishing and Garrison let him handle this line of questioning.

"I never saw the thing, but Billings, he told him it was just a little spoon and he had plenty of extras."

"So did the guy settle down?"

"Not at all, at least not right away. He was on his hands and knees looking all over the place and cursing. You'd think he just dropped a diamond ring instead of a little spoon lure."

"What about their vehicle?"

"That's the car this Billings fellow came in. The other guy showed up in yellow Jeep. A pretty young blond dropped him off and drove away.

Rupert turned to Garrison and asked, "Do you want me to check inside for a registration?"

Garrison nodded and Rupert went to his car to retrieve a Slim Jim from his trunk. He unlocked the car in seconds and slipped on a pair of gloves to open the door and check the glove compartment.

"Nothing. Not a single piece of paper in this thing. I'll run the numbers."

Garrison turned back to the owner of the marina who was still fuming over the loss of his boat but intrigued that there might be more to this episode than just a stolen boat.

"We'll tow the car, OK? Maybe there's something there that could help us. I'll have a tow truck here later today."

Rupert walked back over with a sheet of paper in his hands. "Plates come back as a rental. The renter is a Peter L. Billings with a Tallahassee address."

There were a few other questions and they left the marina owner somewhat comforted that every effort would be made to find his lost boat. Meanwhile, they suggested, he should call his insurance company.

"Insurance? Since Hurricane Charley ripped through here, I can't get any insurance on these boats. I never even filed a claim, but they doubled my rates the next year and cancelled me the year after that. Insurance companies are Class A bastards in my book. I'll just call my accountant; if the boat never turns up, I'll take this as casualty loss."

"Good idea. And that part about the insurance companies, I agree with you."

Garrison and Zell said their farewells and made their way to their cars. Garrison said, "Call for a tow truck but schedule it so you're here when it arrives. We don't know what's happened to the boat or this guy, Billings, so treat it as a crime scene, preserve all the prints you can, that sort of thing, and I'll have Tawanda check out this guy Billings from Tallahassee."

Garrison wondered if there were not two fishermen stranded somewhere on the river or maybe even in the upper part of Charlotte Harbor. Worse, there could be two victims floating around. "I'll ask her to call the Coast Guard and Charlotte County while she's at it. See if there are any stranded or abandoned boats showing up."

Before leaving the marina, Garrison walked over to his Deputy's patrol car while Rupert called the towing service. The call was completed and Zell said, "Twenty minutes. I'll just wait here if that's OK." Rupert made a note on a pad attached to a clipboard.

"Sure, Rupert. One more thing: I want to talk to you about

something." Rupert stopped writing and looked back to Garrison.

"You might have heard this around the department already, but Bud Murphy is retiring the first of May."

Rupert grinned, and Garrison was pleased, as he always was, to see Rupert's toothy smile, implants, crowns and all. "That sort of news travels fast on the underground network." Garrison understood, for rumors made the rounds quickly when he was a deputy as well.

"That means there's going to be an opening at Captain, and I want you to consider putting your name in. No guarantees, because there'll be some competition, but I'd like you to think about it."

Rupert tended to be fairly reserved, but his expression went from broad smile to round open-mouth gape, to raised-eyebrow surprise and finally back to a smile in under six seconds. "I never thought I'd be in the running, Sheriff. But sure, I will put my name in. Thank you."

Garrison put his hand on Rupert's shoulder. "I want you to talk to your wife first before you commit to anything. It means keeping some irregular hours and more responsibilities."

"I will Sheriff, I will. Thanks"

Rupert turned and walked to his vehicle again, this time with a lighter step.

TWELVE

The storm winds that passed offshore and by the latitude of Dodge County stalled off the coast and just to the north, closer to Sarasota, St. Petersburg and Tampa. The Gulf of Mexico was still churning and most pleasure boats, large and small, remained tied to their docks or well out of harm's way. A cruise ship from Tampa and destined for Cozumel had already returned to port to wait out the rough seas. For Floridians accustomed to the ferocious confirmation of nature's power, this storm was a non-event, a source of some occasional downpours and some fronds whipping from the trunks of stately palms. People here tended to understand the rage that accompanies a concentrated area of low pressure, and were grateful but unobsessive about the relative gentility of this weather event. The wind was impressive and the waters white-topped, but the consequent storm surge would be mild and few accommodations would be required.

Fifteen miles east of the Gulf's shoreline, on a small island in the middle of the upper reaches of the Peace River, a seven-foot bull alligator pushed its way out of the wind-whipped water and up the sandy banks. He was attracted to the island by a swirl of turkey vultures and the unmistakable scent of flesh carried over the stiff winds.

The waters of the river were churning now and the mangroves were bending at their knees as the bull lumbered along through the brush in search of the source of the fetid aroma. His feet felt purchase on the sandy bottom and he climbed from the waters up the bank that opened to a clearing. As he moved forward, his nostrils gave him direction. Four blackish-brown turkey vultures hissed and grunted at the disturbance but backed away from the approaching gator. Only one, a larger male, flapped its wings in a six-foot span in a futile effort to establish its rights and discourage the intruder. In spite of their appearance, the gator recognized, vultures are generally non-aggressive and he met no resistance as he approached his objective uninterrupted. A swollen carcass greeted him at the center of the clearing.

The vultures had not been at their task for long, so the alligator still had the intact corpse to himself. He stopped at the foot of the body and glanced left and right. The vultures were gone now, their objections effectively overruled. But the young bull had been interrupted once before by an older and larger bull and that episode nearly cost him his life. Since then, he checked twice before starting to feast.

He didn't take long to survey the carcass and determine its appropriateness as a meal, or even a series of meals. In one loud snap of his jaws, he crushed the right foot and took one more chomp to sever the foot and ankle from the lower leg. He extended his neck and swallowed, then returned for another crunching bite upon the lower leg. The bone was thicker and tougher and the gator took several more crushing and ripping bites before he could tear the limb just below the knee. Again he stretched his neck and swallowed.

This find would take some time to consume and, to the alligator, older and riper was better. Besides, the bull wanted to enjoy his meal in peace and tranquility and could do so only if he could place it somewhere, hide it from other hungry flesh eaters. Almost gently, the bull gripped the remaining foot and dragged the carcass to the edge of the island and into shallow water protected by a thicket. He checked in every direction to make sure that the meal was sufficiently hidden from view. Then, he chopped off the remaining foot in a single bite and swallowed once more. His stomach full from eating considerable sections of flesh and bone, he slid further into the water at the edge of the island only a few feet from this new found prize and slept, his snout protruding from the surface.

The winds continued to course along the Peace River and through the thick vegetation of the islands. Weaker limbs had snapped and splashed into the river the night before when the winds were stronger. On an adjacent island, thick with snowy egrets, the birds huddled in close proximity and held on tight. As the storm continued on its northward trek and the winds along the river began to diminish, the waters started to swell. Some of the lower islands were already fully covered with water and the higher ones were shrinking. The surface remained white capped and choppy.

From another nearby island, five adult alligators, all much older and larger than the seven footer that continued to stand guard over its carrion, swam close by on their way further up river. Their shallow havens where they alternately hunted and rested were inundated and they sought some refuge in one of the quieter creeks that appeared along the Peace River. One paused as if to test the air, turning its attention momentarily in the direction of the rotting corpse and the smaller, younger bull that rested close to the shore watching the passing parade. The young bull considered standing its ground and mounting a stalwart defense if the fearsome larger bull chose to invade his territory, but thought better of it. He reluctantly abandoned his meal and swam out to join the others on the trek up river to more peaceful waters. He'd try to remember, if his tiny brain could do so, where it left his prize when the waters calmed down later on and receded.

Garrison returned to his office and monitored post-storm developments while he stayed in contact with his road units. Only a handful of downed tree limbs caused anything close to serious problems and the utility companies were notified. There were a few isolated problems with flooded property and he dispatched two units to help with evacuations. Compared to a hurricane, this storm was barely a nuisance and Garrison was glad of it.

On a trip to the men's room, he grabbed a newspaper and took it with him. This was a habit he'd had since he was a child and he saw no reason to stop now. When he sat down on the throne, he snapped the paper open to the editorial pages. There was usually some column of interest there and some of the opinions expressed here were directed at, usually against, some branch of law enforcement. Someone felt mistreated during a speeding stop, or expressed outrage at a surprise DUI checkpoint.

The editorial today dealt with the president's recent commutation of a jail sentence for a former crony. The crony was found guilty of four felonies by a jury and sentenced to thirty months in a federal prison, but the president nevertheless saw fit to keep this fine man from the perils of the American penal system. The paper supported the president's decision, but Garrison couldn't help but think that this was one more example of the 'rich white guy provision' of the law; had the criminal been named Jamaal, no such commutation would be expected, offered or granted. Jamaal would have spent six months in jail for jaywalking. Thirty-six months if he jaywalked while he smoked a doobie. God bless America!

Locally, not much was happening to warrant expressions of unfairness, and Garrison tended to believe that no news was good news. Garrison was browsing the sports page when the men's room door opened up and he heard a deputy's voice call, "Chief, Tawanda wants to talk to you about a stolen boat. She said it was found."

Garrison's escape was effectively dashed and he finished, washed his hands quickly and returned to his office where Tawanda stood waiting.

"The boat turned up?"

"Three young boys found it up river, tied off in the mangroves. One of them told his mother about it and she called here. Rupert is on his way to check it out, but it sounds exactly like the boat that was reported stolen."

"How far from the marina is it?"

"About three miles and near the back road that crosses the river."

"Any damage to the boat?"

"No idea. Rupert will look it over, verify the numbers and call in. If it's intact, do you want me to call the marina? The owner will probably be glad to tow it back."

"Hold off. Let's take a good look at it before we do anything."

"It's your call. Let me know."

Tawanda was about to leave Garrison's office when she placed another message on the desk. "You'll want to take a look it this, too." Then she was turned to leave.

"Another message?" he asked?

"This one needs your personal attention." She was gone.

He looked at the name on the message: Ab Swett, oldest living member of the Swett clan and grandfather of the notoriously ill-behaved Virgil Swett. The message included a phone number and read, "Call or stop by when you can." It didn't sound like a command, but the Swett name had enough clout in Dodge County that it grabbed attention. Garrison never met the man but the reputation of Ab Swett was the subject of local lore. As such, the rumors were likely to be largely false, but they were most certainly more negative than positive.

THIRTEEN

Garrison drove the seven miles from his office to the low overpass on River Road and found Rupert Zell and another deputy trudging through the thick brush on the side of the road. "What do you think, Rupert? Is it the missing boat from Peace River Marina?"

"The registration numbers match. I'm getting my evidence kit from the trunk. You may want to look at something."

Together they struggled through the growth back to the shore where the white flats boat was tied off to the sturdy branches of a mangrove. After they pushed their way through the growth and climbed on board the craft, Rupert said, "We bailed some water out but it's still pretty wet. But look at this." He pointed to the knots on the lines that secured the boat.

Garrison looked closely and asked Rupert, "I give up. What am I supposed to see here?"

"Whoever tied this off knew something about knots. A real sailor tied these. Neat and tight. This one is a Carrick Bend joining the two lines together."

Garrison looked at the knot and then at Rupert. "I wouldn't know a Carrick Bend from a ball of yarn, Rupert."

"It's an old sailor's knot and unusual to see around here. Someone with a lot of experience did this. And that other knot is two half hitches. It's more common, but this wasn't tied by a rookie either." Garrison still wondered what he was supposed to gather from this. "Here's what really caught my eye, Sheriff." Zell was squinting and took a flashlight from his belt, aiming it at a point near the front of the deck. "Look at that?"

"What?"

"There's a silver spoon stuck right in that little joint there. See it?"

Garrison followed the beam. "I don't see a thing, Rupert."

"In that seam there, you'll see the end of a treble hook. See it?"

Garrison squatted and leaned in closer. There, lodged in a seam under a bench seat was the treble hook and the edge of a spoon lure.

"You want to get it out of there or do you want me to do it?"

Garrison nodded and gave Rupert the OK.

Rupert slipped on a pair of blue latex gloves and removed a pair of stainless steel pliers and a plastic evidence bag. He leaned over and grabbed the treble hook with the needle nose of the pliers, twisting it carefully as he rocked it back and forth to release its grip. Eventually, the hook worked loose and Rupert held the lure up like a dentist who'd just removed a stubborn molar.

"I'm guessing that this might be the one that our guy dropped. Shouldn't have caused him to curse, though."

"Set it down on that evidence bag and we'll see if we can lift a print."

"It's a good old Johnson Sprite is what it is. Mighty fine for redfish."

"What's that, Rupert?"

"I said it's mighty fine for redfish."

"Before that."

"I said it's a Johnson Sprite. It's been on the market for, I don't know, forever. It comes in chrome, gold and copper. I've had at one in my tackle box since I could hold a rod and reel."

"Thanks, Rupert. You know a lot about fishing?"

"Everything I know about fishing I get from books." Zell's face betrayed his seriousness of tone.

"I'll bet. Thanks for the information."

"You know, you ought to take up the sport. It's relaxing, and I'll bet old Walter would love it even more than you."

"That's exactly what I'm looking for, Rupert, a sport my dog enjoys more than me."

Rupert just winked, smiled, and walked back to his vehicle. Garrison watched him with some sense of pride. Rupert was a man comfortable in his skin. With his combination of intelligence, good sense and diligence, Rupert Zell would make, Garrison trusted, a terrific sheriff one day. He was already a wonderful husband and father. Here was a product of Dodge County who symbolized for Garrison the kind of personal growth in confidence and humanity that required only a bit of mentoring and few injections of higher expectations to develop and flourish. He wished he could spend more time with Rupert and looked forward to the day when he could do so.

Sheriff Garrison took the lure back to his office and placed it, still in its plastic bag, in a clear plastic box with a snap cover. He affixed a label to the box, described the contents, dated it, and added his initials. He would arrange to send it to the Crime Lab in Sarasota tomorrow morning. Meanwhile, Rupert contacted the marina owner who was only too happy to retrieve his boat.

FOURTEEN

Along the Peace River

Tim McElroy was only nine, but he knew more about the sexual habits of river catfish than most marine biologists. He stood twenty feet from his father, both of them clad in waders, as they cast their lines and reeled them in perfect silence.

Tim's father, Ron, was a firefighter with five children, and only Tim, his youngest child and only son enjoyed fishing. The other four, Mandy, Cheryl, Cindy and Ashley, were older and more interested in hairstyles and make up than in the pastime of sport fishing. God bless Tim, he often said to his wife, Jessica, when he considered his situation. Even his dog, Victoria, and his cat, Olivia, sniffed when Ron and Tim loaded the back of the pick up with their rods, reels, tackle boxes and bait for a half-day of fishing.

Tim could almost smell fish under the water. Ron, a fisherman all his life, was never short of amazed when Tim would wander off a few yards and cast into a seemingly hopeless hole and haul in a collection of catfish, trout and bass. This boy, he thought, can teach me a few things.

Tim was starting to get bored and Ron could sense it. He was casting and reeling in a little faster, less patiently than usual. He's getting ready to move, Ron thought. It always worked that way. Some sense told Tim that the fish were biting over *there* and not over *here*. Ron stopped doubting Tim's impatience when Tim turned seven, got a new Sahara casting reel, and brought in a line full of bass from a creek only a quarter mile from the McElroy back yard. Nobody fished that spot, Ron recalled, and here's our little boy feeding the family on a regular basis.

Tim wasn't of a catch-and-release mind. Some people are, but Tim was not. He wanted to fish to eat. Scrupulous about fish length and minimum and maximum daily catches, Tim didn't abide snatching "shorts" or cleaning un-allowed fish to fool the people from Florida Fish and Wildlife. He heard about those non-sportsmen who cheated, and Tim just would not tolerate such a thought to enter his soul.

Sure enough, Tim reeled all the way in, latched his hook on the lowest line guide, and said to his father, "Dad, I'm moving over here a ways."

They were up the Peace River, on the right side, the eastern bank, standing in eighteen inches of water. Ron's flats boat was tied off to a mangrove about fifteen feet away. The water yesterday was extra high due to the storm, and not all the fish had yet settled back into their routines. Tim knew that some of the usual spots were barren and thought he'd try his luck just a few feet over and across the shallow water against the mangroves on the small island.

Tim cast and slowly reeled in. Nothing.

Ron made a comment in conversation, a practice seldom used on these fishing jaunts where silence was preferred.

"These waters get a lot of gators, so watch yourself. If you see one, just yell and get back to the boat."

Ron always carried a .38 police special in his vest for just such occasions. While the .38 might not be lethal to the thick-skinned reptiles, the sound and the impact usually drove them away, at least for sufficient time to allow them to get back into the protection of their flats boat.

Last year, Ron plunked a five-footer that seemed to have a bead on Tim and was swishing its tail through the water in his son's direction. The gator did a full flip, and maybe even died from the wound later on, but Tim hardly flinched. He was pulling in a beautiful snook at the time.

"He wanted my snook, Dad. I just know it. Thanks."

God bless this young man, Ron thought once more.

Ron laid a popping lure about twenty feet away and thought he felt a nibble. He paused for a moment, waiting for the fish to return for a full bite of the baited shrimp so he could set the hook. Then he heard his son yell, an unusual event.

"Dad! Dad! Look at this!"

Ron waded over, one hand holding his rod and the other resting on his pistol. A loud noise on this part of the river was rare enough; such an outburst from his son was astonishing. It was time to get ready.

Tim was reeling something in, his rod held almost straight up but still bent down hard to the water. A mass of . . . some-thing . . . was on the hook. He couldn't tell what it was, but this was no fish. Tim was alternately pulling and reeling in, pulling and reeling in. The mass was still twenty feet or more away.

Whatever Tim had on his line was beige and red, nothing Ron had seen before except . . .

"Tim! Get over to the boat! Hand me your rod!"

Tim wasn't one to yield a great catch gracefully and tried for a moment to ignore his father's admonitions. But even he knew this was beyond his experience and ceded the rod to his dad.

Ron handed Tim his rod and Tim backed off. Ron pulled slowly and thought of a case he'd been on years earlier, almost his rookie year as a fire fighter, when a body was hauled out of a swimming pool after a devastating house fire. Whatever Tim had snagged looked remarkably and terribly familiar. He looked over his shoulder.

"Tim, I mean it! Get back on the boat! Now!"

Tim knew the tone of his father's voice well enough to know when he was kidding and when he was dead serious. He waded over to the boat and got in, waiting.

"Get my cell phone and call your mother. Tell her to call the station house and report a 10-54. Got it? And give her our position; you know it better than I do."

Tim did as he was told. He had no idea what '10-54' meant, but he knew this was serious.

FIFTEEN

The Medical Examiner covering Dodge County was in Sarasota, forty-nine miles away from the Dodge County Sheriff's office. Doctor Ibrahim Parwani was a smallish man with a long pointed nose that Sheriff Garrison found difficult to ignore. The doctor's blue surgical mask, Garrison noticed, was pulled to an abnormal degree of tension; he wondered, do they make them in sizes?

Garrison wore a green paper gown, mask and latex gloves as he stood next to Doctor Parwani, the doctor's gloved hands still spattered with bits of tissue as he wrote down various findings on a clipboard. The air in the room was very chilled so the aroma was less rancid than it otherwise might be. Garrison attended autopsies before that were so horrid that canisters of orange oil were placed about the room to mask the odor. At one particularly nasty one where the body had been rotting in the August Florida sun for four days, he followed the coroner's lead and rubbed Vicks in a thick smudge under his nose. This one wasn't half-bad by comparison.

"This man was dead for approximately twenty-four to thirty-six hours before he was brought here," the doctor said in his clipped British accent, the consequence of his training at the Leicester Medical School.

"I've found a few unusual items so far. Like a false beard for starters."

The body, or what was left of it, lay on a stainless steel table and was bathed in bright overhead lights. The recovered corpse was missing one leg, severed mid-calf. The other foot was severed at the ankle.

"When we got the call, we went out and taped off the area. I had three investigators checking everything in the area where the body was found. Nothing showed up."

"Don't expect to find the missing extremity, unless you're interviewing some of the larger reptiles of the area."

"I was thinking more about a weapon, or maybe a shell if it was ejected."

"Was he found like this? I mean no clothing at all?"

"Naked as a jaybird." Garrison leaned over to look at the bullet wound. "Small caliber, isn't it?"

"I would say yes, but I will excise the slug. It's about an inch behind his right eye. You can see it nicely on the x-ray. I normally send recovered rounds to the crime lab."

"Do the same here, if you don't mind."

"By the way, I know our young fellow here looked better during his lifetime, but look at this. What does this tell you?"

Garrison squinted and tried to figure out the doctor's meaning. He was looking at an area just below the chin, and beyond that he could tell little.

Parwani said, "A small scar."

He pointed with his finger at a neat one inch line below the cleft chin of the deceased.

"Cosmetic surgery, Sheriff Garrison. And look here, just below the brow and at the spot in the middle, what we call the glabella. Again, other scars. Precise and well sutured but still these are surgical scars. Come with me and look at this."

The doctor walked to the side of the autopsy room where a series of x-rays were clipped to a light board.

"Look at the chin area. That, my good man, is an implant. And at the brow, a small implant on each side and one small one in the center." Parwani used a pen to direct Garrison's attention to solid white areas on the film. Then he held up another x-ray and placed it on the backlit screen. "And look at these, the dental x-rays. He's had some work done. You can see the fillings quite clearly here." Parwani used his pen to point out several bright spots on the x-ray. "But I find it odd that the teeth in front are all crowned."

Garrison wondered, "Maybe the result of an accident? I've seen a lot of people lose their front teeth in car crashes."

"Possible, I suppose. But I'll tell you something about this gent's dental work, Sheriff Garrison. It's not North American work. I'd say it's European, but I can't be certain."

"What makes you say that?"

"Dentists in the US and Canada use different materials and techniques. This reminds me more of the type of work I saw in Europe."

"Maybe England? We have a boat theft case involving a man we think comes from England. This fellow could fit the description."

"England is a possibility. We have a man here . . . I'm only guessing at this point, but give me some leeway . . . of about twenty-five years who has been facially reworked. Not so unusual in today's society if we are looking at a man of fifty or sixty years. But twenty-five? Highly unusual. A nip here, a tuck there. A different man. This man reconfigured himself."

"This wasn't reconstructive surgery then? He wasn't injured or disfigured before?"

"No evidence at all of that. Good observation, though. If he'd had bone cancer, for example, or serious facial injuries at one time, then it would explain the plastic surgery. But no, our fellow here appears to have been in fine shape before he had this work done. It was not as if he was bad looking man before-hand . . . weak jaw or jutting brow, for example. He had quite normal bone structure."

Garrison still wondered about the missing parts.

"I see you looking at the lower extremities. I've seen more than my share of such injuries down here in Florida. This was your basic alligator dismemberment. Post mortem, thank goodness."

"I figured as much. The bullet did its thing before the alligator did his."

"Correct. There are other injuries here as well, probably birds. I'll venture some vultures went at some of the flesh before our hungry reptile showed up. But I have to say that the corpse is still remarkably intact."

To Garrison, this was a bulbous mass of waterlogged skin and muscle, a sandy-haired, fair-skinned human being who was walking and talking just a few days ago. Not in as bad of shape as some bodies he'd seen, but bad nevertheless.

"He's still got his hands. Can we get prints?"

Parwani lifted a hand and looked at it. "I'll send a copy to you as soon as they're done. The official cause of death will be catastrophic brain injury caused by gunshot. Sort of like putting a brain in a Mixmaster and setting it on puree. It doesn't do those little gray cells any good, I'll tell you. I'll be able to give you something much more precise when I go in. I'll also do some blood and tissue tests and send those results along to you as well."

"If nothing comes up on the prints, then what? Any suggestions?"

"I would suggest we bring in some facial reconstruction

people from the forensic lab upstairs. You would be surprised what they can accomplish in establishing a likeness of the deceased. They may be able to produce a likeness of the man *before* he underwent this unusual remodeling process. Not my line, really."

"Well, thanks for the guided tour." He took one last look at the remains of the victim. "Poor bastard."

"You have an assassin, Sheriff. I don't envy you."

The remark caught Garrison by surprise.

"The gunshot cases I've seen in this country are usually quite straightforward. Fatal gunshot wounds are usually from a large caliber pistol or a rifle, or even a shotgun in some of the messiest circumstances. This case is more surgical, more exacting, and whoever pulled the trigger knew exactly what he was doing. One round, of sub-sonic velocity I am estimating, well-placed, from behind the victim. He took pains to penetrate enough bone at the entry to reduce the velocity of the round so it would tumble inside the skull. This was no amateur. Yes, I will venture that this is an assassination. Quite professional."

"Not professional enough. The body was found."

When Garrison returned to his office he asked Tawanda to have Rupert Zell come in.

"Tell him it's about the homicide victim we found yesterday. Then check the fax for some fingerprints coming in from the ME in Sarasota."

Garrison closed the door to his office and Walter moved to sit at his feet. Absentmindedly, he stroked the dog's ears and Walter was in heaven. The only thing better than this would be . . . yes! Garrison slid open the top side drawer of his desk and removed a biscuit from a plastic re-sealable bag. The biscuit disappeared in seconds.

The sheriff leaned back in his chair, folded his arms and stared at the ceiling, a signal that Walter understood to mean that this was no time for further interruptions. If the prints on the car matched the prints from the corpse, the swollen carcass belonged to Peter Billings. If that turned out to be the case, and Garrison was confident of the supposition, then where was the other gentleman, the multi-lingual curser who dropped the cheap metal lure?

A knock on the door signaled Rupert's arrival.

"Come in, Rupert. What did you find out about Mr. Billings of Tallahassee?"

"He's quite a guy, Sheriff. He lives in a house in our state's capital city that just isn't here. I mean, the capital city is there, but Mr. Billings' home is vacant expanse of absolutely nothing. The house numbers stop three hundred numbers before his alleged residence."

"I think we found Mr. Billings, Rupert, and I'm guessing he's the same guy we pulled off the island in the Peace River. I had a little meeting with him in Sarasota with the esteemed Dr. Parwani making the introductions."

"The guy with the nose?"

"That's the one. He had our victim on his table, and I'm guessing he'll turn out to be Billings. Did you lift some prints from the vehicle, by the way?"

"Plenty. I sent them to the FBI data base and I have copies here in the file."

Another knock on the door, this time from Tawanda.

"These are what you're waiting for."

She handed the two sheets of paper to Garrison and left. Garrison placed them on his desk and laid the prints that Rupert brought with him side by side. Even to the untrained eye, they were a clear match.

"So our boat renter is found dead. And by a single shot to the brain. Dr. Long Nose says it's an assassin-type killing."

"Assassin?"

"And our Mr. Billings doesn't look anything like he once

did because he's had some sort of plastic surgery and some dental work. All fairly recent. Parwani's a pretty good detective, you know."

"What about the guy that was with Billings? We don't have much to go on except maybe the lure that I found."

"I sent the lure out to be printed and we should have results later on. Maybe that will help."

"So we have a tall assassin of average build who can tie knots like a sailor, is of middle age, who swears fluently in Italian, and has a peculiar attachment to a cheap fishing lure. Should I round up the usual suspects?"

SIXTEEN

Emilio Fortino paced his room at the Gulf Breeze Inn. He was getting tired of making the trip to the secluded island where Alek Mironev was being held, and he could not be sure that some naturalist on the prowl for red crested heron nests or the snow white plumed egret would not stumble across the small bungalow. The island was ringed with a thick growth of daunting mangroves, and except for one narrow and well-hidden channel that Emilio used to access a narrow piece of shoreline, it looked impenetrable.

His patience was wearing thin. He appreciated that the gears of government ground painfully slow, but there should have been some response by now. The faux letter announcing a sudden urge to see New Orleans was found; word would have reached Alek's family; a call would have been made by Vanya detailing the requirements of the Chechens; that was late Monday evening, Florida time, and early Tuesday morning in Moscow. It was now Thursday early afternoon in Russia and . . . nothing.

He called Vanya. "Lido Key. Meet me in two hours."

* * *

The young woman drove her white Hyundai through downtown Sarasota and found a precious parking space along Ringling Boulevard. When she stepped out of the car, passersby paid attention to her, petite, blond hair short and spiked. She ignored the stares and locked the car, then walked into and through the crowds of shoppers and tourists at St. Armand's Circle. Her training and experience provided her with discipline and focus and she made eye contact with no one. Loud tropical clothes and gaudy window displays shouted at her, but hardly a siren song to an individual wrapped in a cocoon as she was. She strode along the avenue, weaving left, then right through pockets of shoppers and gawkers and headed due west towards the rolling surf of the Gulf of Mexico, turning left at the last street that bordered the beachfront of Lido Key. She allowed herself only a single glance over the turquoise waters and the horizon.

Sitting on the hood of his bright yellow Jeep in a parking lot across the avenue was Emilio. He sucked on a small cigar and flicked it over his shoulder in an arc, a splatter of sparks on the pavement when it landed. He was wearing dark sunglasses, as was she. When she was within fifty feet, he slid off the hood and stood tall and slender in his Wranglers and gray polo shirt, a Yankees baseball cap on his head. He cocked his head and nodded, and they walked together to the beach without words. In spite of the warm sunshine, few bathers were on the sand. She slipped off her sandals and they walked together until they reached the limits of the hard-packed sand where the tide had only recently left.

"Thank you for getting here on time, Vanya," he said, leaning close to her, the soft rumble of the waves muffling his voice.

"I understand that signore Emilio Fortino may have questionable ethics, but he has high standards. I have not failed to take notice."

She had still a tinge of an accent, with hints of a coarse Slavic edge.

Emilio's English was as easy and as comfortable as a worn leather jacket, no indication that this was his fourth and most recent language. "Let's walk slowly, like lovers."

"We will walk slowly, like friends."

"Whatever, Vanya. Like friends."

They walked several yards before he spoke again. "What is the status of the arrangement? Neither I nor Alek Mironev can wait forever."

"Things went a bit slow at first," she said in explanation.

"Explain that, please. I'm tending a kidnap victim. There are severe penalties exacted by the legal system of this wonderful country if this victim is suddenly found and he happens to point his finger at . . . who? You? Me?"

"Word of Alek Mironev being held did not reach the President in Moscow until Wednesday morning."

"Moscow time?"

"London time. My colleagues there had a disagreement at the last minute. One faction wished to exact greater concessions than were initially agreed upon."

"Tell me this has been settled." Emilio could taste bile rising in his throat. He did not need this wrench in the gears of his well-devised and, so far, well-conducted operation.

"Settled, yes. There was no change. But the delay was a waste of thirty hours."

"So where does the matter stand now?" He could feel himself settling down, his blood pressure getting back to normal.

"The Russian President was told of his son's situation and he was presented with a list of demands."

"Is everything arranged for the final day? Assuming we ever reach a final day?"

"The boat is ready. My friend leaves me his keys when he

goes away. He is in Costa Rica at the moment and I have access to the boat at any time."

"At the marina?"

She stopped walking, faced him, her arms stiff at her side. "Yes. How many times do I have to explain that?" Vanya Zakayev was demonstrative and her face reflected every shift in mood. This shortage of subtlety was the reason she was great at show business and poor at diplomacy.

"Check, double-check, triple-check. That is a habit I do not break in matters as this. And keep walking. Friends who stand in place and argue will gain attention."

Her nostrils flared and he half-expected snorts of smoke to appear. "The marina is near the mouth of the Manatee River in Bradenton, as you know. By boat, I can make it from the marina to the rendezvous point in twenty-eight minutes."

"And the equipment?" He could see she was calming down.

"Most of it is stowed on board now. The scuba tanks, fins, goggles, the extra clothing and documents in the waterproof bags. It is fueled and the batteries are charged. I start it up every day and run it for a few minutes."

"You are thorough, Vanya. That is a very good thing."

Vanya's smile exposed rows of perfect teeth and a single deep dimple on her left cheek.

"The rifle?"

"I have it in the trunk of my car. Unloaded. Why?"

"We may not need it, but it must be on board that day. Just in case. What about the Sea-Doo machines?"

"I have them on the boat as well. Below. When I meet you at our rendezvous point, they will be sitting on deck, fully charged and ready to go."

Sea-Doo manufactured all sorts of boats and personal watercraft. Jet skis were their biggest sellers. But the firm also manufactured small, underwater propulsion systems. With the

Sea-Doo Explorer, a user could hold on to the handles and travel underwater at over three miles per hour for up to two hours. The devices were inexpensive and readily accessible. For divers, they provided a way to travel with no effort and enjoy the underwater scenery. For Emilio, they represented an ideal escape mechanism; he and Vanya could travel below the surface of the Gulf of Mexico undetected and reach shore where they could dress in dry clothes, gather their necessary personal effects, false passports and an ample supply of cash included, and elude capture.

"After we are done, I will be heading in one direction and you in another. Have you thought about your destination yet?"

"Not yet. I am still giving that some thought. I am thinking maybe out west."

"Reach a conclusion soon, for there will be no time to stop and think about that when the time comes. Meanwhile, we need to impress upon your friends in London that Alek Mironev must be moved soon."

They continued their stroll and she pointed to a concrete bench. No one else was nearby. Vanya said, "Let us sit for a moment. I need to think this through." It came out as "sink dis true" and Emilio smiled. When stressed, her accent hardened a bit. Not a problem for Vanya, he mused, for a touch of the exotic would be an asset in her case.

They took seats adjacent to each other. He kept his face forward but the deep gray of the sunglasses hid his constantly scanning eyes. The closest people were four elderly women at least eighty yards away.

Emilio put his arm around her shoulder. She resisted for only an instant.

"Close friends," he said.

"I think I should make the next call to President Mironev in Moscow. I will make sure that he understands exactly what will happen if he does not move quickly."

"You don't trust your friends in London?"

"It is a matter of control, not trust."

Emilio considered offering a comment on that. Control was valuable, and she was learning quickly. Instead, he let Vanya own that bit of wisdom and said, "I can arrange to get you a stolen mobile phone so it cannot be traced."

"No need. I already have two such cell phones."

"How?" That news took Emilio by surprise and he was genuinely puzzled.

"You told me that I must develop contacts, build assets to help me do what I need to do. I told you that I pay attention, and I have done this. A friend at the circus has less than savory connections. I am sure you understand." She looked at Emilio and he saw the determination on her face. Vanya was eager.

Emilio remembered his own eagerness when he was as young as Vanya. But if he was as eager, he was also patient and appreciative of the broad range of faculties that his career would require. He was willing to learn, and he worked diligently to develop his skills, careful to understand as he learned that he could do only so much; he would never comprehend most Asian languages, so he focused on those he *could* learn well; he was tall and rangy, not a good candidate to engage in close combat, so he either avoided those assignments that required it, or developed alternate tactics to accomplish his goal. He knew his limits.

Vanya brought different talents: Steel nerves, extraordinary human strength, and an actor's capacity to become fully absorbed in her role. Those were powerful abilities, but not enough, he thought, and he told her so. To her disadvantage, history is not always fully absorbed by its students nor does it always transmit the expected lessons. He therefore insisted on repetition. "Let us walk through our plan one last time," he said. Vanya glared, her stubbornness at the surface. To her credit, she surrendered. She did not argue but recited in a monotone every step of their escape plan.

Twenty minutes later, they returned to the parking lot and the Jeep. They were, in her words, "this close to success," her thumb a millimeter from her finger. "I will do my part."

"We will *both* do our parts, Vanya. You and I, we will succeed."

"I will see Chechnya succeed as well. I wish you shared that passion."

"I do what I am hired to do. If you are looking for passion, for commitment to the cause, then you must look elsewhere."

"Of course I understand. Your family was not destroyed. But it would make everything so much easier. You behave as if you have no concern for the plight of those we fight for."

Emilio had come across similar disappointments before in previous assignments. If Vanya indeed saw her future in terms of taking on assignments like this one for other employers, then he might have to share some of his own thoughts on the subject. "Let me suggest something to you. If you wish to pursue this career change you've discussed, you will find yourself in the position of working for people whose aims and ambitions veer sharply from your own. So it may be OK to care, Vanya, but not too much. You must behave as a consultant, not an investor. Your only stake in the arrangement is your fee. You will need to view your various employers with the clarity of an outsider. You can't expect to share the zeal of those who hire you and you can rarely expect neat resolutions. As a result, it is a lonely profession."

"I can be alone. I am used to that. You have seen where I live. It reminds me of the old Soviet style apartments of Moscow. Cold, solitary. I know how to be alone. You?"

He didn't answer. None of us, he thought in silence, is what we imagine. Each of us normalizes the strangeness of our inner lives with a variety of convenient fictions.

Emilio took winding roads back to his hotel in Boca Grande near the southern end of Gasparilla Island. Having been there for three weeks, he was beginning to feel like a native. He knew the usual police hiding places where they set up their speed traps, and he had a good sense for the way the wind shifted every afternoon, bringing a slight drop in temperature. He was accustomed now to slowing his speed before reaching the wide curve after the toll bridge, and he kept a light jacket in the back seat of his Jeep for just these eventualities.

Eventualities. The last time he used that word was with his Chechen rebel employers. He explained his approach to "eventualities". He would study the task, build a strategic operational scheme with all the hiring and training and equipping that the job required, perform the task, and leave with a minimum of mayhem. If you wanted diplomacy, consensus or compromise, you went elsewhere. There were no "legacy costs" with Emilio, no health care plan, no pension benefits, no irrelevant incentives. The tasks tended to be difficult and usually distasteful, but Emilio was efficient and effective.

He drove through the congested city of Venice and turned toward Englewood as he continued south. As he approached the toll bridge that separated Englewood from Gasparilla, the entire tone of the area changed. The condominiums grew taller, the landscapes more lush. The boats tied up at the docks were wider and longer, and the cars in the driveways were recent luxury models. He was not unfamiliar with the US and had been on assignment here as recently as two years ago, but he was not accustomed to such overt opulence and consumption. "Conspicuous consumption" was the way he'd read it described in his preparatory reading, but seeing this up close was nevertheless staggering.

He crossed the bridge and saw the sun beginning its final descent. He looked to his right to see a yellow-orange glow cast over the waters and leading to the horizon. He'd seen this often since he came here, this sun dropping over water, but never tired of the scene. Ahead, he pulled over on the side of the road and leaned over the seat to sit and wait for that moment when the sun made its final plunge and sometimes threw a flash of green-gold into the sky, a last gasp before sinking from sight. When the moment arrived, there was no flash, but Emilio savored the sight anyway.

He prepared to drive on and waited while a Bentley passed by, bringing him fully back to this time and place.

SEVENTEEN

Moscow

President Nikolai Mironev knew his son to be a shallow young man, engaged more in the opportunities for fame and status presented by his father's position than with the enormous burdens that his father might be forced to bear during his tenure. Perhaps he'd change in time, this little piglet, no callouses on his hands or psyche at this early stage. He had seen changes take place in other young men who reached points in their lives where they became serious, not simply playboys. Anything was possible.

But he never expected this. Kidnap. Threat. Extortion. Nikolai Mironev was angry. In this instance he was angry in two directions: First at those who would, for some foolish Chechen cause, elect to capture his son; they deserve only slow and painful deaths. Second, he was angry at his son for putting himself above his country, and therefore putting him and his family in harm's way. Alek's mother, Raisa Mironev, was in a near state of collapse. Their young daughter had taken to locking herself in her room.

Raisa Mironev insisted that her husband dispatch investigators to the US. She was reacting from fear and concern, for she was certain that the kidnappers would not hesitate to kill their son. "The secret police, Nikolai. You can use them! You must find him, Nikolai!"

The president summoned a doctor and Raisa was sedated, at least for now. He must move quickly and decisively if his wife was to regain her bearings, his daughter her inner peace, and his son his freedom.

He placed a single telephone call to Grigori Malko, someone he learned to rely on as his chief aide. Within the hour, the key members of the Russian leadership team were notified and a meeting scheduled. Before the meeting, Mironev spoke with the prime minister about the message he wished to deliver to the world. If there were any objections, Mironev did not hear them. The prime minister understood that his position depended in large part on his acquiescence to Mironev.

It would not be the first meeting in the Kremlin that would deal with a renegade group of Chechens, but some years had passed since the issue of Chechnya was prominent on the Kremlin's agenda. Chechnya. Between 1994 and 2000, that region consumed Russia. Bombings, kidnappings, murders and assorted mayhem ate up a significant portion of Russia's energies and treasure. It was a horrific public relations nightmare for the newly reborn Russia, and only after extraordinary commitments of military might did the Chechen resistance reduce to something manageable. It was never destroyed, but sufficient numbers of the Chechen leaders were dead, maimed, jailed or exiled to make the threat much more a mere mosquito on the neck of the Russian bear. The Chechen rebels, those who were left, were as passionate in their hatred of Russia as ever, but those patriots were fewer and older now.

The Russian president could imagine that this scheme involving his son was hatched elsewhere, probably Paris or London or Copenhagen, where he knew many of the former Chechen leadership met from time to time. Old believers with limited resources who had not seen their rugged homeland since they ran off in the face of Russian tanks and Kalashnikovs, their tails between their legs, their finances already conveyed to numbered Swiss bank accounts. Yes, they were still living and still sitting on some wealth.

If they could visit Chechnya today and see the more recent developments, they would not recognize their homeland. The next generation bore little of their ancestors' ferocity and quasi-nationalism. There was little fervor left in the youth who preferred cell phones and jobs and more modern conveniences. Certainly the Sunni Muslims there were prominent and sometimes vocal, but economics, the pure desire for personal wealth and hope for a better lifestyle . . . the capitalism that Russia once detested to the core of its soul . . . had taken root in a big way. The most recent uprisings were quickly quashed, and more people were concerned with getting a good-paying job rebuilding the nation than were hopeful of another debilitating revolution. The president had heard the American phrase 'It's about the economy, stupid!' and believed that such was the case in Chechnya and elsewhere in Russia. Let them have easy access to capital and goods; let them get good jobs. The old hatreds will die slowly, but they will inevitably die.

Nikolai Mironev poured himself a dram of Glenfiddich . . . bless those Scots, he thought as he inhaled the aroma . . . and sat in his overstuffed leather chair overlooking the inner courtyard of the Kremlin. All will be well, my son. All will be well.

Grigori Malko sat at the far end of the long cherry wood table, polished so bright that he could identify from the reflections the seven men who sat around it. This was a crisis meeting, and the seven were unpleasantly accustomed to crisis meetings. At the head of the table sat the prime minister of the Russian Federation. It was the PM who would carry the summary of this group's discussions to the president, Malko at his side.

Clockwise from the PM sat the minister of Information, the minister of Industry and Energy, Malko, the minister of Finance, the minister of Defense, and the minister of Foreign Affairs. The minister of Industry and Energy had the floor at the moment.

"Why is it that our president is so bent on accommodating our Chechen enemies? Where is this urgency coming from? Is it a threat? Is he being blackmailed?"

The prime minister responded. "That is a strong word, and you can be certain this is not a matter of blackmail. I would advise that you confine your comments to the issue at hand."

"Whether or not there is a threat, the message it sends to the Chechens is catastrophic." It was the minister of Finance speaking now. "They will look on us as an easy target."

"I disagree," the minister of Defense said. "Chechnya at this time is a minor issue. The senior people, those who caused so much of our troubles there, are either dead, in prison or exiled. The rest are merged into the national fabric. I agree with Grigori; we can stand to give some lip service to the Chechens, and the proposal before us is palatable. My colleague from Foreign Affairs will, I think, agree."

He did. "In fact, we can gain by announcing some concessions, if you will, to Chechnya. Let us not forget that much of the world views our past treatment of the Chechens with contempt; we can show that a leaf has been turned in the pages of Russian history. Unless there is some overriding economic argument against this proposal, I agree with the president's approach."

The minister of Finance was expected to add some information, some opinion, but said nothing as he chewed his fingernails, his narrow face pinched with anxiety.

The prime minister looked across the table to Malko. In spite of Malko's relatively low standing in this group, the people in attendance understood the level of trust and confidence that President Mironev placed in him. When Malko first learned from the president that his son, Alek, was being held hostage, Malko's sphincter tightened into a knot. The discussion was held in confidence. No one beyond the president, his family and Malko would be informed. The capture of Alek Mironev was exactly what he was told to expect by his cousin weeks before, yet the reality of the event hit like a hard slap. Nevertheless, at this meeting, Malko was the picture of calm, an unofficial but valued member of the president's inner circle. "I believe the president would agree with my friend from Foreign Affairs. There is only a minor downside to the proposal, and there are some potentially significant gains, especially in our prestige among the world of nations. The president wishes to make a public announcement as soon as possible."

There were more comments but the recommendation was made. Malko was given the task of drafting a proclamation of sorts that would grant the Chechens new rights and privileges, including placing a respected Chechen representative on an important oil exportation board, an increase in government investment in the Chechen region, and inclusion of larger numbers of native Chechens in the pipeline labor pool. Part of the proposal was the immediate release of a score of Chechen rebels, all now effectively broken and advanced in years, from Russian prisons. A small concession, Malko thought, as he invoked the spirit of his dead mother. I am doing my best, he said to her angry soul.

He worked alone in his office for much of the night assembling the key provisions and putting them into a format that would require little modification by the speechwriters on the president's staff. The faint glow of the Moscow winter sun broke through his window as he finished, leaned back in his chair, and sighed. Would his mother be proud of him? Or would she see his participation in this scheme and the resulting concessions as just a hollow victory, nearly meaningless in the overall struggle. He knew what she would think, and he agreed with her.

PART IV

If you feel the urge, don't be afraid to go on a wild goose chase. What do you think wild geese are for, anyway?
—Will Rogers

Who in the world am I? Ah, that's the great puzzle.
—Lewis Carroll

EIGHTEEN

Garrison's drive from the sheriff's office to his apartment did not take him near the narrow road that led to the home of Ab Swett, his morning caller, but he decided to make a turn in Ab Swett's direction and stop by anyway. He hoped that any visit with Mr. Swett would prove to be brief. Today was one of the more intense ones, with reports filed, bulletins sent out and a lot of waiting in between, most of it dealing with the case of the unidentified murder victim. He'd done all he could do on the case to this point, and he made every effort to include Rupert Zell on every aspect of the case. He could envision Rupert as a fine detective one day, and he wanted him to participate in all the steps involved in a homicide investigation, including the drudgery of completing the necessary forms and the tedium of the waiting. Garrison pulled over to the side of the road and made the call to Mr. Swett.

Ab Swett was the scion of the Swett family and the creator of the Swett fortune in Dodge County. Ab Swett started with an orange grove sixty years ago and through some shrewd deals and hard work, he became a significant player in the Florida economy in the years since. In the years that Garrison served as Sheriff, and in the eleven years he lived and worked here, he'd never once met the man personally. By reputation, Ab Swett was a mean old SOB. Some people thought he was already dead or at least confined to a home for the terminally drooling. According to Tawanda, who had likewise never met the man, he was "ninety years old or close enough to spit to ninety and hit it dead center."

Ab made his fortune in at least two known methods and many other suspected ones. There were the orange groves; growing juice oranges was a lucrative business up until a few years ago when inferior but cheaper fruit from Brazil started taking over. Florida orange juice, far sweeter than the imports, was becoming a niche product, and many of the remaining groves in the state were either left fallow or sold off for development. Ab saw an opening in related chemical businesses and decades ago began the business of food related concentrates. Everything from food coloring to flavorings, to air fresheners and furniture polish had some reliance on Swett's chemical firm, ChemAgra.

He also saw an opening in the recycling business long before many others. But instead of recycling household trash, he recycled the houses themselves. Concrete block was the principal form of building material for years, especially in a section of the country noted for termites and moisture, both of which tend to reduce wood construction to sawdust and mold in short order. Add Florida's scarcity of solid rock, and Ab concluded that you could either ship crushed stone in from other parts of the country by rail for aggregate, or reuse the concrete block by crushing it yourself. Crushed concrete block proved an unusually strong agent in manufacturing new concrete block, and Ab had a pair of monster crushers, each forty feet tall and located miles from the population centers that would be bothered by the racket caused by giant steel impellers smacking big lumps of concrete into pebbles.

Garrison exhaled, a sigh that rose from the bottom of his chest, picked up his cell phone and dialed. It was picked up on the first ring.

"Hello Sheriff, thanks for calling me back." Caller ID, Garrison registered. He knew everyone had it, but it still took him by surprise.

After sharing greetings, Ab Swett got right to the point. For a man allegedly well past his prime and rumored to be addled and soon to be stowed away in an institution, Ab Swett sounded healthy and sane.

"Can you arrange to stop by my place sometime? I'd like a chance to chat about something if you don't mind."

Garrison told him he could stop by in a few minutes and Ab said he'd welcome the visit.

At five minutes to five, Garrison approached the address and was surprised to see a rather modest Florida-style home with a wide front porch and mill-finish metal roof. On the porch in one of a pair of high back rocking chairs was an elderly man in blue jeans, plaid shirt and a shawl sweater. On the low round table between the two chairs were two plastic pitchers and two glasses. The man stood when Garrison exited his car and waited at the top of the porch steps with his hand extended.

"Sheriff Garrison, Ab Swett. Thanks for coming."

The man's grip was firm and tremor-free, pale hairs crossed his skull like random strands of straw on an egg. A tanned face full of fine creases was the only indication that Ab Swett was a man of advanced years. He glanced over at Garrison's red Chevy and saw Walter poking his head out the crack of the window.

"Let that dog out of the car, would you? He's not going to

bother anybody out here. Then have a seat. I'm just having a little refreshment. Care for one?"

Garrison asked what it was.

"VO manhattans. I like to have one before I eat my dinner, but I made enough for two. Or, sweet tea, if you'd rather."

Garrison considered the manhattan for only a moment. "Tea is fine." He opened the door of his car and Walter bounded out and deposited a load of manure on the edge of the driveway almost at once. Garrison reddened with embarrassment. Ab Swett just laughed.

Garrison followed Swett to the rocking chairs and Swett poured the drinks. "Cheers," Swett said when he raised his glass to his lips. Walter found a spot at Garrison's feet and fell asleep.

The porch faced west and the sun was encroaching on a stand of pin oaks in the distance. The lengthening shadows and the still warm sun gave a comforting glow to the scene.

"I've been seeing a lot of hawks lately," Garrison offered, scanning the sky for some hint that another might fly by in search of its supper.

"There used to be a lot more around here, then the pesticides nearly killed them all off. I've seen more and more lately myself."

"I think the ones I've seen have been red-shouldered hawks."

"I knew the names of all of them once. Red-shouldered, Cooper's, Broad-winged. I've forgotten most of them."

"You sound to me like you've got a great memory."

Swett took another sip. "I forget a lot of things and some things remain in my head like they happened just yesterday. Getting old does a number on the brain cells." He pointed a bony finger at the small garden of flowers that bordered his porch and walkway. "I even forget the names of some of my friends, or the types of flowers I planted in my garden. Then they remind me: 'Ab, it's us!'"

"Your friends or your flowers?"

Swett took another sip. "They're the same thing, don't you think?"

Garrison was uncertain if the ambiguity was intentional. He still had no idea why Ab Swett wanted to speak with him, but it was nearing the end of the day and he saw no reason to rush the man.

Swett put his glass on the small table and sat back in his seat. "I always liked the Asian custom of sharing a few moments of get-to-know time before I get right into personal conversation, but I understand you're a busy man with a lot to do. It's about my grandson, Virgil. You've met him, I'm sure."

"Yes I have, Mr. Swett." Garrison was not anticipating a comfortable conversation if the subject was going to be the grandson. He wondered how much pressure would be involved to keep the long arm of the law from squeezing Virgil at the throat until his head burst. Garrison at once envisioned Virgil astride his motorcycle and struggled to keep the black thoughts from taking over.

"He's wasn't a bad kid when he was growing up. A little wild maybe, but not a bad kid. I thought he might go to school and then come to work for me when he got out. He did go to college, you know. But then he went into the service. He said he didn't know what he was going to do. What the hell, neither did I when I was his age."

Garrison nodded. So far, the path that Virgil Swett took looked a lot like his own. "How did he make out in the service?"

"Marines. That's what he joined. I sort of lost touch with him then, and I think his parents did too. He was in his own world, I guess. But he stayed with it and I guess he did OK. Never did find out what he did there, and he just sort of dropped out of sight."

"Some kids do that, I guess, Mr. Swett. In a way, that's what I did."

"I thought for a while he was going to make it a career, but then I heard from his father that he was getting out. That was about five years ago. But the kid never did come back to Dodge County, not until six or eight months ago."

"How old is your grandson, Mr. Swett."

"Thirty-five, thirty-six. That sounds about right."

Garrison thought back to his most recent meeting with Virgil Swett. There was no military bearing that he could detect. If anything, Virgil Swett was just another loud-mouthed, shaved-headed redneck with a bad attitude.

Swett kept his eyes focused somewhere to the west. "Look at that eagle over there, would you? There are two nesting pair in those woods."

Garrison saw three soaring high and swooping low and out of sight.

"I blame his mother for whatever shortcomings Virgil developed, but I have to say my son wasn't any prince as a parent either."

Garrison said nothing, still watching the eagles but keeping his ears open to the next Swett observation.

"His Dad, my son Herschel, may not be the most ambitious man in the world, but he's basically a kind and gentle soul. Always wanted to be a history teacher. His trouble is, he wants people to like him, even when they step all over him. Including his bride, the lovely Vella. I call her Vampirella."

Garrison knew Herschel, who'd been a long-time member of the County Commission in Dodge County, and had met Vella Swett a few times over the years. He hadn't given much thought to either one, but could understand Ab Swett's observations. Vella was pinch-faced and carried a permanent sneer. Her husband was quiet and unassuming, given to rare speeches, even during the several campaigns he'd won over the past fifteen or more years.

"Vella is as mean as a viper and has all the sense of a doorstop."

Garrison thought Ab Swett's lack of charity towards his kin stunning.

"I just wanted you to know something about Virgil. How old are you by the way? I'm not nosy, just blunt."

"Fifty-six. Why?"

"I'm ninety. I suppose I'll slip this mortal coil before you do, and I've made some arrangements that you ought to know about. I've got a few questions for you, too."

"I'm not sure I understand what you're getting at."

"Here's the deal. Ab Swett set his glass on the table and shifted in his seat to face Garrison.

"I've got a fairly significant estate, as you might imagine. Or at least I did. I've given a lot away already. Herschel won't be in the chips when I'm gone, but he'll do fine. I'll leave him a little bit of cash, all of it controlled by a trustee who'll dole it out a little bit at a time. He's my son, after all.

"But for Virgil—what a name for that youngster—his Dad really loved the *Aeneid*—he's getting 50 crisp hundred dollar bills and a boot in the ass when I'm gone. That's it."

Garrison's face revealed the sense of surprise that he felt, not just for the fact of cutting Virgil down to a modest sum, but that Ab Swett would reveal himself so.

Ab Swett's firmness of conviction on this matter seemed to abate just a bit as soon as he looked at Garrison. "At least that *was* my plan. I might have to give that just a little more consideration. He's a puzzler, that one."

"How does he afford to live right now?"

"I'm not sure. Vella used to give him whatever he asked for, but I really don't know how he gets by now. He doesn't appear to need cash. That motorcycle he rides must have cost him 20 grand. I was really hoping he'd come back to Dodge County one day, all educated and grown up, and maybe step into the business."

Garrison said, "Education is a good thing, Mr. Swett."

"My family came here from Austria when I was a child and they believed in education. Schwebel, by the way. That's the real name. I was born Abraham Schwebel. Ashkenazi Jews, but we never really practiced. My parents were big on education and I went to Duke. Engineering. Moved here, dabbled in a few things before I bought a small citrus grove. I made a small fortune with that, and then turned that into a bigger one. It just sort of grew. I was a worker.

"But Herschel, he's got a student's mind. Got a degree in history from Florida Southern. Bless him, if he didn't marry Vampirella, he'd still be teaching high school history and enjoying it. Now he's in real estate and he hates it.

"Vella pushed him into that and over the years I've given them some property, a fair size chunk of the orange groves, for income. Vella's mortgaged what she didn't already sell, so when I'm gone, that's the end of it. Virgil's lovely mother won't have anything left to give the child, so the tap will run dry. If she's his source of money, I expect Virgil will need to get an honest job if he wants to keep himself in beer and butts."

Garrison had no soft spot for Virgil Swett, but he wondered how Virgil took this news, or if he was even told. He let it pass for the moment. "How'd the name become Swett from Schwebel?"

"Ignoramus on Ellis Island couldn't read my father's writing. It's been Swett ever since. Name kind of sucks, but it worked out OK, I guess. How about you?"

"Scottish, Irish, a little German, I think. The family was in Brooklyn at first, and then Pennsylvania. I went into the service and bounced around for a while before I moved here."

"Most of us in Florida are immigrants, in one way or another."

Garrison recognized the truth in that and then asked, "Are you planning to tell your grandson about your will?"

"Virgil? I called him up a few weeks ago and asked him to come out here. I'd seen how he treated people since he came back, and damn it, I heard plenty more. So he rode out here on his big old motorcycle and I told him my plans. I wasn't sure what to expect, really."

"What was his reaction when you told him?"

"We sat right here in these chairs, just like you and me. Comfortable, really. He never reacted with more than a nod. I asked him some questions about what he was doing for work, where he was for the past few years, that sort of thing, but he just brushed me off. Non-answers, really. Said he was doing just fine. We just sat here drinking sweet tea like old friends. I told him stories about what life was like when I was his age, and he talked a little bit about his memories of growing up here in Dodge County. We laughed a little and the silences were, well, the good kind of silences. After a good long while, his cell phone rang and he went down the steps and into the yard to take the call. He finished, shook my hand, gave me a hug for God's sake, and then a little peck on the top of my head. He never did that before, ever. Shocked the devil out of me. Then he was gone. I wasn't sure, based on what I'd heard, if he'd show up with a machete, and then I'd be dead meat. I prefer to go out of this life in a more natural fashion, and I expect that will happen soon enough."

"You're ill?"

"The doctors have already taken one lung and both testicles, and my prostate is as big around as your fist. My spleen's gone and I've had three stents and a pacemaker put in. The last time I saw the doc, he told me to get things in order. That's medical-speak for 'You're leaving us soon, old man.' But that's OK. I've had a good run."

There was a question mark on Garrison's face.

"That's one of the reasons I asked you to come out here. You have a reputation as an honest man. You also have a reputation for seeing the potential in people and getting them to take some steps in the right direction."

The question remained on Garrison's face.

"Even an old man like me, stuck out here like a damn hermit, I hear things. I didn't vote for you the first time, but I've voted for you ever since. You, my friend, make a difference."

Garrison fairly blushed at the compliment and said thanks.

"I've still got to give some more thought about Virgil, but there are some other folks around here I'd like your opinion on. You know that family that owns the gas station and minimart on the highway?"

Garrison nodded. They were the same clan that Virgil was engaged in abusing when he last saw the man.

"I'd like to leave them something. Maybe two hundred thousand. That could get them a bigger, nicer store. Be able to serve the area better and give them a good living. What do you think?"

"It would not be wasted. They are good people."

Swett reached for a well-thumbed book from the table. The hardbound cover was faded and the printing on the spine and cover unreadable. "Alex de Tocqueville. Ever hear of him?"

Garrison nodded.

"*Democracy in America.* My old man gave this book to me when I was leaving for college and he told me to read it and understand what the man was saying." Swett opened the book to a dog-eared page near the beginning and read: "'Among the novel objects that attracted my attention during my stay in the United States, nothing struck me more forcibly than the general equality of condition among the people.'" He snapped the volume closed and looked Garrison in the eye. "Can you believe that? What could be less in supply in this country lately than equality of condition?"

Garrison knew the book and the passage.

"So, I've got this rock crushing plant in the east part of the county. There are four families that have worked for me since I started that business. Some of them worked my citrus groves before that. I'm not sure what I'm going to do with that."

"What about leaving the business to them? You can put some conditions on it, like making sure they provide some college scholarships for the high school."

Swett slapped his thigh. "Damn! I knew I liked you."

Ab Swett raised his glass in a silent toast and took a long draft of his manhattan.

"I was thinking about leaving the rest to bankroll a chemical engineering department at the community college on the east side of the county. It ought to be a four year school, and that's going to help them get there."

"Dodge County Community College?" Garrison knew the campus well.

"I call it 'Yucatan U' for short. There should be enough left over for a nice endowment that will keep it going for probably a century, if this fool country lasts that long. This is all between you and me and my lawyer, so I'm trusting you."

"They could even name it after you if you want."

"Shoot. Would you want to wear a shirt that said 'U Swett' on the front?" The man's eyes twinkled at the thought and Garrison could see the spark that drove this man to the kind of financial success he enjoyed. "Maybe they could name it after you!"

"Whoa! That's going way too far."

"One more thing." Swett's voice dropped. "I happen to pay particular attention to a deputy named Rupert Zell. I don't know him personally, but I speak with his grandmother from time to time. He has a fine wife and some wonderful children, from what I hear. I also hear that Rupert holds you in high regard. Says you're one of the most honest men he's met."

The creases on Garrison's face deepened.

Ab Swett kept his eyes straight ahead and focused on the tree line in the distance. "Rupert Zell's grandmother and I, we sort of had a 'relationship' of long standing, if you get my drift. Alma still comes by once in a while for chats and remembering. Rupert, by the way, he gets a little piece of the pie as well. Their youngsters will have their college paid for, at least."

Garrison studied the man's face for some hint of guile and saw none. Instead, he saw an old man's blue eyes alight with mischief and no small bit of rebellion. Ab Swett was his own man. Sensing the stare but never moving his eyes from the eagles that continued to rise and swoop in silhouette, Swett said, "Not half the sonovabitch you heard I was, am I?"

Garrison saluted the man with his glass of iced tea, now half-empty. "I've got to go now, Mr. Swett. It was a pleasure." Walter rose and shook the sleep from his fur. Swett shook Garrison's hand and reached for the pitcher to pour his second manhattan.

The sun arced downward as Garrison drove away, wondering about this curious meeting and this curious man. He replayed the conversation and looked for some evidence of brutality, some indication that might explain the legacy of hurtfulness that appeared to descend on Virgil Swett. Ab Swett was a shrewd man and a man who expected to get his way. But he saw nothing that would predispose his grandson to the sort of behavior he'd witnessed.

NINETEEN

When Garrison walked into his office, Walter trotting at his heels, he scanned the phone message slips that Tawanda placed in ranks on his desk. They were arranged by time so he started, as he did every day, at the lower left, made his way up the row of five messages, and then started at the second row, working his way up from the bottom.

This morning there was nothing particularly unusual in the nine messages. Most of them were from his deputies, calling in with reports or questions. If they were urgent reports or questions, he would have received a cell phone call from Tawanda who would patch in the deputy.

The most recent call was from his doctor. Probably calling with the results of his last physical. Outside of some fatigue and a little numbness in his fingers, he didn't have many complaints when he visited with Doctor Hernandez last week. He set the message aside and would call later.

Outside of the discovery a few days ago of the body on the small island in the Peace River, there was little that demanded his immediate attention. The fingerprint results from the Crime Lab in Sarasota were disappointing. Two beautiful prints but no hits on the state's database. He expected to get the national results from the FBI any time.

Publicly, the discovery of the body in the river was called "suspicious" and the cause of death was "still under investigation." There was little to be gained by releasing more details at this time, and Garrison preferred keeping this sort of information confined to a small circle. Enlarging the circle would serve little purpose.

Doctor Parwani's autopsy results were disappointing. There was little developed in all the tests that he didn't learn from Parwani when they met the other day with the victim on the table. At least he had some photographs to go with the prints of the fictitious Peter Billings. He took another look at the front and side views of the dead man's face and tried once again to place it. He looked familiar, but why? Where did I see this guy before?

Right now, there was little he had to go on. A victim whose name was false and who had no address. No reports of missing persons that might form some connection. A modified appearance for no apparent reason. A missing multi-lingual man who might be a professional assassin. The case was a collection of dead ends.

One message did, however, catch his immediate attention. He pressed the intercom button and asked, "Tawanda, can you come in here?"

Tawanda was standing at the doorway in seven seconds. "What's up?"

"Who is this Dennis Toomey? It says FBI. I never heard of the guy."

"I'm supposed to know? I just get the calls. I don't ask for a bunch of pre-qualifications. He said his name was Dennis

Toomey, said he was from the FBI, said he wanted a call, or he'd be by this way this morning. Didn't I write that down?"

Garrison sighed. Every so often, Tawanda would be in one of her moods. Today, she had that chip on her shoulder and Garrison was getting the brunt of her arrogance. He just thought he'd ask a straight question and have a fighting chance of getting a straight answer. He should have known better.

"So, Tawanda, did he say what his call was about?"

"What's it say on my note?"

"Not a blessed thing."

"Then that's what he told me."

"I'm Special Agent Dennis Toomey, FBI" A short wiry form stood two feet behind Tawanda in the hallway and Garrison thought for a moment that Tawanda leaped three inches into the air.

"Lord, don't you at least announce yourself before you just strut down the hallway and hover over a person's shoulder like that? Well, not *over* my shoulder, but you know what I mean."

"Sorry. I was driving through and thought I'd stop by. I didn't see anybody out front so I walked down here." Toomey had to be five-foot-six and one-hundred-thirty-five pounds. Rail thin, pink-cheeked and with thinning hair combed across his scalp.

Tawanda started to argue when Garrison held up the palm of his hand and said, "Tawanda, that's alright. Let Mr. Toomey in. It's OK."

Tawanda didn't leave at once but stood there, appraising the Special Agent and assessing the need to inject some invective to assert her authority and put the FBI in its place. Tawanda feared no man and no agency.

Toomey took a tentative step forward and Tawanda made a belated step back to let him pass. She held her ground for three heart beats and turned around, letting Toomey know that any future visit to this office would absolutely require a formal checking in, along with Tawanda's vetting procedure.

Toomey remained standing at the doorway, looking at Walter.

"This is my dog, Walter."

"That's great. Does he bite?" Toomey never let his eyes leave the dog.

"If you're not nice to me, he'll sense it, for sure."

"What kind of a dog?"

"Huh?"

"What kind of a dog? Like, its breed."

"Not sure."

"No?"

"He's a dog, for crying out loud. Barks, has teeth, lifts his leg to piss on every tree. He's a dog. What kind of a question is that? What breed? You only have those dogs with papers where you come from?"

"I just don't like dogs, that's all."

"I thought the message said you were FBI. Is the FBI afraid of dogs?"

"It's personal."

"Well, Walter won't bite. Just walk in here nice and slow with your hands in front of you and palms open. You can sit over here."

Toomey did precisely as he was told, and Walter stood at attention and watched every move that Toomey made without blinking. When Toomey took his seat, he sat straight up.

"Walter. Good boy." Garrison opened his top drawer and removed something beige from inside. He slid it over the surface of the desk in Toomey's direction.

"Take that biscuit and whistle. Watch what happens."

"I . . . I can't whistle."

"What?"

"I can't whistle. Never could. My sister Maureen can hail a cab from three blocks through her teeth. I never could get more than a squeal."

"Then just make one of those sounds like you're calling a cat. You know, purse your lips and make that squeak thing. Watch what happens."

Toomey took the dog biscuit and made a noise, to which Walter responded by darting immediately to Toomey's feet, rolling over on his back, his tail wagging and his tongue lolling.

Toomey was dumfounded.

"Well, give Walter the biscuit, for crying out loud. He's not doing this for nothing."

Toomey held the bone down to Walter who snatched the biscuit, sat upright and chewed it. When he swallowed, he sat at Toomey's ankles, tail wagging.

"See? Walter likes you. Now, what's the FBI doing visiting the Dodge County sheriff? Must be a slow day at headquarters."

"It's this," Toomey said, sliding a paper from his pocket. "It's the report on the fingerprints we got from the body you recovered from the Peace River and from the lure you found on the boat."

Garrison reached over and looked at the report. It was brief and to the point. Neither print yielded any results. No hits on any data base that was connected to or maintained by the FBI. Much of the report was in alpha numeric code, but the bottom line was clear. No match was found among the millions of prints on the enormous FBI data base.

"So you're here to give me negative information about a case when I could have found that same information by checking my fax or my email? What gives, Special Agent Toomey?"

"You will see a code at the end of each response. All those numbers and letters mean something if you know how to read them."

Garrison looked and saw what appeared to be random combinations of letters and numbers. "And what do they say?"

"There's a code for every data base that was checked. For example, the first code indicates that the Integrated Automated Fingerprint Identification System was consulted. This is the Bureau's national . . ."

Garrison cut him off. "This isn't East Podunk, Special Agent Toomey. We know what IAFIS is."

"Sorry. The second series indicates that the Canadian data base, CPIC, was consulted."

That drew a nod from Garrison and a question. "There's a big 'but' coming. Where is it?"

"Sheriff Garrison, the report shows that only those two data bases were used. But the fingerprints you sent us were never checked against Interpol or other European data bases."

"Not that we have much experience with international crimes here in Dodge County, but tell me, Special Agent Toomey, why would I care about an Interpol data base?"

"Before I was transferred to Florida, I was assigned to the Boston and Chicago offices where the FBI had more frequent contact with European investigative units. I know the codes."

"There's a point here, right?" The skepticism on Garrison's face was apparent to his visitor.

"I know the people who are working on the remains you found. They're working on reconstructing the skull to see if they can ID the guy."

"I met a woman who does this stuff for a living. I haven't heard anything yet. You have?"

"Martha Mary Egan. She should be able to narrow it down better when she's done. Now, you know about the dental capping, but the teeth underneath were in good shape, nice and straight, but they crowned those perfectly good ones with crooked teeth."

"You're getting my attention."

Toomey assumed the pose of a professor and held up one finger. "First of all, American dental work is different from the work that's done in most other countries. This guy's work was definitely done overseas."

"OK. Go on."

"Second," he said, adding another finger, "the medical examiner's report describes the victim as uncircumcised. The vast majority of males of the victim's approximate age in the US are circumcised. Just the reverse in Europe. Plus, the supporting information that you sent in with your request mentioned that one witness thought he had an accent, maybe an English accent. You also mentioned in your report that the other print likely came from someone identified as being able to curse in Italian. That's just a few reasons why Interpol and other overseas data bases should have been consulted."

"I'm not sure I buy that as much as you're selling it, but I'll agree the odds are in your favor. So tell me, if going to Interpol is such an obviously good idea, why don't you just put in the request?"

Toomey appeared to wrestle uncomfortably with the answer. He shifted in his seat, crossed and uncrossed his legs. Then he said, "It's not my call, Sheriff Garrison. That has to come from somebody higher than me in the Tampa Bureau."

"How long have you been with the Bureau, Special Agent?"

"Twenty-eight years."

"You used to be in Boston and Chicago and now you're sitting in my office in Dodge County Florida. I would have thought you'd be the Bureau's top guy in Tampa, or at least somewhere near the top."

Toomey's discomfort level increased and Garrison detected the start of a blush. Another shift in his chair was followed by, "There is a personnel issue, Sheriff."

Garrison considered that. "So I need to find somebody farther up the Bureau's food chain to get agreement to resubmit these fingerprints to the data bases you described. Is that correct?"

A nod from Toomey.

"So, Dennis, if I can read between the lines, your recent reassignment to the Tampa Bureau of the FBI was not exactly a promotion."

Another nod. Toomey's discomfort remained on the surface.

"And because your name is mud at the Bureau's Tampa office, you want me to ask somebody there to check prints overseas?"

"Exactly."

"And I shouldn't mention you or your visit, right?"

Toomey stood from his seat and stepped over to the window that looked out on an open field. "I've been with Bureau a long time. I love my work. But Sheriff, under the circumstances, it would be better for all of us if you didn't mention my name. Your going to get the same negative results from the Bureau on the fingerprints any minute now by fax. They may already be here. I'm suggesting that you call the Bureau and say that you recognize the codes from some cases you worked on before, and that you recognize that some important European data bases were not cross-checked. You can add that you have reason to believe that the decedent was from overseas. You can mention the dental work and the lack of circumcision, if you need to."

"And your boss, the Special Agent in Charge, he won't think I'm blowing smoke?"

"If it comes up, tell him your brother is a dentist and you discussed this same matter before on another case. Tell him your brother looked in this guy's mouth and confirmed your suspicion."

"And what about the circumcision?"

Toomey returned to his seat. His lips curled and his eyes travelled around the room. Garrison could see the man was running possibilities through his mind. "Tell him you were circumcised five years ago and did a lot of reading on the subject before you went under the knife. So you know that the percentage of uncircumcised males is far higher in Europe than elsewhere."

Garrison nodded with some vigor at that suggestion. "I would have done that reading if I faced that situation, I certainly would have."

"He probably won't ask you any questions anyway, but it's better to be prepared."

"Why doesn't he do the European cross check on his own? Why does he need a special phone call from me before he does it?"

"Money is one reason. He's the brand new Special Agent in Charge at the Tampa Headquarters, and one of his jobs is managing the budget. Also, since he's new here, from Memphis, I don't believe he understands yet that there is a significant European population on Florida's west coast, Germans, Austrians, Brits, Swiss, who either live here full time or spend at least part of the year here. To him, the likelihood of a European being found that far up the Peace River is remote. Further, there were no missing person reports."

Garrison turned the information over in his mind. He reached for his telephone and said, "You're going to give me some more details on your recent difficulties with the Bureau, but right now I'd like you to get Martha Mary Egan on the phone. I'd like to talk to her."

Toomey checked his PDA, looked up a number, and punched it in. Martha Mary Egan picked up on the first ring.

"Egan."

"Martha, it's Dennis Toomey."

"Great. Just what I need. A call from a disgraced Bureau employee on my telephone line. Not that this line is being tapped, of course. This will do a lot for my career. What's up, Denny."

Toomey's complexion had flushed to a deep rose, but he never lost his composure. "That skull that you're working on."

"Give me a hint: I've got six in process."

"Male, pulled out of the Peace River in Dodge County."

"I'm looking at the young man as we speak, Dennis. His whole face was surgically altered a few months ago."

"You already told me about the surgical scars and the teeth."

"This guy's got a small prosthetic mental protuberance, what you'd call a chin implant. The superciliary ridge, his eyebrows, were built up as well. This guy went through some serious remodeling. But the medical examiner in Sarasota already put most of this on his report. It's not exactly breaking news."

"I'm with the sheriff in Dodge County right now. Can I put you on speaker?"

Garrison had two questions.

"When you rebuild the skull and come up with a face, are you going to do the rebuilding with or without the prosthetic chin and brow?"

"I'm going to make both. I'll be making two casts and I'll work on them side by side, so you'll see the before-and-after versions. If you want them fast, they may look a little unfinished."

"OK, that's fine. Special Agent Toomey tells me that one of the reasons we can't run his prints by Interpol is primarily budgetary and secondarily a result of a level of ignorance on the part of the new Special Agent in Charge in Tampa. He apparently has not yet learned that there are high numbers of Europeans who live on the west coast of Florida."

The response was slower this time, and Toomey was slouching in his seat.

"Well, I'm sure Special Agent Toomey explained that . . ."

Special Agent Toomey jumped in.

"It's OK, Martha. Sheriff Garrison and I have talked."

Martha came to Toomey's defense. "Sheriff Garrison, Special Agent Dennis Toomey is a superior member of the FBI, and I've known him for many years. For reasons that should embarrass his superiors, Special Agent Toomey was transferred and effectively demoted. The new Special Agent in Charge in Tampa is a first class jerk off, pardon my French, and I don't care who's listening in on this line."

"Why don't you make the suggestion? You already have some evidence that the victim is from overseas."

"Because I'm known as a FOD, a 'Friend of Dennis'. Technically, I'm not supposed to even know about the fingerprints and the data bases they've been run through. Dennis is right, Sheriff Garrison. If you make a call and toss in something about the teeth, he'll probably agree to take the next step."

"And if the Special Agent in Charge disagrees?"

Toomey interjected, "Maybe the circumcision angle will put him over the edge. Grown men are naturally sympathetic as soon as the word is mentioned."

Martha Mary added, "I'll bet you boys have your legs crossed at the mere mention of the word."

She was right. Garrison uncrossed his legs. "Let me think about this for a minute, OK?"

Martha Mary signed off and Toomey sat in the chair across from the Garrison's desk. The natural light coming in from the window dimmed dramatically and the sheriff looked out to see a passing series of dark clouds. In the distance, he spotted a flash of lightning. "Oh crap."

Toomey was perplexed. "What?"

Suddenly, Walter rose from his position at Toomey's feet and began a curious pacing routine, his tail down. The dog walked to a corner of the room and returned, then walked to another corner. In a combined growl and whine, Walter seemed to be saying, "Oh, no. Oh no." It was a low, plaintive, depressed moan, almost a lament.

"What's wrong with the dog, Sheriff?"

"Thunder. Poor Walter is afraid of thunder. He does this every time. He'll be alright."

Walter kept up the routine as if he was seeking some refuge, all the while muttering his woeful, "Oh no. Oh no." Eventually he went to the space under the sheriff's desk and huddled, still unnerved and wary of the thunder so distant it barely registered to the human ears in the room.

"In the summer when we get thunder storms almost every day, Walter really gets worked up. Loses weight and everything, don't you Walter?" The sheriff patted the dog on the head and tried to offer some comfort.

"OK, Special Agent Toomey, punch in the number for your office and I'll talk to this guy."

Toomey reached for the desk phone and punched in the numbers.

"This is the main line into the Tampa office. Ask for the Special Agent in Charge."

TWENTY

"J. Edgar Hoover used to wear women's dresses and high heels and they kept him in the job until he died. So what on earth did you do to get rewarded with a demotion?"

Sheriff Larry Garrison and FBI Special Agent Dennis Toomey were sitting at a booth in Cattle Driver's Diner having coffee when the question arose. Toomey's necktie was loosened, his navy blue suit jacket was on the bench next to him and the sleeves of his starched white shirt rolled up.

"I was the number three guy at the Chicago office and I was on a case involving a kidnapped twenty-year-old woman. This was three months ago. She was from the south side of Chicago and I traced her and her captor to a warehouse in Gary, Indiana. It was her ex-boyfriend. I called for back-up and it took almost two hours for anyone to show up. When they did, we got into the building and got the boyfriend, but by then, the girl was dead, suffocated by the duct tape that her boyfriend used to bind her.

"I was pissed off like I was never pissed off before. Why did it take so long for back-up to get there? I was screaming. It turns out the new head of Homeland Security was giving a speech at a resort just north of Chicago when my call for back-up came in. The Chicago office of the Bureau had most of its people there and they didn't leave until the speech and the ceremonies were over.

"So I was ranting about this at the scene when the Special Agent in Charge came over and told me to shut up, but a reporter got everything on audio and video and it really caused a stink. It was all over TV that night."

"Was it that bad?"

"I think one of the words I used was 'confuckulated'."

"O-o-o-h. On video?"

Toomey nodded. "The Bureau decided I wasn't a 'team player' and I was pulled off active investigations for three weeks until they sent me here. So I'm supposed to be humbled and I'm supposed to rehabilitate myself. Meanwhile, my new boss in Tampa is keeping me under his thumb."

Toomey waved to the server and asked for a refill on his coffee. When it came, he dropped in two sugars, stirred it, and the cup was half-empty, all in the span of about forty seconds.

Garrison considered the man's explanation. It was sufficiently self-deprecating that it rang true. In that case, Dennis Toomey had Garrison's sympathy.

"So, if your job is walk the walk and talk the talk, why get your nipple in a wringer over this? You'd be better off keeping your eyes straight ahead and your mouth shut."

Toomey shifted in his seat and leaned forward. "I just don't like the way this is being dismissed. The Bureau ought to just do the right thing." He sat back in his chair and took another sip of coffee. "But look, I've got enough time in the FBI to retire, and if I get canned over this, so what? I've always done what I thought was the right thing, and I don't like working with one hand tied behind my back. Besides, I've got an ex-wife in Boston and a grown son who lives in Denver. I have no ties to anywhere right now. I'm flexible and maybe even a little past my prime. Maybe I should buy a place around here and enjoy the sunshine."

Garrison was looking at someone who ran on nervous energy. A quiet retirement in a rocking chair was not in this man's future. "This call for re-running the fingerprints could develop absolutely nothing. You understand that." He was careful to manage the level of expectations.

"Absolutely. It happens all the time."

"If I find out anything, how do I reach you? Just call your office?" Even before he asked the question, he'd guessed the answer.

"I'd rather check back in with you, if you don't mind. And please, call me Dennis." Toomey stood and extended his hand. Garrison felt a firm handshake.

"I'm Larry from now on, and I'll tell Tawanda to expect your call and to patch it through when it comes in."

"Thanks. And tell her I'm sorry for sneaking up on her like I did."

When Garrison returned to his office, Tawanda was on the phone and jotting down something on a telephone message pad. As he walked past, she glanced up but gave no clear indication that the call she was taking was urgent or needed his personal attention. The file on the autopsy report was still on his desk and he opened it when he sat down. Next to the file was the official print-out from the FBI, the same report Special Agent Dennis Toomey showed him earlier. Garrison opened the file and looked at the face of the deceased. The face. Where did I see this face?

Tawanda tapped the doorframe lightly and said, "Sheriff, two messages. The FBI called and said you'll have a report soon on the fingerprints that are being run against some European data bases. And I got this message a few minutes ago." She walked to his desk and put the note in front of him. "Dr. Hernandez called again. This was his second call. It must be important because he left his office number, his home number and his cell. No doctor I know gives out his home or cell numbers."

Garrison wondered what was so important.

"He won't tell me anything, not with all the privacy laws, but he sounded a little anxious. By the way, is this the guy that got fished out of the river the other day?"

"That's him. Handsome devil, eh?" They were both looking at the photograph of the bloated man's face.

"He's not in great shape, but I'd swear he looks like somebody I've seen before."

"Like who? I had the exact same reaction."

"You still have no ID at all?"

"He used the name Peter Billings when he rented the boat, and he had a Florida license with the same name, but it's phony. We can't find out anything about him. I'm sure you saw the report from the FBI. So far, they can't put anything together on this guy either. And by the way, if this Dennis Toomey happens to call in, patch him in, OK?"

"I will, but don't forget to call Dr. Hernandez."

Tawanda was almost in the hallway when Garrison said, "By the way, Toomey said he's sorry he made you jump out of your skin when he showed up."

Tawanda smiled. "No harm, no foul."

Garrison picked up the phone and called Dr. Hernandez. Whatever glow the sheriff enjoyed moments earlier was dashed.

"Why do you want more tests? Your people drew plenty of blood when I was there a few days ago."

"I want to see an MRI of your head, Sheriff, and a lumbar puncture, what we used to call a spinal tap. I think it would be a good idea to have them done the same day."

"So, tell me, what's your thinking? You must have some idea."

"Let's get the tests done, then we'll talk."

Before he could respond the doctor cut back in, almost as if he could sense the reason for Garrison's reluctance. "I have my suspicions, but I'd like to be sure. Until I get the test results, it's just guess work."

"But you suspect something. Otherwise, why the tests? A spinal tap?"

Garrison listened to empty noise, holding out for a response that did not come.

"I know I've got some arthritis. I can feel it in my joints. Is that it?"

"Could be related."

Garrison understood when he was getting the stall. He waited for the doctor to continue.

A long pause was followed by a softer, lower tone of voice from Hernandez. "Look, Sheriff Garrison, I've seen this before and it turned out to be MS. I'm not saying it is, but you need to know what the likelihood is. I won't be sure until I see the results of the tests I'm ordering."

Multiple Sclerosis. The thought of it took Garrison's breath away. He'd seen other people with the disease and it was never pleasant. It got worse as you got older, until you ended up unable to control your muscles.

Hernandez could discern the effect his words had on the sheriff. "I want you to understand that this is only a preliminary diagnosis. But your reflexes are off, you have some creeping neuropathy, and your gait is awkward."

"My gait?"

"You're walking off balance. Impaired coordination. Not so pronounced that most people would notice, but I see it. And when I asked you to close your eyes and tell me when you felt anything, I was using a pin on the soles of your feet."

"I remember it hurt when you stuck me."

"I stuck you seven times, Sheriff. You only felt the last one."

"O-o-ooh. I failed that test, huh?" Indeed, his emotional self-image fell to the floor with a thud.

"D-Minus."

"Why couldn't you tell me this when I saw you last time?"

"Because I wanted to see your blood test results first. I can't tell everything from a blood test, but I can rule out some things. There was nothing that would lead me in any clear direction. Let's get these tests done and go from there."

Garrison agreed to have the doctor make arrangements for the tests at Sarasota Memorial.

When he hung up, Garrison spun his chair around and stared out the window. The doc was right, of course. Run a few more tests. Any fretting he did in the meantime would be pointless. He determined to get busy and stay that way.

His intercom buzzed and he was glad for the distraction.

"What is it, Tawanda?"

"Dennis Toomey is on the line. You wanted me to put him through."

Toomey was checking in to ask if he'd heard from the Tampa office about the fingerprints against the larger data base.

"We should have something from them later on. But here's something strange."

Garrison described how he and Tawanda and Dr. Parwani saw something familiar in the face of the deceased. "Dennis, we know this guy was professionally remodeled. We think his features were changed to look like someone else."

"Can you send me the autopsy photos?"

"Where? Give me a fax number."

Toomey recited the number and told Garrison he'd be at his office in Sarasota in about forty minutes. "I'll pick up the pictures then."

TWENTY-ONE

"I have good news and bad news. What do you want to hear first?"

Vanya was becoming more westernized. She and Emilio were sitting at a small circular cocktail table on the veranda of the Gulf Breeze Inn sipping glasses of iced tea. Emilio asked for the good news first.

"The police are not looking for Alek Mironev. I have my scanner turned on and there have been no bulletins, nothing to indicate any concern. I believe they are content in the knowledge that Alek Mironev is on his way to New Orleans."

"I suppose that's good news. It means that President Nikolai Mironev is keeping information about his son's kidnapping to himself."

"That is also my assessment. I would expect that there would be some obvious signs of police activity around Tampa, especially the interstate highway heading north and in the direction of New Orleans if they were concerned about a possible kidnapping."

"And the bad news, Vanya?"

"Ah, the bad news. Nothing has yet been resolved with respect to the Chechen demands. There has been no announcement from Moscow."

"They are making our job more difficult than it needs to be. I want to deposit young Mr. Mironev before the end of the coming weekend."

"Not likely, I'm afraid."

"Every hour that passes makes life that much more complicated." Emilio was staring off into the sky over the Gulf of Mexico but his mind was on his captive and the pressing need to complete the assignment.

"I told them that. When Alek Mironev does not appear soon in New Orleans, people are going to become suspicious."

"The FBI will be among the first to start searching. No one wants to be known as the agency that was duped by a simple scam. They will begin to retrace every step from the time Alek got on the Planet Capital plane at Heathrow. Eventually, they will focus on the mysterious lady at the Sarasota Airport who interrupted his arrival."

This notion seemed to catch Vanya off guard but she revealed little beyond widened eyes.

"Every peculiarity will set off alarms, and taking a young and important lad into a ladies' room would certainly be seen as peculiar. Don't you agree?"

"So should I just stay out of sight until this is over?"

"You can't. There are too many things to be done. Your preparations remain vital if we are to conduct the drop off and departure as planned. Today should be your last visit here to Boca Grande, but if you just drop out of sight entirely, it draws its own suspicions. Your neighbors will notice your absence."

"Pah! My neighbors do not know me and I do not know them."

"Vanya, if you look in a mirror, you will understand that you are someone that everyone will notice. Your neighbors, especially your male neighbors, will expect to see you going about your daily business. They want to see you as they usually do, going from your apartment, returning home, acting as you would under the most mundane circumstances." Emilio was certain he caught the beginning of a blush cross her face.

"I will do that. Meanwhile, have you seen any television?"

"I avoid it when I can."

"The celebrity television programs have crews staked out in New Orleans waiting to catch a glimpse of Alek Mironev."

"The celebrity press corps will have less patience than law enforcement. Make certain you emphasize the urgency in your next communication. We must resolve this soon."

In a small apartment in Sarasota, the shades were drawn across the windows to keep out the bright sunlight and peering eyes. The only light inside came from the glow of a laptop computer sitting on a table in the kitchen. The operator, thick set and dressed only in worn jeans and a scruffy tee shirt, sat hunched over the screen, his right hand manipulating the mouse and his fingers tapping out messages.

There was news and the news demanded a response. If the report about the fingerprints was correct, he could be called upon with little notice to change his plans.

He used a small notebook to take down some pertinent information. He finished his communications, logged off and turned on the ceiling light in the kitchen. Then he looked over his notes.

They were brief. "Sheriff L. Garrison, Dodge County. Tampa Bureau FBI. Homicide: James P. Finney." The words represented a major departure from the original plan, but he was accustomed to sudden lurches in assignments. He could ill afford to drop everything concerning his original task, but this was a serious development and demanded his attention.

From the refrigerator, he removed a quart bottle of milk, unscrewed the top, and took several gulps. He grabbed an apple, took a candy bar from a cabinet drawer, shut off the light in the kitchen, and left. It was time for some serious looking around.

TWENTY-TWO

Sheriff Garrison turned off the television news and walked to his bedroom. His apartment was a Spartan affair with two bedrooms, one reserved for his home office, and one bath. He was not a finicky housekeeper, but there was little sign of life in the space. All of his dishes were washed and put away, and there was no clutter.

On one wall of his living room was a framed print of an El Greco painting, *Knight with His Hand on His Breast.* It was a dark, serious, almost somber work, with a handsome bearded gentleman wearing a formal jacket and white ruffled collar. The subject stood alone and faced the painter squarely, the ornate gold hilt of his sword standing straight up in front of him. Garrison spent many hours at Madrid's Prado admiring El Greco's work, and felt particularly drawn to this portrait. He received this print as a gift from a friend when he left Spain years ago to return to the US. Since then, he always recognized his Knight with a slight nod as he passed through his apartment, an acknowledgement of the man's valor and commitment to his fellow man, whether lord or vassal.

Next to the painting was hung a long and broad sword manufactured at one of the great sword makers of Toledo and also a gift from his days in Spain. It was four feet long with a handsome gold-plated hilt and leather-wrapped handle, a reproduction of an ancient original allegedly owned by King Solomon. Garrison kept the sword polished to a high gloss and spent a week's pay when he first moved to Dodge County to have it custom-mounted on a velvet background and bordered in a sturdy oak frame. The print and the sword always took Garrison back to a sweet time of his life that he treasured. They reminded him daily of duty and wisdom, courage and fairness, qualities he admired in others and considered worthy aims to emulate in his own life.

His apartment was in a cluster of four six-unit buildings about two miles from the Sheriff's Department, and his neighbors were a mixture of young couples, older retirees and a few small children. It was a place to start out or to wind down; few were here for their middle years.

His bedroom nightstand carried some evidence of human habitation, with a few books with bookmarks in various locations. For reasons he considered on more than one occasion but could not parse, he rarely read one book at a time. He moved from one genre to another and was as likely to have at least one book of poetry as well as a recent release of current fiction. Tonight he was too preoccupied to pick any of the books and he opted instead to try to get to sleep quickly.

He set his alarm clock and whistled for Walter who had been asleep on the kitchen floor. Walter appeared, rear legs stiff from a combination of sleep and advancing years, and took his place by the doorway on a large plaid dog bed. In less than a minute, Garrison could hear Walter snoring.

Garrison turned off the bedside lamp and put his head on the pillow. Walter's snoring was loud, as usual, but Garrison could hardly blame his canine companion for the night's fitfulness. He spent most of the uneasy night in a confused fog, only part of this world, trying to manage his way through the jungle of thoughts about the conversation with Dr. Hernandez. The doc was no alarmist, but Garrison did not mistake the real sense of urgency in the man's tone. Whatever it was, he'd go through the tests and then get more information. He shook his head more than once to clear it, knowing he could not at this early stage of knowledge, of speculation, share his fears with anyone else. Except for Walter, there was no one with whom he could talk about his feelings of dread at the doctor's news.

There was a person in his life once. To Anita McGovern, Garrison could reveal his innermost thoughts and fears and hopes. Anita was patient with him, and kind. She was far from beautiful on the outside but gorgeous on the inside. In fact, until he got to know her, he would have said she was just short of ugly. Skinny and tall, with mousey brown hair that hung limp to her shoulders and teeth that belied her childhood of poverty, she was an elementary school teacher in Fort Meade, one of those dots on the map of central Florida. A sort of female Ichabod Crane.

He wondered anew how he could have missed the signs of Anita's own demons. Garrison knew he was only intermittently given to self-examination, real introspection, before he met Anita and in her found a person who probed and prodded and enforced a strict code of honesty within oneself. "Tell me what you're feeling, Larry. Be honest with me, or at least be honest with yourself." And he did, and he was.

They met at a County Commission meeting, he there to defend a budget request, she to speak in favor of paving a rural street. She was born and raised in Maine and moved to Florida six years ago. A few meetings with her for coffee on weekend mornings led to a lunch date and then dinner. For Garrison, who subsisted on a combination of diner food and his own cooking, and always alone, dining out with a friend was a welcome change. He never believed the saying about having a "soul mate", at least not in the mythical sense of there being some perfectly complementary being on the planet. But with Anita McGovern, Garrison found someone with whom he shared an unusual affinity, some bond of friendship, love even, and to whom he felt such compatibility that he could expose elements of himself that he'd never shared with anyone before.

To Anita McGovern, he poured forth, almost spewed thoughts-into-words that until then he kept harbored and secured in some hidden niche of his psyche. How his father had beat him and his brother and his mother so badly and so regularly that they shed not a tear that night when the word came from a State Trooper that he'd been killed in a rollover on the way home from a bar. How he himself had sunk into drunken stupors almost every night for years to ease the pain and deny the memories of the mother and brother he abandoned when he joined the service and escaped the agony of a lost adolescence. How he feared that he might carry the birthright of violence into his later life, and vowed to reject his heritage of inflicting pain. How he sometimes felt his control was tenuous and just below the surface.

Garrison shared himself and his insecurities in ways that made his soul soar. He let her into his being and felt better about himself, almost elated with the sense that he'd unburdened his soul. So many nights she'd listen to him. If confession was good for the soul, Garrison thought, he was in a divine state of grace when he was with Anita.

Their lovemaking was cautious and unhurried, a merging of body and spirit. With Anita, he was not the Sheriff of Dodge County, but Larry, the uncertain child whose principles and good heart led him to a degree of respect and praise he felt he never deserved.

He learned the lesson, though, that talking was one thing and communicating another. All the while he was unloading his own onerous baggage, he failed to pay attention to Anita's private suffering. His sense of renewal was a one-way street, and he was the only car on the road. So when he found her hanging from the oak tree on the far side of the barn, a small step stool knocked over on its side beneath her feet, he felt such shame, so much greater than the loss of his dear Anita. He felt such anguish that he'd taken her encouragement and advice for granted, had not made the time or the effort to give back some of what Anita had so generously given him.

Anita had her own demons, and he learned later what they were. Her slowly eroding heart, her constant state of physical pain, her deterioration of mind and spirit, the wrenching loss years before of her only child to cancer, her guilt at the thought that she contributed the fatal genetic markers to her dead child. Anita had lung cancer, the doctor told Larry after the autopsy, and it spread sufficiently through her body that it reached her brain.

Garrison never knew, nor had he asked her state of mind and body while she was alive. He would punish himself, lapse back into the depths of Dewar's bottles and jugs of cheap wine. He awoke one morning two months after her death and two months after a daily regimen of booze and self-pity, with a resolve that he would do his level best to never take a person like Anita for granted again. Like Garrison's, Anita's life was chockablock full of potential grievances, but unlike him, not one gram of score-settling poisoned her memories. What he failed to recognize in her lifetime, he would try hard to appreciate in her death.

Her death was now ten months past. Tonight he thought a lot about Anita, and he jotted a note to himself on his small note pad that he always kept on the nightstand next to his bed: "Call Dr. Maria Albano" he wrote. Tomorrow morning, he would see that note and make the call. He felt himself settle when he put the pencil down.

He looked forward to the busywork that would certainly consume him when he eventually got to work. The result of the FBI prints came in late in the day and pointed a finger in an unusual direction. The victim had a long history of criminality, and a fingerprint on the lure came from a suspected participant in more than a few homicides across the globe. The basic information was sketchy, but he should get much more clarification tomorrow.

When he arrived with Walter at the office the next morning, Tawanda was there, "Catching up on some paperwork," she said before he could ask. He could sense her preoccupation with something undefined, but no remnants of the tough attitude she wore on her sleeve the day before.

Without looking up from her sorting and filing, she suggested that he rearrange his schedule to arrive earlier. "Your colleagues in other law enforcement agencies apparently take their jobs seriously, Sheriff. You've had two phone calls while you were getting your beauty sleep. One from Dennis Toomey and another from somebody named Rene Royale from Paris. He's a big fromage at Interpol. That means . . ."

"Cheese, Tawanda, I know. He called from France?"

Tawanda ignored his question and resumed in a mock French accent. "Varee saxxy. I almost have what you say, a climax of some magnitude?"

"Come on, Tawanda. You know how I get when you talk dirty."

"He faxed a file and it's on your desk. And Toomey said he'll call again at eleven. Are you guys like phone buddies?"

"I got some results back from the FBI late yesterday. They identified the victim from the Peace River. James Philip Finney is his name. Apparently a very bad guy with a long sheet, including sexual abuse of minors. And with all the plastic surgery and the dental work, it smells bad. The shooter's fingerprint leads in another direction, but it looks like that man has a long history of his own. Plenty of aliases and plenty of dead people wherever he showed up. I'm hoping there's a lot more detail in that Interpol file."

"Toomey seems like a nice guy, by the way. I mean, for a Feeb. The ones I've met from the Bureau were usually pompous and overbearing."

"You sound like you like the guy. Almost."

Tawanda ignored the comment. "I'll leave you and Walter to your file."

Garrison had never seen an official Interpol file and was intrigued by the one in front of him now. He could tell it was an extract from another larger case that was developed in large part by UK law enforcement personnel. Consequently, it was written in English, but he wondered if he'd be able to navigate a file in another European language. Garrison spoke Spanish well, but his French and Italian were rusty and he remembered only a smattering of German.

This file concerned a male adult individual known under various names. He was a suspect two years ago in a murder in Marseilles but never captured. In the US, he was implicated in the death of a street thug with connections to the Irish Republican Army. Most recently, he was using the alias Patrick Keough when he was interrupted in an assassination plot in the UK. The man known as Patrick Keough was captured but escaped from a prison hospital. In spite of rigorous efforts by law enforcement to seal off every port, air field and ferry service, he was never seen. Bulletins were posted at every point of entry and exit in the European Union and no positive sightings were reported. The man simply disappeared.

The file suggested that the man had operated in several countries over a long period of time, and he blended in well. He was assumed to be fluent in at least French, English, Italian and Spanish based on the various locations where his presence was verified. A photograph was in the file, but it showed a battered face, swollen by the injuries he sustained when he was captured in England. He was listed as 190 centimeters and 90 kilograms. Garrison did a quick calculation and estimated the man to be about 6'3" and 200 pounds. There was no age given, but Garrison saw a man of approximately middle age, maybe close to his own. A cover letter with the file suggested that this suspect should be considered armed and very dangerous.

Garrison propped the photograph of the man once known as Patrick Keough on his desk and studied the face. He would arrange to get some copies made. What would possess such a man, not a particularly young man, to become involved in yet another murder, and in Dodge County? The man was apparently intelligent, multi-lingual, comfortable in various disguises and situations, and moved easily through several countries. If he was so successful at his craft, as the Interpol file suggested, he was probably a man of some wealth. Murders of the kind described in the file did not come cheap to those who ordered them. And if he failed in his most recent task, why get involved in yet another? At what point do a man's skills, however considerable, begin to wane? This man had a curious sense of morality, a twisted ethical compass, and a pathology that a skilled psychiatrist might enjoy for research. But why, if he had success and money, take on one more assignment, and risk capture? Garrison gave this considerable thought as he probed the lines and creases of experience on the face of the man known as Patrick Keough.

An hour went by and Toomey called the sheriff back.

"I looked over those autopsy pictures, and I can't see any resemblance to anyone I know. You have any guesses?"

"None. But Tawanda is certain it's somebody famous. By the way, I'm looking at an Interpol file of our suspect. You'll want to take a look."

"I will." Toomey didn't follow up those words right away, but paused for a moment. "Look, Larry, I've been thinking about taking some time off and, besides, my boss would like to see a lot less of me than he does. Do you mind if I stop by your office?"

Garrison's mind was never far from his conversation with Dr. Hernandez, but the events and discoveries today were great therapy. As soon as he thought of Dr. Hernandez, Garrison remembered the note he'd written to himself the night before and made the call.

"Karen Albano." Her voice clipped and professional.

"Doctor, this is Larry Garrison. I thought I'd get an answering machine."

"I started having office hours on Saturdays a few months ago, but don't tell anybody. I usually have a secretary taking calls, but she decided to have her baby three weeks early. What can I do for you?"

"I need to see you. Can I make an appointment?"

"Are you feeling OK? Do you need to come in right away?"

"I'm OK. Nothing dangerous. But I'd like to talk with you."

"Tomorrow I'm not free until five. Can you stop by then?"

"Tomorrow? It's Sunday."

"Right. I've got a family thing going on, niece's birthday. But I'll be back by five.

"Are you sure?"

"I'll be here."

TWENTY-THREE

"I need to stop by the repair garage and check on my regular vehicle. They had to ship it to a body shop to get the frame straightened. Up for a little ride?"

Toomey took a long look at the Chevy Super Sport and climbed in. "Can we cruise for some babes while we're at it?"

"We pass by a school on the way. St. Agnes' Academy for the Terminally Unattractive. They might be hard up for a couple worn out old lawmen and we could get lucky."

Toomey didn't notice Walter in the car until he felt hot breath over his shoulder. "Is it legal to take your personal pet on law enforcement calls?"

"Dennis, I've got special dispensation. Walter here is a certified police dog."

"Really?"

"I certified him myself. He comes with me on most of my calls. Tells me if somebody has a criminal mind. Smart as a whip and almost never wrong."

"Sure. Does Walter still like me, by the way?"

"I'm not a betting man, but I'd put money on the likelihood

that Walter loves you. He even says you're OK, for a Yankee. Did you have coffee?"

"It was crap, but I had a cup anyway." He was looking over his shoulder at Walter when he answered.

Garrison turned to enter the Dunkin Donuts drive-through lane.

When they drove off, Toomey was surveying the scenery. "I'm still new here, so tell me more about this place, Dodge County."

"You tell me. I'll be interested in your reactions to what you've seen so far."

"I spent most of my life in big cities . . ."

"Try." Garrison was smiling.

Toomey turned in his seat and studied the people and businesses they passed by. "OK. Going down some of these streets reminds me a little of the Wild West. I did a little reading about this place before I moved down to Florida, and what I read about this part of the state seems to ring true. We just passed a bunch of corrals and a sign for a rodeo coming to town. Florida had its cowboys and they worked this area for a long time."

"Maybe for not as long as you might think, but basically you're right."

"There are some farms and orange groves, and I see a lot of workers in the fields." He pointed to his left. "There are some Hispanics and African-Americans in front of the convenience store waiting to be picked up, probably for constructions work or odd jobs."

Garrison nodded and appreciated Toomey's perception.

"There are clusters of houses where the people are either mostly of one racial minority or another. It's probably like most cities, but on a smaller scale. Ethnic enclaves."

A group of motorcyclists were headed in the other direction and Toomey commented, "I'll bet that group has more tattoos than teeth."

Garrison couldn't suppress a guffaw as they approached an intersection and waited for the light to change. In his rear view mirror, Garrison spotted the infamous Virgil Swett behind him and astride his silver and purple Harley, revving it and making enough noise to cause Toomey to turn around in his seat and check out its source. Beside Swett was another rider, the same beefy man that Garrison saw with Virgil a few days ago. Virgil had a black jacket, black bandana tied around his shaved head and a pair of large extra-dark sunglasses. Apparently going for the Darth Vader look.

Toomey saw Garrison staring at the rear-view mirror. "I hate the damned things."

"I love them, myself. It's some of the riders I can't stand."

"Is the guy behind us familiar? I see you checking him out in your mirror and you aren't smiling."

Garrison nodded his head. "Gives Harley riders a bad name. Just one of many, I'm afraid. I'm sure there's some heavy-duty drug dealing going on, but we don't have the personnel to chase it all down. The two turkeys behind us are probably into it up to their eyeballs. I've asked for help from the feds and the state, but you know how that goes. We try to do our best, but there's more going on than we can handle on our own."

"Get in line along with everybody else." Toomey looked around and continued his observations. "Putting worn out appliances and junk cars in the yard is commonplace down here, but that reminds me of a lot of places up north in New England, too."

"Really?" Garrison's surprise was genuine.

"Really. There are plenty of people who have a couple cars without wheels sitting on concrete blocks, plus a pit bull roaming the property to guard all the valuables. Not all the rednecks live south of the Mason-Dixon Line."

"And here I thought everybody up there sat around in white

clapboard houses and discussed Thoreau every night in front of a blazing fireplace."

"They do that, too, but not if there's a pit bull in the same room. Pit bulls hate Thoreau."

"You already met Tawanda. Any opinions there?"

"We didn't get off on the right foot, but I've talked to her on the phone a couple times since then. A nice lady. Smart, quick-witted. And she set me up at the Dodge Budget Motel at a special weekly rate."

Garrison turned to Toomey at that revelation.

"I figured I'd take a few days off from the Bureau. Maybe find out if I'll like the retirement gig." Toomey's matter-of-fact words did not disguise the interest he was developing in the case or in Dodge County.

"That motel is the only one around here, by the way, unless you count a couple of love nests along the highway. I don't trust the sheets in those places."

"Well, at the Dodge Budget Motel, so far so good."

"Then you haven't seen any Palmetto bugs yet."

"What's a Palmetto bug?"

"You'll know one when you see one. Imagine a cockroach you can saddle up and ride away on."

"Sounds delightful."

"They've got them in the best hotels in Sarasota and the worst hotels in Jacksonville. Palmetto bugs don't discriminate."

They were silent for several minutes until they reached the Interstate and Garrison looked at his gas gauge. "I need some gas. There's a place just before the on ramp.

Toomey offered to pump the gas but Garrison waved him off. "You could buy me an orange juice, though."

Toomey entered and picked out two cartons of juice and approached the counter. When he reached into his pocket to pay for the purchase, some coins came out with some folding money and landed on the floor, rolling in every direction. The customer behind him, a tall dark-haired man, snagged two of the errant coins and placed them on the counter. Toomey retrieved the rest and thanked the man for his help, paid the counter clerk and left. As he stood next to Garrison at the pumps, he said thanks once again to the man who nodded in return, climbed into his yellow Jeep and drove off.

Toomey and Garrison went to the repair garage and stopped once more for coffee on the way back to the sheriff's office. When they walked in, Tawanda was just passing by on her way to her desk.

"That coffee mine?" Garrison handed it to her.

"I visited my SUV. She's going to be tied up for another few days."

"Poor baby." Tawanda turned to Toomey. "How is the Dodge Budget treating you?"

"Fine, but the Sheriff was warning me about Palmetto bugs."

"They'll keep you up at night when they start their war dance. But they only bite if you snore loud. You don't snore, do you, Agent Toomey?"

"Agent Toomey and I will be in my office, Tawanda." Walter remained in the reception area where Tawanda was spoiling him with a biscuit and some ear rubbing.

When they entered Garrison's office, Toomey asked, "How long has Tawanda been here."

"She's started as a deputy about twelve years ago. She was a widow with a small child, the first woman and first African-American in uniform here. She passed all the tests, did a good job, took some courses, got one promotion, and absorbed a lot of grief. Then she went to a bar fight and took two rounds in the side from a .44 while she was protecting her partner. Got a new hip and lost half a stomach."

"You get the guy who shot her?"

Tawanda appeared at the doorway, a message slip in her hand. "I did. One round in the chest that lodged in his spine. He'll be paralyzed from the neck down for the rest of his life."

"You look fine now."

"I can't pass the physical so I can't be on the road, but this desk job is OK for now. By the way," she said as she turned her attention to Garrison, "Martha Mary Egan called. She's faxing some photos of the reconstruction within the hour."

"Will you bring them in as soon they come in?"

"Sure enough." When she walked out, Toomey noticed a limp he had not seen before.

Garrison waited until she was out of earshot before he continued. "Tawanda's going to law school nights. She graduates in the spring and takes her bar exam in July."

"So you'll lose her soon."

"She wants to work as a prosecutor at the State Attorney's office, so we'll probably see a lot of her even after she graduates. One day, this woman is going to run for State Attorney, maybe even Attorney General, and she'll win. She just doesn't know it yet." Garrison leaned forward and asked another question. "So any more impressions of our fine county?"

"It's not the Florida we see on the postcards."

Garrison leaned back in his chair and stared at the ceiling as if considering an answer from a wide range of possibilities.

"You're right. No ocean waves, no broad sandy beaches, no high-rise hotels."

"And there's poverty. I see it everywhere and you probably have the problems that come with it."

"Poor people do tend to drink cheap alcohol in large quantities, and we've got that. And they smoke too much and some have poor hygiene. Pregnancies by close relatives are not nearly as rare here as they ought to be, and a lot of our people have low expectations for themselves and those around them. They're probably a little sadder and fatter than they should be, and they're probably too easily reconciled to the suffering that's been delivered to them by themselves and others."

Toomey was stunned by the frankness and even more stunned by the sheriff's cynicism. "You sound bitter."

"Sometimes when I wake up on the wrong side of the bed, I get resigned to the futility that so many of these people here face. It can wear on you."

"So what do the people do if they want to get ahead?"

"The ambitious ones move away. The money's on the coast. Places like Naples, Sanibel and Sarasota. We're too far inland to get attention from good employers. We also don't have the major land developers here yet, but that's going to happen one day."

"When I first moved down here, I heard that the millionaires live in Naples but the billionaires live in Sarasota."

"Lots of money in both places, but I'd say that's more than half right."

Just then, Tawanda knocked on the door and stuck her head in. "The fax you were waiting for just came in."

"Let's take a look."

Garrison accepted them and looked them over. There were frontal photos plus left and right profiles. In addition, there was a photograph of a reconstructed smile to illustrate the altered front teeth. Garrison had seen examples of facial rebuilds at various criminology lectures and presentations, but this was the first instance where he was directly involved and he was impressed.

Tawanda was standing over the sheriff's shoulder, anxious for some reaction. The sheriff handed the photographs to Toomey and noticed Tawanda standing very close.

"What is it Tawanda?"

"These pictures. Aren't they incredible?" There was excitement in her voice.

Toomey said, "Martha Mary is one of the best at this."

Garrison rubbed his jaw as he studied the photographs, unsure why Tawanda was acting like a juvenile, bouncing on her toes. The photos showed a young male, probably between twenty and thirty years of age with dark hair parted on the right and a slight widow's peak. The lips were thin, the jaw prominent and with a noticeable cleft in the chin.

Tawanda could hardly contain herself. "Come on, Sheriff, you know this guy!"

"I know. His name is James Philip Finney and he's an ex-con from England."

"But you know who he looks like. Everybody does."

Toomey was still focused on the photographs. "I know I've seen the face somewhere."

Garrison felt left out. "Give me a hint, Tawanda."

"That is Alek Mironev, I swear."

"Who?"

"Alek Mironev. Son of the Russian President and most eligible bachelor in the world, if you trust the judgment of *People* magazine."

Toomey handed the photos back to Garrison. "Tawanda's right."

"Alek Mironev? I should know this fellow, right?"

Toomey punched in the number for Martha Mary Egan and pressed the button for the speaker.

"Martha Mary, I've got some folks here who tell me that we're looking at a guy who bears a remarkable resemblance to a young man named Alek Mironev. Tell me what you think."

"In my job, Agent Toomey, I'm not supposed to make those kinds of suggestions. It skews my work product. But . . ."

"But if I put sharp things under your fingernails . . ."

"It looks like Mironev, but Alek Mironev's fingerprints are on file because of his passport and international travel, and they don't match with this fellow's. This guy you're looking at was remanufactured to look like Alek Mironev. No doubt about that. He had a passable job of cosmetic surgery and some so-so dental work. Take a look at the fourth photograph I faxed to you."

Garrison flipped through the pages and found it. He turned it around so Tawanda and Toomey could see it.

"There are three smooth blue crescents, two small and one slightly larger. These were surgically implanted to give the victim slightly heavier brows and a more prominent chin. You can even see how the implant was creased to form a little dimple."

Toomey asked how the implants were secured.

"Surgical cement and a few plastic clips. If they stayed inside long enough, the bone would start to grow around them, but these were still resting right above the surface of the skull and jaw. I'm estimating that these were implanted twelve to sixteen weeks ago. I can get a firmer estimate if you want. We have an orthopedic surgeon available and a plastic surgeon in Naples has done some consulting for us before. You've got all the reports and the photos. I'll hold the model here unless you think you need it right away."

Garrison said, "If we need it, we know where it is."

"By the way, you need to speak to Sue Benidt over in Ballistics. She's got something for you."

"Benidt?" The name caught Toomey off stride.

"The same one you worked with up north. She works here in Sarasota now." There was a pause. "And I know everything, Dennis."

Sheriff Garrison and Tawanda Bradford were in the dark. While the phone call was being transferred, Toomey turned three shades of crimson.

When he spoke he was stammering. "I knew Sue Benidt from my years in Boston."

"Evidently." Tawanda's voice was laced with mockery and she enjoyed Toomey's discomfort.

The phone was picked up on the other end and a woman's voice came across the line on speaker. "So, Dennis, do your colleagues in Dodge County have a full dossier on you yet?" She laughed. Toomey sat stock still.

"I can fax them everything, Dennis, including all the gory details. You were quite the dude back then."

"It was another life, Susan. I've settled down." Toomey's voice was barely a mutter.

"I'll believe that when I see it. Who am I speaking with, by the way?"

Garrison introduced himself and Tawanda to the disembodied Susan Benidt.

"Someday I'll have to tell you two about those Christmas parties with Special Agent Dennis Toomey. Meanwhile, let me tell you what we found here." Benidt's tone suggested she was ready for business.

The trio in Dodge County could hear papers being shuffled. Benidt started. "The round that was removed from the decedent's skull was fractured into two pieces. It was too damaged by ricocheting around the skull cavity to get enough information from the lands and grooves to match it to a specific weapon, but I will tell it is a .22 caliber round and it was made overseas by Fiocchi, the Italian ammunition manufacturer."

"Fiocchi makes ammunition here, don't they?" Tawanda knew her ammo.

"In Missouri, yes. But they don't make this caliber in the states. Someone went to Europe to get this particular round."

When she hung up, Garrison asked the key questions: Why was a criminal from England named James Philip Finney modified to look like Alek Mironev, and why was Finney killed on a remote patch of the Peace River in Dodge County?

No one in the room had a good answer, but Toomey stood up and removed his cell phone from his belt. "The Tampa Bureau ought to know about this." He walked toward the door. "Alek Mironev was in Tampa for the Super Bowl. We didn't have a specific detail assigned to him, but we kept close watch. The day after the game, he took off on his own for New Orleans. He never told anyone ahead of time."

Garrison turned to Tawanda once again and they waited while Toomey stepped into the hallway to call the Tampa office of the FBI.

"Well, that answers a few questions, doesn't it?"

Tawanda asked, "But why kill someone who's had all this surgery to look like Mironev."

"Maybe Finney outlived his usefulness. Maybe there was a plan to do a switch with the real Alek Mironev and it got botched up, or maybe the plans changed. Whatever the reason, our dead guy was expendable."

Tawanda suggested, "Maybe something went wrong, but the murder was performed according to a plan. The shooter knew exactly what he was doing and he did it neatly and well. So that leaves us with a professional assassin, whoever he is. What was he doing down here?"

Toomey stepped back into the office and Garrison asked, "You've had to cover plenty of high profile people over the years. What kind of security do they usually bring with them?"

"If it's a foreign diplomat or some VIP like this, you can bet that they have their own version of our Secret Service around them, some more than others. If it's a head of state, we supplement that country's security with our own, whether it's Secret Service or FBI or both. At the Super Bowl there were loads of Bureau people, Homeland Security, plus state and local police, private security, the works."

"So there was a blanket around this Alek Mironev."

"In his case, he doesn't like having a swarm of people with earpieces and dark glasses around him in a protective circle. He's got a reputation as a party animal, and I guess it cramps his style. At least, though, there would be some professional security people in his vicinity, and they probably would have had some training from the Secret Service. With high profile people involved, there's a certain protocol. He's not the first child of a political leader to demand some freedom of movement, but there would be at least a few people around him at all times."

Tawanda asked, "So what did the Bureau say about this carbon copy of Alek Mironev laying on a slab in Sarasota?"

"I got half way to first base before I got stuffed. They can't believe that their security was breached. Alek Mironev was the guest at the Super Bowl of a big financial firm, Planet Capital. They had a private suite for the Super Bowl and they figured they could have Mironev rub shoulders with some of their prized clients. Mironev was watched by Planet security people and the Bureau watched over him from a distance. There were no incidents and everything was fine. When I told them about the plastic surgery and the capped teeth, they just snickered."

"They can't believe it?" Tawanda was amazed.

"They told me that Mironev was followed back from the Super Bowl to his suite at the Don Cesar and he was in perfect health. They have videos and photographs of him looking just as happy and alive as you please."

"But what about this supposed trip to New Orleans? Doesn't that raise a few eyebrows?"

"Not enough. They know that he likes his freedom and they have no reason to believe that he's not safe and on his way to New Orleans."

"Hubris." It was Garrison making the comment, and Tawanda nodded in agreement.

Toomey heard the word and said, "In a way, I can't blame them because the security was incredible."

"And they're sure that Alek Mironev is on his way to New Orleans?"

"Mironev has a reputation for slipping out of his security

202 / P.D. LaFleur

net and getting away on his own. The Bureau is keeping an eye out for him, but they're not chasing after him. He's an adult and he can do what he wants. Plus, no one from his family is saying there's any problem."

Garrison followed up with another question. "Let's say that Alek Mironev is not in New Orleans. What then?"

"Good question, but not one the Bureau is concerned with right now. As far as they're concerned, he's either already there or on his way, and probably in the company of a lovely young woman. That's also part of his reputation."

Tawanda asked, "So what do we do now?"

"Sheriff, maybe you should talk to the Bureau yourself? Show the Special Agent in Charge what you have. The fact that one known criminal from England who was modified to look like Mironev is dead and another known criminal from somewhere in Europe was with him and can't be located ought to count for something. They won't listen to me."

Garrison looked over to Toomey. "I could go there this afternoon if I had to."

"Take the pictures with you and make your point. You've also got the Interpol report showing that a known assassin was in the vicinity. You won't be telling them anything that I haven't already, but maybe you can get through to them."

TWENTY-FOUR

The next day

Garrison and Toomey drove together to Tampa. While Toomey waited in a coffee shop, Garrison went alone to the FBI office about a mile south of the Tampa International Airport.

"I'm Sheriff Garrison, Dodge County, here to see the Special Agent in Charge."

He was speaking with a heavy-set woman of indeterminate age who held forth at an enormous desk in large reception room. Without saying a word, she turned to her computer and typed, then waited for a response.

"He's busy at the moment in a meeting. If you'll take a seat, he should be available in a few minutes.

The Sheriff sat on a leather sofa in front of a coffee table strewn with magazines.

Before Garrison could get comfortable, a stout, florid-faced balding man in a navy blue suit walked into the area from behind the receptionist's desk and put his hand out.

"Martin Weatherbee, Sheriff." Garrison suppressed a smile.

He just knew the man's name would be 'Martin'; he just expected the surname would be 'Chuzzlewit'.

"Good to meet you. I'm here about the report I sent to you by fax. I haven't heard from you and I was in the area."

"Sure, sure."

"Since time is of the essence, I wanted to see you personally and talk to you about the suggestions in the report."

Weatherbee took a deep breath and folded his arms as he spoke. "Sheriff Garrison, your report did come in and I glanced at it. Quite a plot of intrigue you wove together."

"Not something we wove together out of straw, sir. We have evidence that points right here to Tampa and the Super Bowl."

"Sheriff, I'm sure you're doing a fine job over in Dodge County, and I would never doubt your motives." Garrison detested the man already. Smarmy, self-righteous, smug, all the qualities that made him want to rabbit punch the man square in the nose. "You guys are right there on the street in the war on terror. Believe me, we at the Bureau understand and appreciate that."

Garrison recognized the bum's rush when he saw it.

"But please, we are the FBI and we had more resources from more agencies swarming all over the Super Bowl, all coordinated by the Department of Homeland Security. We had instantaneous facial registry scans on every single person who went through those turnstiles. Think about that for a second. Nobody escapes technology. We had four security trailers at the scene, all with access to every criminal data base, including some terrorist-related data bases I don't even know about.

"There were 900 additional forces from state, local and federal agencies who were assigned to everything from moving traffic to undercover surveillance. We constructed a special Super Bowl Command Center to coordinate every detail. I shouldn't even be telling you this, but since you are a sworn officer, I'm taking you into my confidence."

Yada-yada-yada, Garrison thought as his gaze wandered from Weatherbee to the painting on the opposite wall that depicted an American flag draped over the remnants of the World Trade Center.

"Normally, Sheriff, we assign as many as 15 security personnel when a Level Four foreign dignitary, that includes their family members, visits this country. On Alek Mironev, since he was travelling alone and had his own security detail from Planet Capital, his hosts, we had FBI, Secret Service and other assets keeping an eye out for him and still maintaining some distance. Even the Department of Defense. So, look, we had all the bases covered. The place was scoured every day for the ten days before the Super Bowl as well. Alek Mironev was at several parties before the Super Bowl, and we kept him in sight at all the events.

"And believe me, we had more on our plate than just this playboy son of a foreign head of state. There were 67,000 people at the game, including movie stars, singers, scores of senators and representatives, a passel of governors, and a thousand corporate CEOs. These are all A-list people, believe me.

"Now, if you told me that you had evidence that a rocket was poised off the Gulf Coast that was aimed at the 50-yard line, then I'd make some phone calls. DOD handled the airspace and the sea-based threats. But after an extraordinary event where no major security issues arose, all you have is a single guess, based on some possibilities, all founded on a supposition. Not to mention that you are asking me to misuse important federal investigative resources based on the advice of a disgraced federal employee."

Garrison's fists opened and closed, either in an effort to relieve tension or to prepare for a frontal assault on Weatherbee. He could feel the blood rushing to his face and he was reminded of his confrontation with Virgil Swett. He suppressed the same inclination to lash out with a hard punch square to the nose and told himself to remain calm. When he left the office, he walked down the broad granite steps and placed a call to Dennis Toomey. By this time, his blood pressure was back to normal.

"I guess I just had one righteous ass whuppin'. I am so deeply embarrassed to have to tell you of the depths to which my integrity has fallen."

"You want to talk about this?"

"If you don't mind being seen with the Sheriff of Dogpatch, there's a little joint over in Ybor City, sells great cigars and beautiful brandy, doesn't have any televisions, and the owner has access to the real Cuban stuff."

"How?"

"First, you arrange for someone in Cuba to send some Cuban cigars to Canada or any other country where there's some enlightened trade practices, which means anyplace on this earth except the United States. Then slip some bands on those cigars that identify them as Honduran or Dominican or whatever country you want, except Cuban. That's what my buddy does."

"So we'll be aiding and abetting in a federal crime?"

"Basically, yes."

"With a glass of brandy? I assume the liquor is legal?"

"Two wrongs do not make a right, Dennis. Of course the liquor is legal. What do you take me for? I'll meet you at my car."

Garrison and Toomey puffed on Churchill-sized cigars, leaning back in the oversized stuffed chairs and they held their cognacs to the light, swirling the contents and inhaling the sharp aroma. Garrison had slipped a light sweater over his uniform shirt and looked like just another customer. He and Toomey were the establishment's only ones in the place at the moment.

"Tell me, what do you want to do now?"

"I suppose I could go to the newspapers. It would make a catchy headline: 'Local Cop Senses Super Bowl Kidnap Plot; FBI Calls Report Incredible.'"

"It was *that* insulting?"

"I try to look on the bright side. Martin Weatherbee insulted me in complete sentences. I'm not used to that." He closed his eyes and tried to keep his heart rate under control.

Toomey took a long drag, blew it out slowly, and leaned forward. "I've been doing some thinking about this and I have a couple of ideas."

Garrison leaned forward. He would welcome a fresh approach. "Is this going to be some sort of life-changing epiphany?"

"I'm thinking apocalypse."

Garrison faced his friend, an aura of Cuban smoke surrounding them from the shoulders up. "So, tell me, O Wise One."

TWENTY-FIVE

When they returned to the Dodge County Sheriff's Office at the end of the day, Toomey gave the sheriff some space and took a walk outside while Garrison answered his phone messages and caught up on some paperwork. Standing alone at the edge of the department's shell parking lot, Toomey gazed at a flat expanse of light brown with a scattering of low green palm-like shrubs. Dotting the terrain were occasional clumps of greenery sporting bright colored flowers. The brilliant yellows, the brightest purples. He considered the contrast with the brittle mid-winter landscape where he lived up north. There, the last specks of summer green and the dazzling spray of autumn leaves were buried under a layer of dirty snow and crusty ice. The roads were spread with coarse sand and ice-melting chemicals that streaked the cars and tainted the soil.

This day was coming to a close and the sun threw long shadows, his own stretching several yards across the lot. The air was cooler now, but he was still comfortable in shirtsleeves. The sky changed colors, from orange to pink to muted purples and a few stray clouds scudded slowly to the east. The air was dry as ash and as he walked across the shell lot, puffs of dust rose and settled. He was standing not many miles from the outer edge of the Everglades, that enormous river of grass that collected surface waters from a hundred miles north of Dodge County to the Bay of Florida, three hundred miles south, in spreading fingers that gave refuge to an astounding collection of flora and fauna.

Toomey wanted to learn more about this land and knew only that the Everglades were threatened. He'd read of the phosphate mines that despoiled central Florida with settling pits of poisoned waters and clay stacks that soared a hundred feet into the air and gave the radioactivity that came from the mining operations some opportunity to dissipate and foul the atmosphere; of the sugar cane farms and other agriculture that spread chemicals to maximize yield and criss-crossed the landscape with irrigation pipes that stole precious waters from the Glades, only to spew the filthy proceeds further along in the system. In this rugged but fragile fragment of the Sunshine State, the pay was lower, the cancer rates higher, the education poorer, and those who owned the mines and the fields lived in the rarified atmospheres of the mansions and luxury condos that lay along the two coasts. Their children would not be schooled here, or swim here, or work in these fields.

Toomey turned and meandered back to the sheriff's office, saddened by his thoughts and sharing some sense of the same cynicism he'd noted earlier in Garrison. He reached for the door handle and was met by Tawanda, just leaving for the day.

"Taking in some of our Florida air?"

"This is quite a difference from where I come from."

Tawanda set her briefcase on the walkway. "Come with me."

Toomey glanced at her briefcase; was she going to just leave it there in plain sight?

Tawanda saw his glance and reassured him. "Don't worry. It'll be here when we come back."

Tawanda led the way along the side of the building and stepped onto a path worn bare of vegetation. They went about fifty feet when Tawanda stopped and pointed to a clump of tall trees in the center of a field. Toomey looked but was unsure why. It was, after all, a clump of twisted trees, some scrawny pines with irregular branches, a few pin oaks that spread their gnarled arms in every direction. He searched the scene to the horizon and sought in vain for some curiosity in the surroundings that ought to catch his attention. Tawanda could see that Toomey was looking without seeing.

"Look up." He did. In the sky, now a dim mix of pale gray and lilac, he saw a pair of shapes soar in lazy circles. "Those are bald eagles. Until last year, we saw a handful once in a while. For a long time, we never saw a single one."

Toomey stared at the spread wings, indistinguishable to him as eagles. They could have been osprey, or even vultures. Then they swooped lower, soundless, coming closer to the trees. In seconds, one alit on an upper branch of an oak and Toomey could appreciate the size and nobility of this beast. With white heads and tails, they stood erect and side by side as they scanned their environment.

"They're nesting in that group of trees. And over there at the edge of that field," she pointed along a fence line, the other side of which was covered with an assortment of tall trees, "we have panthers and coyotes and all sorts of stuff. And bats. Look up at the bats over there."

Toomey followed her finger and saw a cluster of darting figures, silent and quick as they cut left, then right, then up or down as they feasted on some form of insects.

"We're lucky here."

Toomey tried to follow the dipping and flicking of bats as

they seemingly stopped and started, zigging and zagging on a dime as they ate their evening meal. In the distance he heard some low grunts. "Panthers?"

"Gators. There's a slow creek at the edge of the field. They travel back and forth and sun themselves once in a while along the banks."

"How big do they get?"

"I've seen a few around twelve feet, but they can get a little bigger than that."

Toomey looked at Tawanda, her face bearing a broad smile as she surveyed the landscape and the sky, enjoying the activity that the unawares would pass by.

"You really like this place, don't you?"

She looked at Toomey, her smile still in place, and started to walk slowly back to the department office and her briefcase, Toomey close behind and noting once more the hitch in her gait.

"It's beautiful in its own way. Sometimes that's easy to over-look it but I try not to take it for granted. Yeah, I love it here."

"It shows."

"I'm sure there are things about the places you know that wrap you up and make you happy, but this is mine. It's still wild, and I try to keep that in mind every day. It might be ge-netic."

Toomey's eyebrows raised and Tawanda saw his puzzle-ment.

"With a DNA genealogy test, I learned where my ancestors were living when the first one was snagged by slavers in Africa and shipped over here. I saw photographs of the area, and hon-estly, it looks a lot like this. Rugged and dry and wild."

"So your attachment to this place is deep."

"I just know that I've always loved this place, in spite of the problems we've had here. Sheriff Garrison could tell you stories, and I can tell you a whole lot more. But I hope the land stays this way long enough for my grandkids to see the same things."

"Grandkids?" Toomey thought her too young to have any.

"Someday, maybe. I'm just hoping that we don't screw things up so bad that they never get to appreciate this. There are politicians here who are more enthusiastic about developing Florida into condos and shopping malls than they are about preserving what we have."

"Human beings have a way of finding the path to self-destruction at every turn, and we seem intent on taking it."

Toomey shifted the focus. "The world could use more people like your boss."

"You're right. What's he doing, by the way? When I left, he was making phone calls. Did you guys discover anything today about this case when you went to Ybor City?"

Toomey was caught off guard because neither he nor Garrison ever mentioned to anyone in the department where they were, but he was a trained professional and assembled the evidence with alacrity. "We smell like cigars, right?"

"Reeking. When the Sheriff goes to Tampa, it's not unusual for him to make a stop at Ybor and smoke one of those ugly things. So what did you come up with?"

"I suggested that if a switch with Alek Mironev never took place, and if he really is somewhere between here and New Orleans, then no sweat. Let him have his good time in the Big Easy and call it a day. But if the switch did take place, then it probably happened early, probably right after he arrived."

"Why do you say that?"

"It would not have happened in England before he got here. Alek Mironev is too well-known there and even the slightest hint that the fellow was a phony would have caught someone's attention. An unexpected gesture, a mispronounced word. Anything. But as soon as he's on American soil, he's just another celebrity that most people here have never seen up close. He could have been switched with Finney and most of us wouldn't pick up on the tiny nuances that would give Finney away in an instant as an imposter back in London."

"But his face was all over the news when he was here. He probably had his picture taken a thousand times."

"Still photographs and a few seconds of video clips on the news. But what about the timbre of his voice, his personal habits, the little tics that we all have and that define us. From a snapshot or a quick scene on television, no one would suspect."

"Assume you're right. Now what?"

"We have a list of every stop on Mironev's itinerary from the time his plane arrived in Sarasota. On the way back from Ybor City, we stopped at Sarasota International Airport and walked through the motions. I even phoned a man who was a member of the Planet Capital security team hired to watch over the man."

"And?" Tawanda's attention was rapt.

"When Alek Mironev walked into the Sarasota Airport, before he reached the waiting limo out front, he was met by a 'damsel in distress'. Those are the exact words of the security guard. She dropped her purse, spilled the contents, Mironev stopped and helped her, and then went with her into the ladies' lounge to calm her down. The guard thinks he might have got his first taste of American hospitality while they were in there. Those were not the exact words of the security guard, by the way, but we caught the drift."

"I'll bet."

"A few minutes later, out of the ladies' room comes a smiling Mironev with the young lady on his arm. She gave him a fairly long goodbye kiss . . . not just a modest peck on the cheek . . . and Mironev went on his way in the back seat of the limo to the Don Cesar hotel at St. Pete Beach and to all the Super Bowl parties." Toomey kept his eyes on Tawanda as he described the scene. He paused for a few seconds to let her digest the sequence of events before he asked, "What do you think?"

"Switcheroo. If it happened at all, it could have happened while they were out of sight." Toomey's smile reflected a sense of self-satisfaction.

Tawanda's eyes were focused someplace else and she ran the sequence of events through her imagination. "The Planet Security guy spent all of thirty seconds with the real Alek Mironev before the incident with the girl. Not long enough to get such an impression of the real Alek Mironev that he couldn't be fooled by a phony Mironev. Good plan, if that's what happened. So what did you find at the airport? Was the real Alek Mironev stuffed in a trash can?"

Toomey's smile broadened. "No such luck. Not that finding him in a trash can would have been a particularly good result for Mironev. But we did look around and ask some questions. Your boss, by the way, speaks Spanish like a matador."

"That's one of the reasons he likes living here. He can speak to everyone."

"The question is, if a switch did take place, how did they get the real Mironev out of there?"

"You're thinking it was a kidnapping and that Alek Mironev is being held somewhere."

"That's my guess. We looked for people who might have been at the airport at the same time. Who would you think of?"

"Airport staff, ticket agents. You said you talked already to the security guy assigned to Mironev."

"What about cleaning people?"

Tawanda gave that suggestion some thought. "And most of them speak Spanish."

"Your boss asked around and found the names of some people who were working in that area during and right after all this took place."

"Did he talk to anybody? What did they say?"

"He did, but I didn't understand a thing except 'hombre' and 'aeroporto'. But he's probably speaking to some others right now on the phone."

They stood together in silence and watched another eagle spread its wings and fly with seeming effortlessness to another more distant perch. "Sheriff Garrison is a hard working guy. What do you think of him?"

The question caused Tawanda to gaze off in the distance in another direction before she responded. "When I met Larry Garrison for the first time I was not exactly awestruck. If anything, he was unremarkable. He was a deputy assigned to road patrol and I only worked with him a few times before he ran for Sheriff. The old sheriff had one of those military buzz cuts and a gruff manner; he always made it clear that he was in charge wherever he happened to be. I expected the same thing from Garrison when he took over. Instead, he was un-sheriff-like. I was sure he'd be gone by the next election."

She paused in her description but her eyes never lost their far-away focus.

Toomey asked, "So you didn't expect much?"

"I expected something different. He's not perfect, mind you. I've seen him get millimeters away from knocking someone's block off. He stopped before he went too far, but I sense there are powerful and dangerous forces inside that he reins in." She tried to suppress a chuckle.

"What?"

"A few months after he was first elected, he found that a deputy was accepting bottles of booze from a downtown business every Christmas. Sheriff Garrison called on the deputy in front of the entire office, demanded his weapon, his badge and his resignation. Everything was so quiet you could hear a pin drop. When the deputy walked out, his career ruined, for good reason mind you, Sheriff Garrison called me into the office and gave me the weapon and the badge for safekeeping. I asked him then why he did all this in front of everybody. He said, 'Tawanda, there's nothing like a public execution to get peoples' attention.'"

"He's right."

"But then there's a softness about him, as if he accepts the fallibility in all of us. He also has a degree of humility that baffles me. He listens to people with a curiosity you usually see only in a child."

She turned away from the sky and faced Toomey directly. "Sometimes I get a catch in my throat because I'm sad I didn't see him all along as an extraordinary human being. I know I give him a hard time, pull his leg and all that, but it was a singular moment of discovery for me when I came to realize just how special the man is. We were blessed when he entered our lives."

Toomey said nothing but let her words sink in. Her remarks were delivered in a thoughtful, measured manner. It was clear to him that Tawanda Bradford had answered his question many times in her own mind.

The sky had grown dusky and darkness was creeping across from the east. Toomey looked at the Sheriff's office and saw the glow of lamplight. "I think it's going to be a long night."

"Well, I've got a long night ahead of me, too. I'm your basic single parent with a child at home and a test on criminal trial procedure that I need to study for." They reached her briefcase on the front walkway, right where she left it. She picked it up, extended her hand to Toomey and walked to her car. "Will I see you tomorrow?"

"I hope so."

TWENTY-SIX

Establishing an overseas telephone connection was uncomplicated, but for good reason, Vanya insulated herself from discovery. With the help of a fellow circus worker with black market connections, she acquired a pair of stolen cell phones. Tracing her call, if that was possible, would lead investigators to either an elderly woman living alone in Atlanta or a shoe store manager from Pittsburgh. From her Chechen comrades in London, she received the private number in Moscow that she needed. Vanya made certain that all the arrangements were made before she picked up the phone.

The voice on the other end was pure Mother Russia.

"This is Nikolai Mironev?"

"It is I, President Mironev."

She could envision the President sitting bolt upright at the sound of her voice. "How is Alek?"

"President Mironev. I will make this very brief. Your son is well and safe."

"But when will he be released? His mother must know."

Vanya kept her voice level and restrained, but she used a bit of added volume to step on his pleadings to deliver her message. She wondered, though, why the man's voice carried no edge of personal anxiety; it sounded to Vanya that he was pleading on his wife's behalf rather than his own. "You have received clear instructions, Mr. President. As soon as the demands have been met and the Russian Federation makes it public, your son will be released, unharmed. I understand you cannot place great faith in my words and all I can add is that you must trust me."

"The policy." Mironev was matter of fact. "It is being changed, I assure you ..."

The last words were spoken to no one. Vanya had hung up.

In her Sarasota apartment, Vanya poured herself a glass of Evian water and took a seat near her window overlooking the parking lot below. Soon, she was confident, such an unpleasant view from her living room would be a thing of the past. She was planning a more attractive sight, perhaps of the Rocky Mountains in Montana. She'd read of the area and thought it would remind her of her native land. Of course, sunshine was now a welcome part of her life, so perhaps Santa Fe or Taos, someplace further south where grand snow capped mountains could be seen and the warmth and sun were not so remote. Yes, New Mexico it would be. A cabin, something rustic, nothing pretentious, but with a beautiful view. She could rest there and give some thought to her next move, for there were contacts to be established and plans to be made if she was to enter the high-stakes world she sought. With Emilio's help, she would have in her hands some forged documents plus some cash and credit cards to give her the flexibility she'd require. With some of her own contacts, she could go on to the task of making herself available to perform tasks that others could not, or would not.

She sipped the water, reminiscent of the flinty water on which she'd been raised. On the dining table, in parts, every spring, screw and lever arranged in careful rows on a large sheet of white paper, lay the Blaser, the high-powered rifle she'd be-friended and come to love. Emilio remarked to her often, and with some sense of awe and respect, that she was astonishing in the way she kept her breathing controlled while she shot the Blaser in practice. She held her hand out from her body and looked at it. She did not expect to feel any tension during the telephone call to Nikolai Mironev, as she used the same breath-ing techniques she'd practiced since childhood to moderate her and maintain absolute focus and control. Neither a twitch nor a quiver. She'd just finished a conversation with one of the most powerful human beings in the world. It was a conversation that she initiated and concluded on her terms. One might be al-lowed a bit of nervous energy under such circumstances, but Vanya made demands on herself, physically and emotionally, that spoke to her success in the dangerous activity of trapeze. She would be as controlled and as successful as she began her new career path.

PART V

A hard beginning maketh a good ending.
—John Heywood

There will come a time when you believe everything is finished. That will be the beginning.
—*Louis L'Amour*

Begin at the beginning and go on till you come to the end; then stop.
—Lewis Carroll

TWENTY-SEVEN

Toomey stepped back into the sheriff's office, fully expecting Garrison to be engaged in conversation on the phone. Instead, he sat, in silence, back to the door, staring out at the darkening sky.

"What's up?"

The question brought Garrison back to the present and he spun in his chair to face his guest.

He pointed to some paperwork on his desk. "Oh, I just sent a quick memo to my crew supervisors and department heads. I'm supposed to have a meeting with them in the morning and I'm turning everything over to my Department Major. He'll handle it."

"Any news from anybody? The cleaning people from the airport that you wanted to track down?"

Garrison picked up a pad of ruled paper filled with notes. "I found a lady who cleans restrooms at the airport, among other things. Juanita Gomes is her name. Nice lady, and she remembers some odd things about the day Alek Mironev flew in."

"Like what?" Toomey leaned forward in his seat.

"Like the young lady who evidently stumbled, literally and on purpose, into the path of Alek Mironev. She remembers the woman—a 'rubia', she said, and she called her a 'duendecillo'—a little blonde pixie. She was in the waiting area at the airport for almost two hours before the Planet Capital jet carrying Mironev came in. Señora Gomes said she looked preoccupied, maybe a little nervous. Then there's the fellow who came in about an hour or two later from an outside janitorial supply company. Tall guy, floppy hat, dark complexion, bushy mustache, Hispanic, wheeling in a large blue plastic barrel of industrial cleaning detergent on a dolly from his van. He went to the ladies' room, put an orange warning cone at the entry, and then spent a few minutes inside. He told Señora Gomes that he had to do some special cleaning in there for a few minutes."

"Wasn't that unusual?"

"Not particularly. She told me the airport has some contracts with outside firms to do some heavy-duty cleaning and deliver bulk supplies. But here are a few things to think about. One, this man in the floppy hat was very tall. Señora Gomes thinks he was well over six feet. Let me ask you, Dennis, how many very tall Hispanics you've seen since you've been here?"

Toomey shrugged. He couldn't think of a single one. Most of them, in fact, were quite short in stature.

Garrison continued. "Z-e-e-e-ro. And get this. He spoke beautiful Spanish, so beautiful that Juanita could hardly understand him."

"What do you mean?"

"Spanish, like English, has different dialects depending on where you're from. Like a farmer from Scotland would have difficulty understanding an oil rigger from west Texas, even though they both speak the English language. It's the same with Spanish. Someone from Guatemala might have a hard time understanding someone from Madrid, at least at first. In Spain, there are dozens of regional dialects, practically separate languages. Señora Gomes told me a few words he used and the way he pronounced them."

"And?"

"This guy was speaking the dialect of the Spanish upper crust from Barcelona." Garrison reached for another piece of paper. "By the way, my little visit to the FBI apparently did get the attention of Mr. Weasel Weatherbee, the Special Agent in Charge. His office sent out broadcasts to all law enforcement agencies to watch for Mr. Mironev at every point between Tampa and New Orleans and report all sightings back to him. I'll bet he's nervous that we might be right, but he won't admit it."

"That sounds like something he'd do."

They sat in silence trying to assemble the information into plausible explanations. Toomey idly picked up a snow globe, studying the enclosed scene of a log cabin surrounded by fir trees. He tipped it upside down and righted it, mesmerized by the flakes drifting down and catching on the boughs of the trees and the cabin roof. Garrison entered the office and stood at the doorway watching Toomey. When all the snow had settled inside the globe, Toomey picked it up again and repeated the upside down motion.

"Maine. Ever been there?"

Toomey watched the snowfall when he answered. "Many times. You?"

"Only in my dreams. A good friend visited her family there and she brought that back for me. I always thought I'd like a little cabin like that in the mountains or on a lake."

"It is beautiful up there, but I think I'd rather have a nice little place down here in the sunshine. After you've experienced packed snow and ice on a steep hill, and you fall flat on your ass often enough, the concept of 'warm and flat' has its attractions."

Garrison changed the subject back to the new information.

"I think this cleaning man is Patrick Keough from the Interpol file, the same guy who went on the boat ride with our Mr. Finney. Whatever his real name is, he's our killer."

"It's making sense."

"What do you think he's like?"

Toomey sat back but continued to turn the snow globe upside down and watch the flakes float down. It was hypnotizing. "Smart, experienced, resilient. He's a chameleon who can adopt different disguises and personas to fit in and do his work."

Garrison leaned back in his chair and stared at the ceiling, focused on some vague, distant portrait of the man he was seeking. He was silent.

Toomey set the snow globe down and focused on Garrison. "You're trying to imagine what it would be like to meet the guy, right? Does he enjoy what he's doing? Is he cold, friendly, introspective . . . ?"

Garrison leaned forward in his chair and stared directly into Toomey's eyes. "I'm thinking that, yes. He's intelligent, well-traveled, and someone who pays attention to detail. But this man also has some inherent evil that I can't comprehend." He took a piece of blank paper from his top drawer. "If I could draw a mental picture of this fellow, I'd say he's a gentleman, what you'd call a 'man's man', someone who'd be interesting to talk to, someone you could share a drink and conversation with, maybe even get to like." He jotted some notes on the paper as he spoke.

"But he kills people for a living."

"Exactly. He kills people for a living." He slammed his fist on his desk. "What makes a man do that, Dennis?" Garrison kept on jotting notes as he spoke.

"There are psychiatrists all around the world trying to figure out what makes people do the things they do." Toomey stood up, walked to the window and stared out at the palmetto-strewn landscape, his mind grasping for an explanation. "In the early days, I'd come across people I knew as a kid and wonder what happened between the time they were eight and the time they reached twenty-eight. Like Brian and Steve Sullivan. They were a year apart and I used to play stickball in the streets with them. Tough kids. Street-wise kids.

"Today, Steve is a priest and runs a homeless shelter in Boston. He's a gentle soul who wouldn't think twice about giving you the shirt off his back. Brian took a different path. He started boosting cars when he was fifteen and feeding them to chop shops. Then he branched out into all sorts of things, including arranging the murders of maybe a dozen people along the way. Today, Brian Sullivan is number three on the FBI's most wanted list. Same household, same parents, same teachers. Both of them were altar boys and both of them are interesting, intelligent men. You tell me what bent Steve one way and Brian another."

Garrison had stopped writing and pondered Toomey's words, drawing parallels to this current case. "This guy is well-read, probably speaks several languages, and I'll bet he enjoys going to the finest museums and reading poetry. I'm guessing he's a passionate guy and doesn't enjoy the dirty part of his work. There was nothing cruel about how he shot our victim. It was probably painless except for that first nano-second. And the victim, this James Philip Finney, was a sexual predator that we're all lucky to have gone from the world."

"Was Jay Finney a loss? Is the world better off without him?"

"I'd say the world is a little safer, and he won't pass his infected genes to another generation."

Toomey chewed on that remark for a moment, his gaze rising to the ceiling. "If our killer has scruples, he's comfortable enough to bend them when he feels the need to do so. Besides, who is supposed to judge if the world is better off without the people he's taken out."

"We don't judge. We just shrug and take a guess."

Toomey took time to consider the idea and Garrison questioned his own outlook on the human condition.

Their silence was broken by the ringing of the telephone. Garrison answered and nodded, mouthing the words "Highway Patrol" as he listened. When the conversation ended, Garrison said to Toomey, "That was a friend of mine at Florida Highway Patrol. I called him when I saw the FBI request. Alek Mironev hasn't appeared yet in New Orleans. There are people cruising every highway and asking questions at every point between here and there, but no sightings yet."

"And I lay dollars to your doughnuts that there *won't* be any sightings, Sheriff. What do you want to do?"

"I need a few medical tests. I have an MRI tomorrow and the next morning I have the pleasure of undergoing a spinal tap. When I get here tomorrow, you and I are going to call on Planet Capital and then drive back to the airport and take a closer look at that ladies' room. I have an idea that we'll find something. I'll call Planet now and let them know we're paying them a visit."

"Then maybe we can have dinner?"

The restaurant was a combination eatery and mercado, with groceries in the front and four mismatched tables and chairs in the back. The menu was a chalk board tacked to the rear wall and the server did double duty at the front register.

Garrison ordered for both of them and chatted with the waiter in Spanish with ease and speed. Toomey said, "I'm impressed."

Garrison pushed the food around his plate. "I spent a few years in Spain during my years in the service and stayed there afterwards for a while. I learned the language and loved it."

Toomey studied Garrison's face. Tawanda told him that she saw softness in Garrison, and he could see what she meant. He guessed he could ask the sheriff almost any question and get a straight and honest answer. He put his fork down, wiped his lips with a napkin and leaned back in his chair. "You told me you're going through a few medical tests." Toomey watched for signs of dismissal and felt the vibrations in Garrison's manner and speech. He decided to push just a bit with a combination of concern and general nosiness. "I'm not a doctor, but you look like your coordination is a little off. I hope it's nothing serious."

The comment took Garrison by surprise. He was not accustomed to this kind of conversation and the discomfort registered.

"It's none of my business." Toomey backed off. To him, prying was a habit but not a sport.

Garrison said nothing for several moments, wondering what he might or might not reveal. The decision was not difficult. "We are all of an age, Dennis." Garrison placed his trust in this new friend. "I'm told I should expect I have MS. Maybe it's more obvious than I thought."

"That sucks, Larry."

"It's part of life. Just look at all the suffering that goes on around us. Young people getting horrible diseases. Terrible accidents that maim and cripple. If you want fairness, then life on this planet just isn't for you. I've been lucky to get this far without getting hammered over the head by something."

"Part of it might be luck, but only part of it. I can tell just by watching you and the people around you that you're a decent person. I'll tell you this. If you asked your staff to run through a brick wall for you, they'd argue over who'd be first to try. They love you."

"You've been listening to Tawanda."

"I shouldn't?"

"Her high opinion of me may not reflect the rest of the people who know me." He looked directly at Toomey when he said, "You ought to know, by the way, that she asked more than a few questions about you."

Toomey stopped chewing.

"More than a passing interest, if you ask me."

Toomey reddened and Garrison saw that the interest might be mutual. He said nothing more about the subject. If he considered himself inept at matters of the heart, he knew enough to recognize that there was a time for talk and a time for silence. He changed the subject.

For the rest of the meal, they chatted about everything from their personal and professional backgrounds to recollections from their personal experience. From there, the conversation deepened, with Toomey telling the story of the loss of his partner to murder by a dirty cop, and Garrison sharing the blunder he'd made in his relationship with Anita. The dinner and the dialogue established a foundation that would hold them fast.

Garrison paid the tab and they drove to the Dodge Budget Motel. Across the street was a country western bar and Toomey suggested a nightcap. The place had a honky-tonk look and the sound from the jukebox was of the wailing truck driving brand. "Maybe another time."

"If I take a walk over there by myself, will I live to tell the tale?"

"Just like anywhere else, Dennis. You don't tug on Superman's cape without expecting a little payback. You'll figure it out."

"I shouldn't order a Campari and soda?"

"Who knows? Culture does get here, Dennis, even if it takes the slower back roads."

Garrison shook hands with Toomey, reminded him that Tawanda would be at the motel in the morning to pick him up, and the grips of both men were firm and sincere.

TWENTY-EIGHT

Toomey strolled across the road to the "Cattleman's Bar" and stepped in through the swinging café doors. A few patrons turned from their swivel stools at the bar to check out the newcomer and Toomey felt himself being examined. He'd had this same self-conscious feeling on other occasions and felt not unlike a patient in a hospital johnnie.

A pair of men in black tee shirts played pool under the smoky glow of an overhead lamp and Toomey walked to the first empty stool and took a seat.

"Scotch on the rocks," he said when the short, stocky woman in a plaid shirt and jeans who tended bar appeared, damp rag in one hand.

"Any one in particular?" The bartender stood aside and pointed in the general direction of the shelves. In the dim light, Toomey could identify all of the popular brands.

"How about a Johnny Walker?"

"Black or Red? I like the Black myself."

Toomey agreed and she free-poured into a rocks glass. She didn't name a price or leave a tab in a sign that said that there was no shortage of trust here. Toomey inhaled the peat and smoke of the drink and took a sip, enjoying the warmth and the sensation of the liquor as he swallowed. He closed his eyes and replayed his experiences since he first stopped in to visit the Dodge County Sheriff. The cause of his concern that led to that visit was the tiny detail of the fingerprint matching request. In his career, details played an important part, and he took some pride in his ability to spot the small aberrations, the little things that popped up from the page and led to deeper investigations. Sometimes his curiosity led to dead ends, but his questioning of this detail proved to have merit. He just had no idea at the time that his own life might be so affected by that almost casual visit to Garrison's office. The occasional thoughts of retirement were now deeper reevaluations, for example. Part of that thinking was driven by a growing friendship with Sheriff Garrison. Another was his own growing appreciation of this part of the country, this otherwise flat and unattractive landscape that he'd never consider as home. He could now appreciate its hidden beauty and the grip that it could have on one's soul. For that, he thanked Tawanda Bradford.

Now there was a human being of note, he thought. Tawanda Bradford was a woman whose depth, character and bearing caught him by surprise. She was a woman who wore her attitude on her sleeve, and she was neither unafraid nor reluctant to express herself. At another time in his life, he would have found that off-putting; in Tawanda, he found it captivating, and he shook his head at that realization. He wanted to know her better, to maybe spend time with her beyond the confines of the sheriff's department's walls. He had little confidence that such a possibility existed, and the Irish in him would be unlikely to accept his good fortune if it did. He took another sip of his drink and the bartender approached.

"You look deep in thought," she said as she wiped the edge of the bar with her towel.

He looked up and smiled. "I guess I was." He chanced a question. "Do you know Tawanda Bradford?"

"Sure do. Why?"

"I just met her a few days ago and she's one powerful personality."

"That she is. You're the FBI fellow, right?"

Toomey's eyebrows rose. Was his appearance in Dodge County such public fodder?

"Word travels fast around here. We tend to pay attention to the little things that seem out of the ordinary."

The conversation was interrupted by a confrontation that arose at the bar's pool table, an argument over the rules and an accusation of marital infidelity. Voices were raised and the bartender walked around the end of the bar and approached the pair, both of them in posturing mode and both holding cue sticks.

"Knock it off or take it outside, boys. You know the rules."

Neither one moved, their eyes locked like roosters in a cockfight. After a moment's pause, the tension thick with pheromones, the bartender, at perhaps five feet tall and with her gray hair pulled back in a ponytail, approached one of the men, the taller of the two, a broad-shouldered man with a shaved head. She snatched the cue stick from his hand, and said, "Virgil, whenever we see an argument in here, you're in the middle. Why is that?"

The man named Virgil started to complain and the woman cut him off. "No more excuses. Just leave."

Toomey glanced over at the commotion and watched the bartender intervene. She'd done this many times before, he could tell. Not a single soul in the area, comprised mainly of large men with tattoos, muscles and missing teeth, raised any objection. The bartender spoke and her rule was law.

The man named Virgil grabbed a jeans jacket from the back of a nearby chair and stormed out, cursing the woman and his pool-playing rival under his breath as he crashed though the saloon doors. Something about the man made Toomey look twice. He could have been the motorcyclist that was behind him and the sheriff earlier. Same size and demeanor. But something in the man's face was distinctively familiar. He'd seen this man before, but in different circumstances. Not in a darkened tavern and not dressed like a biker. Somewhere.

In a minute, the sound of a revving Harley ripped through the air as it tore through the parking lot. Most of the people shook their heads as if accustomed to the childish bravado of a grown man on a loud machine: The universal symbol of bluster, the definition of self-doubt. It was the same personality glitch that afflicted bullies, rapists and those who poked cruel fun at the mentally retarded. It was, Toomey concluded long ago, some deficiency that prompted the need to display power. Fortunately, he mused as he took another swallow, the onset of adulthood takes care of the matter with most individuals.

"Is he a regular?" Toomey asked the bartender when she walked back to the bar.

"Comes from an important family around here, but just started showing up here a few months ago." The woman came around the back of the bar and poured another shot of Johnny Walker Black and slid it in front of Toomey. "On the house."

"Thanks, but I didn't do anything to deserve this."

"You did. You just don't know it yet."

The woman walked away, expecting no response. Toomey overheard the low murmur of conversation from an area further down the length of the bar that included words like "Virgil" and "Larry Garrison" and "Tawanda", and he wondered where the talk started and where it was headed. He sat and sipped, left a generous tip under his glass and nodded his thanks to the bartender on his way out. She returned the gesture and added, "Take care of yourself, Special Agent Toomey."

Toomey smiled all the way back to his room at the Dodge

Budget Motel, more convinced than ever of two principles: That the world was small indeed, and most people, left to their own devices, are basically good and decent.

While this speculation was going on in Dodge County, a young man sat on an upended plastic bucket and pondered his condition. Alek Mironev still had no idea where he was, nor that he was being sought in the city of New Orleans a thousand miles away. Now with a thickening beard after nearly two weeks of imprisonment, as best as he could guess, he bore little resemblance to the dashing young bachelor whose image made women swoon the world over.

He'd never been alone for such a long time, never experienced such desolation. He recalled a brief encounter with a young woman in Bologna who was a yoga practitioner as well as a wonderful romp in the hay. He remembered a night when she described the perfect state of nirvana that could be achieved by meditating. He tried it here with limited success. The incense, the low chants, the extraordinary peace. The entire experience drove him batty.

He closed his eyes and tried to blot out the scene of his current surroundings and replace them with more pleasant visions. His mind riffled through remembered episodes like a Rolodex, dismissing some (like a gentle hike through the Italian Alps) as too carefree, others (like his experiences one drunken evening with multiple nymphets in Majorca) as too hedonistic. He wanted to dwell on those moments painted with contentment but which delivered some sense of personal growth. "Personal growth" was a term his father used often, and ironically, it was an episode at Torquay, at a summer holiday cottage when he was perhaps eleven or twelve, with his mother that settled in on his vision.

His mother had only months before, given birth to his younger sister and he watched his mother rock the new baby to sleep one afternoon under the dappled sunshine that filtered through a tall tree. She placed the child in a cradle and sat with Alek on a garden bench, within earshot of the cradle, but far enough to have a quiet conversation with her son. When she took her seat on the bench, she leaned over, rubbed Alek's shoulder and closed her eyes.

"Do you think we will leave this world a better place than when we arrived?"

He felt he should answer something with depth and thought of a few alternative responses; he was his father's son. Before he formed an answer, she said, "My sense is that we are marching steadily to annihilation. Your father thinks I am too full of negativity. Perhaps he is right."

His mother rarely shared her thoughts of her husband with Alek, and this unusual revelation caused him to turn to his mother with questioning eyes. His mother's eyes were closed, her thoughts far off in some distant place.

She continued, "We do our best to speak in elevated tones, but what century was crueler than the twentieth? I'm sure you've read of those events; your grandfather was badly wounded in the war, you know."

Alek knew, but he never heard the details. A grenade, he recalled. His grandfather used a cane and always wore a heavy boot on his left foot. Alek wondered where his mother's thoughts were taking them.

"We live a bit longer and we travel faster and in more comfort. Diseases have been conquered, but man's cruelty to his fellow man never seems to me to improve. Perhaps we are doomed to be barbarians." She opened her eyes and looked at her son, a smile appearing on her lips. "Oh, women as well, Alek. Some believe that women are the crueler of the species."

There was a silence and she closed her eyes again, wrapping her arms around herself as she drifted far away once again. For the moment, he considered the coy smile that had appeared and then left. He wondered if it was that smile that attracted his father to her. His father was away again today, some important meeting that would keep him from his family for two more days, at least.

When his mother reopened her eyes, there were tears forming and Alek saw beads trickle down her cheeks.

"There are now two children in this family, hundreds of millions in our human family. My generation works diligently on one hand to improve the world as the other hand tries to blow it up. I hope, Alek, I hope that you and your colleagues in this adventure do a better job. Does this make any sense to your adolescent ears?"

"I think it does."

The scene evaporated. Alek had recalled this event before and was struck by its ability to hold on to a corner of his memory bank with such tenacity. He wondered about its relation to his situation now. What caused this one episode to recur at this moment? He could feel tears well up in his own eyes. How he wanted to hold on to his mother, how desperate he was for her comfort and her understanding.

As Alek Mironev sat alone and wept, a telephone call was being placed from a cell phone in Sarasota to a telephone in Russia. It was early morning in Moscow, but the President had enjoyed little sleep for days, and his stamina was at a low point. Raisa Mironev was relentless in her insistence that her husband take action, that he order an immediate sortie by covert operatives to go to the US, find their son, retrieve him, and end this episode. Gone was the bright-eyed enthusiasm of the nation's leader who climbed to the top position in his government on the strength of his youthful, energetic optimism. Nevertheless, his heart raced and he grabbed the phone quickly when it rang. On the other end was a woman's voice.

"How is my son? We want to hear his voice!"

"We?"

"His mother. She is frantic, as you can guess."

"He is fine, Mr. President. You will have to trust me on this issue. I just wish to advise you that a decision must be made quickly. The announcement we expected days ago has yet to be made."

"I understand, but I've done everything you have asked. An announcement will be made soon. Surely you can allow my son to speak to us."

"Unfortunately, Mr. President, until that announcement is broadcast, I suppose we just continue to wait. And hope."

"But I must speak to Alek. Let me speak with him, please."

The line was dead.

When she finished the call, Vanya dialed another number.

"Anything?" Emilio was anxious for some word from London—or Moscow—or Grozny—anywhere, so that he could conclude the captivity of Alek Mironev, drop him off safe and sound, and get on with his life. In spite of his chosen profession, he detested intrigue.

"Two things to report. First, there are many members of law enforcement on the highways looking for young Mr. Mironev. I am guessing that they are covering the roads from Tampa to New Orleans and stopping at every place in between looking for Alek Mironev."

"Great. We don't need this attention. What about word from the boy's father?"

"I just spoke to the great leader. He says that an arrangement is in the works."

Emilio was not satisfied with words like *in the works*. "There are risks that only increase as time goes on."

"But Emilio, all of the efforts are being wasted on the phony trip to New Orleans. That is a good thing for us."

"A charade. In time, law enforcement will see Alek's failure to appear in New Orleans as a stalling tactic. We cannot hold onto Mr. Mironev forever."

Emilio wanted to place further emphasis on his point that some conclusion had to be reached immediately, but the line was dead. Emilio stared at the phone and thought that young, petite Vanya was taking her role in the espionage trade a bit too seriously for her own good.

TWENTY-NINE

Moscow

The gaggle of journalists gathered in the anteroom of the Blue Room at Novo-Ogaryovo, the official residence of the President of the Russian Federation. Two stood apart, both clad in blue sport coats with shiny elbows, both smelling of tobacco and not a little alcohol, both staring at the younger members of the TV and print media who elbowed for position among themselves, waiting for the moment when the doors opened and prime seats were taken.

"Ten o'clock in the morning and the Kremlin wants to make an announcement. Have they no sympathy for the frail? I just got home from last night."

"So what are we here for? You have any idea?"

In decades past, this pair would be loath to share interesting tidbits that could spell the difference between meeting a deadline for the morning edition and ending up buried in the afternoon edition. Now, those competitions buried by waves of electronic 24-hour news, and instant blogging, they recognized the futility of keeping secrets from each other.

"Chechnya. That's what I hear. Some concessions to help ease the tension."

"Tension? Chechnya is ancient history. If seventy-one percent of American ninth graders don't know where Iran is on the world map, eighty-one percent of the Russians couldn't find Chechnya if you offered a million ruble jackpot. Who gives a crap?"

"Makes you wonder why they'd get this kind of crowd together, doesn't it?"

"A subtext?"

"There has to be more to the story than making a few concessions to a group that nobody knows or cares about."

"What? You think there's something sneaky going on in the Russian government?"

"Right. How long will this take?"

"Ten minutes, even with Q & A. Where are you going after?" 'After' meant after the announcement and their reports were sent in.

"Petro's. They've got free snacks at happy hour, and happy hour is all day long."

"It'll barely be noon when we get this wrapped up and sent off." He saw the shoulders of his colleague rise in a shrug that conveyed less caring for personal health and hygiene than might be acceptable in other circles. "See you there."

The President of the Russian Federation entered the room alone, as he usually did, from a side door after everyone was in position. Entering this way, he felt, always added some small sense of drama to press conferences and other announcements. Of no small benefit was that entering alone and with everyone seated, his short stature was less noticeable. He detested those events where he stood in crowds and his nose reached the neckties of his colleagues.

His Russian was polished and bore less of the consonant-soaked brutality than many. Making the Russian language sonorous was a difficult task, but he came closer to achieving a level of audible comeliness than any of his predecessors who ruled the country and the Soviet Union before that.

"I wish to make an announcement," he began, "that will demonstrate to the world, especially those vocal critics of our nation who claim that the Russian Federation is devoid of compassion and is rooted in the past, and will bring rays of economic sunshine to an area of our great nation that has been shrouded in gray clouds for decades."

He went on to explain his five-point plan to "invigorate the great Chechen peoples" by bringing jobs and economic opportunity to the region. It was a brief, organized presentation with several charts to illustrate and emphasize the "elegance of a strategy that recognizes the contributions of the great Chechen people and simultaneously shares the immense riches of our nation's reserves in ways that enhance the entire Federation." Words like "equity" and "glorious" and "opportunity" appeared throughout the presentation. The follow-up questions were few, and only one, the last one and from one of the pair of grizzled members of the printed press, was pointed. The President acknowledged the questioner with a grimace.

"Why, Mr. President, are you making this announcement when there has been little pressure of late from the Chechen people, when the resistance has been effectively quashed? Why does this announcement come today and not ten years ago, when it would have meant something?"

The response from the President was a clever reworking of the same words used in the announcement. Words like "atonement" and "justice" were strictly avoided. "It was time," the President said as he concluded. "It was simply time. Thank you." He stepped away from the podium, a process that involved stepping from the eight-inch riser cleverly hidden behind it, and left the room, a wave and a smile evident as he made his exit.

Greeting him inside a hallway immediately adjacent to the Blue Room was Grigori Malko. As usual, he said little, offering only a nod and a quarter-smile. The President, in a personality trait not shared by many of world leading fraternity and sorority, detested fawning and false bravado. "Just do your job and do it well," was a common phrase spoken by the President.

"Do you have my wife on the line, Grigori?"

"Yes, Mr. President." Grigori led the way to a small anteroom decorated in tones of taupe and teal. On the oak desk, an artifact preserved from Czarist days, was a note pad, a pen, and a telephone, red light blinking. Grigori motioned to the desk and said, "I'll be out here," as he closed the door to leave the President to his task.

Sarasota

Sheriff Garrison sat alone in his car at the Sarasota County Memorial Hospital. He didn't want to draw undue attention to himself today by showing up in a law enforcement vehicle and dressed in his official uniform, so he was clad instead in chinos, a plaid shirt and a windbreaker. Now that the tests were completed and after a brief conversation with Dr. Hernandez, he was still in shock.

The MRI was done as soon as he showed up at the hospital. Ten minutes in and out. Dr. Hernandez showed up a few minutes later and they found a vacant examining room where they both took seats and faced each other. Hernandez placed a thick file on the paper-covered examining table.

Hernandez expressed no regret for his tardiness. "I was tied up with a patient. An eleven-year-old boy with lymphoma." With a nod at the file on the table, he added, "That's the kind of thing that gives you perspective."

Garrison rued his self-pity. "I understand. You see a lot of suffering."

"And you don't? In both our businesses, we get to see some things we'd just as soon miss. But let's talk about you. I just looked at the MRI and my opinion still stands. This looks like MS and I'm going to treat it that way. I have a colleague in Neurology who should also look at these results plus the spinal tap you're getting tomorrow morning, but I'm certain enough to tell you. MS eats away at the myelin sheath that surrounds the nerves in your body. The myelin is sclerotic. It's scarred."

The news from Dr. Hernandez was delivered in a flat voice, as if the diagnosis was a bad cold that would resolve itself within a week, given rest and sunshine. Garrison tried to form words but his mouth was dry and uncooperative.

"I know this isn't the kind of news you wanted me to confirm, but I can't think of another way that would make the news more palatable."

"Is that what's causing the numbness in my fingers?" Garrison formed his first sentence.

"And your feet. It's progressive. Your symptoms can be slowed down with medication, but you're not going to get better. Do you understand?"

Garrison nodded yes.

"Are you experiencing any excess fatigue?"

"Not really, but how quickly should I expect changes?"

"A few lesions showed up on the MRI, all small, but they could show up in healthy people as well. I'm going to prescribe something for you and I'm referring you to my friend in Neurology to talk about progression of the disease. I don't think we're looking at rapid progress. This could go on for many years, but frankly, Sheriff, I want you to be prepared."

"Do I need to make arrangements?"

It was Hernandez' turn to be stunned. "Do you mean . . . *arrangements*?"

Garrison caught the reason for the confusion and almost smiled. "Not *those* arrangements. I mean, about my job. Can I still work?"

Relief crossed Hernandez' face. "Goodness yes. In fact, run for reelection! I'm not the expert on this, but I don't think we're talking about any drastic changes, at least in the short term."

"What's the medication?"

"Interferon. It doesn't cure a thing, but it slows down the progress of the disease. Do you use the internet a lot?"

"I do."

"Then look at the MS sites and download the brochures. The better informed you are, the better off you'll be. You'll also have better questions to ask when you visit with the neurologist."

"I understand."

Hernandez put his hand out to shake and Garrison took it. The doctor was out of the room and on his way to his next patient, leaving Garrison alone to consider the news.

Another call was being placed inside Moscow, ironically within minutes, and the voice of Raisa Mironev was cracking with emotion when she answered. The caller was her husband.

"The details have been worked out and I just finished speaking to the press."

"Thank God, Nikolai."

"The announcement will reach the ears of the kidnappers within minutes of my speaking. We will hear soon, Raisa, and I am certain that the news will be good. They have no reason to harm him and every reason to protect him and release him."

"I hope you are right. Was the phone call you received from the kidnappers traced? Was it recorded?"

"I don't know if the trace was successful, but we know it was made from Florida again. The same young woman. Definitely Russian. We expect it was from a cell phone, though, and the phone will prove to be either stolen or false, just as the last time."

Special Agent Dennis Toomey was considering turning in his retirement papers, his badge and his weapon, but even if he made up his mind today, the paperwork still had to inch its way through the federal labyrinth. That could take at least several days, maybe weeks. Meanwhile, he was still active FBI, still had access to some important people, and one of those important people received a telephone call this morning.

"I need to reach him," he said into cell phone. Toomey was insistent, but trying to conceal the urgency that he felt inside. At this point, he just wanted some rather routine information; he wanted to avoid raising red flags that would only erect barriers and he'd be unable to get simple answers to even the simplest questions. "I know he's in Florida. I saw him last night."

And he did. Putting the pieces of his memory together took a little while. There was a segment here and a fragment there, and they kept on meeting in his mind throughout the night and disturbing a sleep that should have been fairly routine, especially with two hefty drinks of Scotch whiskey before he put his head on the pillow. By the time the sun rose and the morning light sliced through the narrow slats of the blinds, Toomey had the name fixed in his brain.

From there, it was a short leap to the man's past and the experience the man brought to his position. Most of the assignments involved complicated undercover operations. The man he was looking for was not in some backwater like Dodge County with no reason at all. If Toomey could reach him in time, then this could prove to be a valuable asset to have on the side of Sheriff Lawrence Garrison.

Toomey listened to computer keys being tapped somewhere in Washington. Connections were being made and information transferred. He waited for a voice to give him what he asked for.

"I apologize for the delay, Special Agent Toomey. I cannot verify that the person you seek is above the table." Toomey recognized the code that the man he wanted to reach was operating under cover. Getting a message to him, if it was possible at all, would take time. A formal request would have to go through the man's handler and that presented too many opportunities for more red flags. Toomey would have to keep this simple.

"I will give you a telephone number. If you could just pass on my name and the number, I will appreciate that."

"I cannot guarantee that there will be a response. Is that alright with you, or do you want to submit this through NSA?" The National Security Agency was the repository for all sorts of undercover operations that even the President may not ever learn about. Often referred to, without a shred of humor as 'No Such Agency', the NSA data bases could be searched only by certain individuals with extraordinary high clearance levels. Gaining approval (via a trio of federal forms, each with federal identification numbers, and appropriately hand written and witnessed federal signatures at higher levels than Toomey could ever secure) would be impossible.

"Just give him this name and number."

Toomey waited for the message to be transcribed, hung up the phone and wondered how long the connection would take. If he was right, he could speak to the man and perhaps gain an upper hand in the process of solving the curious murder that was consuming his new friends in Dodge County. He waited for ninety minutes before the call came in.

* * *

Vanya Zakayev was chopping celery and onions for a tuna salad which she would have with cold vegetables for her dinner when CNN announced the provisions of the new arrangement in Russia to benefit Chechnya. The knife she held in her hands clattered to the floor as she rushed into the living area and turned up the volume.

"The President of the Russian Federation this morning pledged an extraordinary degree of support for the people of Chechnya during his remarks, and reports here in Moscow indicate widespread support for the President's decision. It is one more mark, another positive mark in this President's quest to bring the Russian Federation forward and to further establish compassion as a hallmark of the nation's persona. This is Theresa Garza-Levin reporting from the Kremlin, Moscow."

The scene changed to Washington where a reporter cited the US President's acclaim for the Moscow announcement. What the US thought of the announcement was immaterial to Vanya and she raced to the telephone and called Emilio. "Turn on your television. The Russian President made the announcement. It is everything we hoped for. A great day for Chechnya! I will speak to you later." She never waited for any response from Emilio but went immediately back to her TV. She sat, phone in hand, leaning forward on the sofa, waiting for the usual CNN loop of taped reports and perhaps some additional details about the announcement. Her telephone rang and she held it to her ear, fully expecting Emilio. Instead it was London.

"We are dancing, Vanya. Dancing! You have heard the great news?"

"Why are you calling me here at my apartment? This is an international call and everything is monitored. We have rules for a reason."

"I've been trying to reach you all day! The announcement was hours ago! It is such a cause for celebration. I had to call you."

"I have been busy." Checking the boat, making certain the air tanks and other gear were on board and secured. Timing her travel routine. Practicing with her Blaser, getting more comfortable with the recoil, perfecting her aim. "Please let our colleagues know that the plan will proceed. Release will be very soon." She was careful to avoid any names.

"Who cares, Vanya? Kill the little boy! We have won!"

"Who cares? I care!" With that, she slammed the phone down, forgetting for the moment that there was no cradle at hand in which to slam it. She pressed the "end call" button instead and flung the handset across the floor.

Kill the boy? But we have a plan! We will complete it and fulfill our bargain. Kill the boy? Who were these people?

THIRTY

Garrison was finishing a telephone conversation and placing the handset back in its cradle when Toomey appeared at the office door. "I called the Tampa office of Planet Capital. They were not pleased to hear from me, but I'm sure they have some photographs, probably some video."

"Can we take a look?"

"They told me in very polite terms that they prefer that I stick my request to view any such material in their possession where the sun doesn't shine."

"They were that blunt?"

"Almost." Garrison stood up from his chair, reached for his hat and said, "It's a beautiful day and I have my trusty SUV back. Wanna take a ride?"

Toomey sat in the passenger seat, energized by the course of the investigation. Part of him was enjoying the fantasy that his boss at the Federal Bureau of Investigation would be embarrassed by a small time sheriff solving a crime that the Bureau did not even consider was ever committed.

They were nearing Sarasota when Garrison pulled into the

same convenience store they stopped at the day before. The gas pumps were on the side, and while Garrison filled up, Toomey went inside and bought some soft drinks and a bag of chips. Like every convenience store, this one had the cold sodas near the rear so that customers would have to walk past every over-priced doodad to get the single can of soda they came for. When he reached the counter, he was second in line behind a tall man. Not for the first time, Toomey thought if he ever came back in another life, he wanted to come back as a taller man.

This one was buying a large bottle of Evian water and two cans of Altoids. For an apparently bright man, he took a long time counting out money to pay for the items, Toomey saw. After a frustrated effort, the man dumped a pocketful of coins on the counter and picked out the appropriate amount as the bored counter clerk with the tattoos on his neck and two piercings in his left nostril waited.

When the transaction was completed, the man slid the re-maining change in his pocket, picked up his purchases and turned from the counter, spotting the waiting Toomey for the first time. "Scuzi," he said almost inaudibly.

Toomey put his sodas and chips on the counter and the clerk said, "Happens every time he comes in." Toomey heard the young man's tongue bar click against his teeth as he spoke. "You'd think the guy had never made change in his life." Toomey muttered nothing, maybe a slight, "um," as the clerk rang him up.

He left, noting that the previous customer, the tall man, was just pulling out of the lot in his yellow Jeep. He saw the same man before, on his last visit to this store. He was the man who picked up the coins that Toomey had dropped. Something made Toomey focus longer on the man than was necessary and Garrison noted his distraction. "You see something?" Toomey shook his head and climbed into the vehicle.

*　*　*

In Tampa, they found the Planet office in a slick building faced in reflective glass and introduced themselves to the shirt-sleeved manager, Brent Duchovny, who was flanked by a pair of attorneys, one blond, one with a shaved head, both in expensive navy pin-striped suits. Garrison nodded to Toomey, indicating that the conversation could become contentious.

Duchovny led the way to a conference room overlooking Tampa Bay and the quintet took leather seats around a dark cherry table.

"Sheriff Garrison, as I explained to you on the telephone earlier, Planet Capital is not prepared to release any materials related to the Super Bowl."

"Customer privacy is something the firm takes seriously," Attorney Blond added.

Duchovny continued. "Obviously, any photography or videography would reveal the identities of selected clients of the firm."

Toomey's and Garrison's eyes met, both marveling at the rehearsed legal linguistics.

"This is not to imply," Attorney Bald interjected, "that there is any such material."

The Planet trio leaned back, smug in their conclusion that the meeting was over and the request successfully denied.

Garrison cocked his head and stared at the ceiling for a moment as if composing his thoughts. When his eyes returned to Duchovny, they bore in like lasers.

"Mr. Duchovny," he began, enunciating every syllable in the name, "this unofficial visit is apparently sufficiently bothersome to the senior management of Planet Capital in New York that there are two members of the Florida bar in attendance. I am guessing that the folks in New York would not spend, say, over a thousand dollars per hour unless there was some concern that client confidences could be compromised." Garrison looked in turn to Blond and Bald before focusing once more on

Duchovny. Toomey almost sensed a smile start to appear until the words began.

"On the other hand, I am here investigating a homicide. That means, for those of you in corporate law, that a human being was killed, and I, we, have very good reason to believe that the victim was the very official and visible guest of your firm about forty hours or so prior to his untimely demise."

Duchovny almost choked. "Who? Who was killed?"

Bald held a broad hand up and said with authority, "Planet Capital has no knowledge . . ."

Garrison slapped the table and spoke in a far louder and more insistent voice. "Gentlemen, this is a 'come to Jesus meeting', and one would be wise to be found standing at the foot of the cross when attendance is taken. Otherwise, I will be officially forced to seek an official order that Planet Capital release all material, audio, video and otherwise to assist in the official homicide investigation, an order I assure you will be most swiftly granted by the courts. Such an official order would, of course, be public record and I suspect that some clients of Planet Capital will conclude that their confidence in the firm may have been misplaced, especially when they find that one of their social companions at the Super Bowl did not return safely home after the event. I think they would consider that as a rather unsavory aspect of their financial relationship with the firm, wouldn't you agree?"

Garrison paused for a moment to let that sink in. The silence was a tool in Garrison's hands and he used it.

"'Why? Why would my investment manager allow this to happen,' they may ask, and rightfully so. 'How could they let my name, my very image, for goodness' sake, be made public in such a horrendous affair.'"

Garrison paused just a beat.

"'Why did the firm not cooperate with the authorities in such a way that would keep my name and my image out of the public eye?'" Garrison was on a roll. He modified the tenor of voice. "'Why yes, they could have, Mr. Client, but the firm chose not to. It chose not to permit two members of law enforcement to view the material in question, within the confines of Planet Capital's office in Tampa and under the watchful eyes of the Tampa manager and two respected attorneys. That would have kept you out of the public eye, but your firm chose not to do this.'"

Garrison paused once more and looked at Toomey. Toomey added, "What a thing to have to explain, Sheriff, when everything could be handled right here right now without the attendant public scrutiny."

The silence was hanging heavily. Blond asked, "If you can view the material here, with one of us sitting in the room, would that satisfy you?"

Garrison nodded. There was no further denial from Planet that such material may not even exist.

Fifteen minutes later, Garrison and Toomey were alone in the conference room watching a video monitor. Duchovny periodically looked in the room, but otherwise, the pair was alone.

Toomey was pressing the buttons on the video deck. "I love this high-tech stuff. Where was all this crap when I was starting out?"

"Here comes the video."

The recording began somewhere after the game started. Toomey would have guessed somewhere in the second half. It began with a woman just taking her seat after returning from the bar. She was, Toomey guessed, about forty-five, but makeup and Botox can work wonders and distort things. She smiled at the camera and took a sip. The audio was garbled and indistinct with all the crowd noise in the background.

"I wish the operator adjusted the gain," Garrison said, eliciting a blank stare from Toomey. That he had no clue what adjusting the gain meant, or why one would want to do so was apparent by the questioning eyes and the jaw low enough to leave the mouth open. "Look, Dennis, if the person making this tape adjusts the gain, it effectively limits the range of the microphone so it doesn't pick up every bit of noise in the background. Wait a minute, I think that just happened. Listen."

The voices of the people in the luxury suite were more distinct now. Whoever was operating the camera was doing a slow pan of the room. Leaning forward in his seat at the very edge of the room overlooking the field was a very heavy man with sagging jowls. To Toomey, he looked like a walrus and he said so. The camera caught another man, very tall and dressed in a dark suit. "Probably one of the Planet Chief Something or Others ... CEO, COO, CTO ... I can never keep them straight," Garrison said. A blur passed as someone moved directly in front of the camera. Another man in a shiny suit, this one small, wiry and with thinning hair slicked back across his head was ordering a drink, a Sambuca, Toomey thought he said. The man was focused on the action on the field and did not appear particularly pleased.

"You'd think the guy would at least pretend to enjoy prime seats at the Super Bowl and free cocktails."

Garrison nodded and counted nine different people so far, but no sign of Alek Mironev yet. A slim woman in a beige pants suit walked from the bar area to the window and glanced down at the field. The camera operator stayed focused on her and for good reason. She was stunning. She made a remark to the skinny man in the shiny suit who just looked at her, his sneer of displeasure unchanged. Toomey and Garrison strained to hear the exact words in the conversation, but only a few words were discerned. In context, it appeared the man had a lot of money riding on the game and his team was behind.

The camera panned again to a pair of men watching the

game on one of the large flat screen monitors in the room. In another corner, two men were chatting, and the one with his back to the camera caught Garrison's attention. "That's him, I'll bet. That's Alek Mironev." This was confirmed when the camera stayed on him and the voice of the operator said, "Say hello, you two. This is for posterity." The man turned to face the camera and smiled and Mironev's identity was established.

"That's your man, Sheriff. Enjoying a drink and making conversation. Looks like he's having a decent time."

"What do you think he's drinking?"

Toomey squinted. "I'd guess a vodka tonic. It looks clear and maybe has a lime on the top."

"That's my guess. Except it's probably gin. He's English, you know."

Mironev gave a slight wave to the camera but said little beyond, "Hi there." Then there was a roar from the crowd and the skinny man walked over to the bar, obviously disgusted by the way the game was going. He was going to take a seat near the television when Alek said, "Enjoying the game?"

"The refs are ruining it." Toomey thought he discerned a few muttered curses as he waited at the bar for his drink.

Another man walked over with his own freshened drink and said to the man, "I'm loving it! We're up by nine and your quarterback can't throw the ball within ten yards of his receivers."

"Vaffanculo," the thin man said.

"What was that?"

The man didn't know what the phrase meant and turned to Alek Mironev and the other man. Both of them just shrugged their shoulders and shook their heads as if to say "You've got me".

The camera made another pan to the left and another pair of guests, this time two women who were more interested in whether or not George Clooney was in the adjacent luxury suite than in the game.

"Wait as minute," Garrison said. "Let me rewind that." And he played the scene back.

"I thought so," he said when he saw and heard the exchange again. "Do you know what the man just said, Dennis?"

"I've heard it before. It's an Italian curse, but I couldn't tell you what it means."

"Literally, he's suggesting that the other man perform a sexual act on himself, if you get my drift. It's not a term of endearment."

"I knew a guy on the force years ago used to say that to me all the time. He never liked me."

"So why does Alek Mironev not know what it means?"

"Because he's from Russia?"

"And how did he get through the University in Bologna without speaking Italian? And believe me, he would have heard this phrase many times in his college career."

"He's just shrugged, like he really doesn't know."

"Alek Mironev would know the words better than me. That man on the video is *not* Alek Mironev."

THIRTY-ONE

Moscow, the same day

The phone said "unidentified caller" but he took the call anyway. It was a familiar voice, that of his Chechen cousin.

"Grigori, how good of you to take my call. I have been listening to my radio all day. I am calling to express my gratitude, without you, well. Your mother would be proud." The line went dead.

Malko didn't have an opportunity to even acknowledge the call and probably would not have responded if presented with it. There would be some cheers in Grozny, fewer but no less fervent in London. Malko found no cheering in his heart.

Hollow, almost pointless, a small meatless bone for the benefit of whom? His mother, Malko was sure, was observing the action from somewhere above, or perhaps from below, and shaking her head in disgust at her son's empty gesture. He was a Chechen with no reason to celebrate.

Sarasota

When they arrived at the Sarasota Airport, Garrison and Toomey went straight to the ladies' room. Garrison knocked, cracked the door open and called inside. "Men coming in. Security Check." There was no answer.

They walked into the space and scanned their surroundings. There was a short hallway that opened to a larger area. Stalls, sinks, the usual dispensers, a wastebasket. Affixed to one wall was a diaper-changing station. They looked in each stall. Either the place was rarely used or it was cleaned thoroughly and recently. There were no signs that anyone had used the restroom in a while, no balled up paper towels in the trash, no water droplets splashed on the counter near the sinks, every faucet gleaming. The pair stood back to back in the center and looked around. Garrison glanced at the lighting in the ceiling, bright fluorescent bulbs in two-foot by four-foot fixtures set in a dropped ceiling of white acoustic panels. Toomey was turning around, still looking for some ideas when he saw Garrison looking up. He reached the same conclusion five seconds after Garrison. "I'll go find a janitor and ask for a ladder," he said, trotting down the hallway and out the door. Garrison's eyes never left the ceiling. Three minutes later, Toomey returned.

"Sheriff, what's the Spanish word for 'ladder'?"

"Escalera." Garrison was staring up at the ceiling, just as Toomey left him.

"Well, I said 'scala' but the guy figured out what I wanted. He'll be here in a minute."

"Look at the corner of that panel, Dennis." Garrison pointed to a panel to his right, about four feet from the edge of the room.

Toomey looked up and squinted. "Looks like it was bent or chipped off. We'll start there."

A small man entered the room and carried a six-foot step ladder.

Garrison pointed to a spot on the floor. "Justo aquí." The man opened the ladder and Garrison rose to the third step. Toomey held a flashlight in his hand.

"Me voy a pasar este panel, señor." Garrison had his latex gloves on in the event there were latent prints on the ceiling panel that might prove valuable. "Hold that light right here, Dennis."

The Spanish-speaking worker asked, "¿Estás seguro?"

"¿Por qué pedís?"

"Te parece inestable." The worker held the ladder steady.

The mono-lingual Toomey said, "Fill me in. This guy looks worried."

"He just thinks I'm too old to be up here."

He raised the panel an inch, and then another. No barrier.

Garrison slid the panel slowly to one side and let it rest on the adjacent panel. The light in Toomey's hand illuminated an odd contraption of belts and pulleys.

"Bingo," Garrison said at the sight.

"Bingo," Toomey echoed.

"Si, Bingo. Por favor paso por ahora, Señor." He held out his hand and led the Sheriff back to floor level.

"Let's get some pictures of this thing and then call the FBI. They have to pay us some attention now."

A stainless steel and brass pulley with sturdy nylon ropes was attached to a heavy eye-bolt affixed to the concrete ceiling. Attached to the ropes were yellow nylon straps. A black carrying bag with two yellow straps attached sat empty on an adjacent ceiling panel.

Garrison could barely contain himself and said something in Spanish to the man who brought the ladder. The man responded and Garrison asked something more.

"Si, si. Juanita."

Garrison said something more and the man left in a hurry like a man on a mission.

"He's going to find Juanita Gomes and bring her here. I want to ask her something. What do you think of this?"

"Same as you're thinking."

Juanita Gomes entered the ladies' room, the ladder carrier at her heels but remaining at the door. She and Garrison spoke rapid-fire Spanish while Toomey tried to follow the staccato exchange and picked out a stray word here and there. Garrison removed a photograph from his wallet and showed it to the woman. With a pencil, he converted the battered face of Patrick Keough taken some years ago in England into a mustached man with a floppy hat.

"Si. Si."

Those words Toomey understood. The man who was once known as Patrick Keough and who escaped could be the same tall man, if Juanita Gomes had a discerning eye and if Garrison's artwork was at least passable. Garrison thanked the woman and asked Toomey to retrieve a digital camera and an evidence bag from the back of his Sheriff's vehicle. When he returned, Garrison slipped on a pair of gloves and carefully stowed the pulley, ropes and other evidence in the bag. In minutes they were off and on their way to the Crime Lab to drop off the material they found in the ceiling.

"So tell me. What happened?"

"Senora Gomes says we're on the right track. Same guy. Drove here in a dark green van."

"What picture did you show her? What was this business with the pencil?"

"It's the photograph of our guy Patrick Keough that I got from Interpol. It's a few years old but with a floppy hat and a bushy mustache, it's our guy."

"Photograph? What photograph? I didn't know you had pictures."

Garrison pulled a notebook from his breast pocket and passed it to Toomey. I've got a couple of copies in there. Not great copies, but passable. You never saw the photos?"

"Never. You must have taken them from the Interpol file before I had a chance to look it over."

Toomey fumbled through a series of assorted photographs inside the flap of Garrison's notebook. Most were from other cases his Department was investigating. Garrison saw him flipping through them and offered, "Look for one in black and white. Face all bruised up, one eye swollen shut. I should have two or three copies in there."

Toomey found it and angled it to get a better look under the streetlights they were passing. Garrison switched on the overhead light.

Toomey tilted the print until he could get rid of the glare and focus. After a few moments, he muttered, "What the hell? I saw this guy! I even said thanks to him! He was at the convenience store! Twice!"

He explained about the tall man in the convenience store. We're going to stop by that store on our way back from the Crime Lab. Maybe that kid at the counter can tell us something else.

Garrison dropped the evidence off at the Crime Lab in Sarasota and they drove back to convenience store near the Interstate exit ramp.

Yes, the tattooed and pierced clerk said, the tall man had been here before, maybe a half-dozen times in the past several weeks. No, he didn't know his name and the man always paid in cash. Yes, he seemed to take a lot of time with his change. Except for one time when he came in with a young woman, a tiny blonde, he was always alone. Garrison left a card and told him to call if he saw either one come in.

"By the way," Garrison said when he was leaving the store. "Do you have surveillance cameras in here?"

The clerk leaned far over the counter to whisper his response. "They haven't worked in two years, but don't tell anybody."

When he reached his vehicle, he called Tawanda Bradford.

"I'm glad you called. Everybody is convinced that Alek Mironev is shacked up in a No-Tell Motel between Tampa and New Orleans. What else do you have?"

Garrison, in a calm voice, explained the findings and asked her to call the FBI with the information.

Garrison drove while Toomey used the laptop computer attached to the Chief's vehicle to look up some information. When Garrison hung up, Toomey spoke, the laptop opened in front of him. "I've been checking on line. The gear we found in the ceiling is called a Rescue Positioning System. Big with building contractors, mountain climbers, ski patrols, people like that. Runs almost two grand for the stuff we found in the ceiling."

"So our little pixie gets Alek Mironev into the ladies' room, disables him somehow, and Mr. Finney is already there, probably brought there in the barrel by our mystery man earlier."

Toomey added, "Then, up into the ceiling goes Alek Mironev and off to the waiting limousine goes Mr. Finney. Our tall Hispanic gentleman shows up later, closes the ladies' room for another cleaning assignment, and removes Mironev from the ceiling and puts him into a blue plastic barrel. Voila!"

"You speak French?"

"Then, after Finney leaves a note saying that he's going to the Big Easy, he sneaks away and goes on a short fishing trip in your county. His use as a decoy is finished, and he'd be a real threat to our killer if he's allowed to live. So he's gone."

Garrison nodded, his attention fixed on the traffic ahead. "And the real Alek Mironev is someplace else. Any ideas?"

"This is your territory."

"Someplace remote. He can't be kept in a barrel forever, and he can't be in a place where there are a lot of people."

"He could be bound and gagged, you know."

Garrison got quiet. After a few moments, he said, "I really don't think this guy would keep him bound and gagged. He's not that kind of guy."

"You seem to know him better as every minute goes by."

"You're right."

They continued in silence and arrived at the Dodge Budget Motel at midnight. Garrison said, "Thanks for everything today, Dennis. I mean that."

Garrison smiled at the thought. "Tawanda is going to pick you up tomorrow around nine, if that's OK. I'll be in around ten. If you want a car to use tomorrow morning for a while, Tawanda will take care of you."

"I'll be ready. She'll take me for a Dunkin's coffee, right?"

"Extra large, plus you get a donut if you want. It's on the department."

"In that case, I might get two. I'll probably just stay in the office, though, if you don't mind."

"In fact, maybe you can sit in on the staff meeting for me."

"Maybe I will. Good luck with your spinal tap."

"Ugh. Thanks."

"Getting old sucks, Larry."

"*Not* getting old sucks even more."

THIRTY-TWO

Emilio Fortino worked quickly but methodically, starting from the far corners of his hotel room and working his way to the door. With a slightly damp cloth, he began to wipe every surface. In a small plastic bag, he placed every small item that might be tied to him. He'd dispose of those items somewhere along the way after he left. He'd already paid for his room, by credit card connected to a bogus account, and thanked the hotel manager for his hospitality. His luggage was already in the rental van along with the bicycle he'd been using during his stay. These would likewise be wiped down and disposed of today. The Jeep he left when he picked up the van rental was already methodically wiped down. He arranged with Vanya to stow sealed packets of clothing for both of them along with bogus passports, some cash and other counterfeit credit cards in waterproof plastic bags. They'd be on the boat. When Emilio deposited Alek Mironev in the drop off point and they finished their day's work, he and Vanya would leave on the boat, enter the waters of the Gulf, swim to shore with the aid of their underwater equipment, change into their new clothing and identities, and be off as silently as they arrived. Vanya was to split up with him at once and make her way elsewhere.

They could not be seen together ever again. If Vanya, for her own twisted reasons, chose to pursue the career path she desired, he would never know. As far as he was concerned, he'd be fully and irrevocably retired, tending his olive trees. Where Vanya went was entirely up to her.

Emilio was about to close the door behind him when he heard his telephone ring. Not daring to reenter the room, he paused for some moments and opted to check at the front desk for a message, which he did. Probably another frantic call from Vanya, in either some state of exultation or despair but rarely in between. When he checked with the front desk, the number he was given was not Vanya's but his contact in Italy. This must be serious, he thought. He used his cell phone to call back and was given yet another number. He reached his Italian contact who told him, "The caller said you should phone at once. He had such a distinctive voice, signore, a voice so low, like a basso profundo without the rich melody."

Emilio knew. The deep voice was unmistakable and unforgettable. It was a voice dragged through the gravel, as low in range as a human voice could be and remain audible, one that spoke power and authority in most cases. He'd last heard the voice in France, Perpignan, when he scanned the Interpol files and made his selection of Finney for this assignment. When he placed the call, the voice spoke to Emilio with resignation.

"You are warned. I can say little else."

"Is that why you wanted me to call? For you to warn me?"

"Ah, Marcel, or Patrick, or Gervasio, or whatever name you prefer to use at the moment, I have my own concerns. If you hear the hounds from a distance, be assured that those dogs are nearly at our heels. I'm afraid my days at Interpol are over."

"They know that you gave me access to the data base?"

"Only that I gave someone access when I should not have

done so. But they will assemble the pieces soon enough. They can calibrate the date, time and sequence of every keystroke, no? And the name of James Finney was prominent. I'm afraid they will be on to you soon."

"You will tell them?"

"If they but show me the thumb screws, I will tell them the sins of my grandmother. I have never claimed courage as an asset. But the information on you was already sent to the states, to Florida I believe."

This information rendered Emilio speechless.

"You are still there, my friend?"

"Yes. Yes. But a file on me?"

"A complete file from our Interpol friends, I'm afraid. From that brief but unfortunate confinement in England before you managed to escape. You may not recall, in the condition you were in at the time, that you were photographed and finger printed."

"Where in Florida? Who has the file?" Emilio needed to know.

"I don't recall the name. It was a Sheriff. Dodge County. Is that familiar?"

Emilio knew of the county too well.

"When was it sent?"

"On the weekend, I believe. Yes, on Saturday morning."

Emilio thought back. For three days his Interpol file was in the hands of a local sheriff in an obscure county. Emilio's temporary lodgings in Boca Grande were in Lee County, but Dodge County was barely an hour's drive. Where had he been since Saturday? Back and forth on the Interstate to Sarasota once, with Vanya into the unpopulated interior regions of the state for target practice, over to Charlotte County to arrange rental of the van he'd need to transport Alek Mironev . . . He considered the likely damage and thought it unlikely that his own convoluted activities would be unraveled in such a short span of time. He relaxed before he spoke. "Perhaps that is not so bad, my friend. If they have been looking at the file for three days, then perhaps I remain at little risk."

The man with the low voice almost harrumphed. "Hah! You'd better rethink your comings and goings. They are likely much closer than you would like to believe. I can almost hear the bloodhounds from here. For my part, I think I shall go. I have a place to which I can retire in some comfort. Beaches, co-conut trees, some maidens who see no need to walk the earth fully clothed. I don't expect we will meet again."

"I cannot contact you?"

"Contact me? I think not. Your last contact with me is the cause for my current troubles, although I must say it only ac-celerates plans I made long ago. Good by, my old friend. It has been . . . interesting."

"But if I need to reach you, to trace . . ." The line was dead and Emilio listened to the dial tone.

THIRTY-THREE

Tawanda was waiting out front when Toomey walked out the front door of the Dodge Budget Motel. "I hope you weren't waiting long. I've been up for a while and was just reading the paper."

"Sheriff Garrison is accustomed to more civilized schedule and he expects others would follow his example. I guess he thought you'd be sleeping in, like he usually does." Tawanda poked fun at her boss, even as she adored and admired him.

"We didn't get back until midnight last night. We had quite a day. And I thought he was having a medical test this morning."

"That man will do anything to stay away from work." Tawanda pulled into the Dunkin's drive through and handed the coffees to Toomey. "Hold on to these, please, and I'll tell you what's been happening this morning. The Bureau in Tampa called first thing and faxed some information, too. They wanted to speak with the Sheriff but I convinced the guy I was the detective on the case."

"What did he say?"

"There were two sets of prints on the pulley you dropped

off. One was from the victim, Finney. The second was from an immigrant from Russia, Vanya Zakayev, who came to Sarasota a year ago and works the trapeze at the circus."

Toomey considered this news, understanding Vanya's double value as seductress and agile performer; her strength and training would have come in handy in getting Alek Mironev stowed in the ceiling of the airport ladies' room. The tall fellow could show up a bit later, use the barrel to stand on, open the panel, remove the drugged Mr. Mironev, and put the panel back in place. Great plan.

"Where does she live?"

"In Sarasota. The Bureau is sending someone out to check her out. The Sheriff also called and said he'd try to get in by ten."

They entered and Tawanda suggested he use the Sheriff's office if he wanted to make any calls or do whatever he wished. He had yet to reach the Sheriff's chair when the intercom came to life and Tawanda's voice came across.

"The Bureau is on the line and the agent wants to talk to you. Just press line two and pick it up."

"Thanks," Toomey said, not realizing until he said it that Tawanda couldn't hear him. He pressed line two and took the call.

It was a friend of Toomey's, one of the few he made during his brief tenure at the Tampa Bureau. "Did Detective Bradford fill you in about my earlier call?"

"About the Russian lady? Yes."

"She left her apartment early this morning. The apartment manager was surprised to see her so early and asked her where she was going so early in the morning. She mentioned she was headed to Boca Grande."

"So what's next?"

"The Bureau is still convinced that Mironev is OK, but I'll

bet they're wavering upstairs at this point. The family in Moscow has been contacted by the Bureau and everybody else about where Alek might be. They're not saying they're alarmed, but if my son was kidnapped and being held for ransom, I'm not sure what I'd say if I thought talking to the authorities would put his life in jeopardy."

Toomey agreed.

"The fact that the prints came back to a Russian immigrant is raising eyebrows upstairs, though. Put that together with a murder victim, the whole ladies' room thing, and your suppositions aren't quite so far-fetched. I'll keep my eyes and ears open."

The conversation ended and Toomey sat at the Sheriff's desk and looked out the window, trying to make sense of the information he'd just received.

The intercom came to life again and Tawanda told him to pick up line two once more. "It's somebody from a convenience store that you spoke to last night." Toomey picked up.

"She was here, the little blonde."

"When?" Toomey grabbed a pencil and a piece of paper.

"Around seven."

"That was over two hours ago!"

"And it was busy! And I'm not allowed to make personal phone calls on company time, and I just finished a twelve-hour shift! I've put in thirty hours in the past two days. Did you want to know or what?"

Toomey knew when to back off. This was someone with information and rousing him to anger would solve nothing. "Sure, sorry. Tell me."

"She came in around seven. Alone. She bought a muffin, if you want to call what we sell in a cellophane wrapper a 'muffin'. It's processed wheat flour, high fructose corn syrup, and preservatives. She also bought a container of orange juice. The real stuff, from right here in Florida, not from concentrate. She paid in cash and left."

"Did you see her get in a car?"

"She parked right in front. It was a white or light gray Toyota or Honda or something. No one was in the car with her."

"Plates?"

"What?"

"License plates. The kind on the back of the car. Did you get a number from her plate?"

"Oh, we call them tags. Not plates. You from around here?"

"No." Toomey's frustration level was at the edge. At the best of times, he was not a patient man; at times like these, he wanted to scream. "*Tag* number?"

"Seven-Zero-Eight-Four-Four-Nine."

"Super. Thanks. Anything else?"

"One thing. She wasn't here, if you know what I mean. I mean, she was *here*, but she was like zoned, wandering in another universe, like drugged or something. Does that help?"

"It might. Was she nervous? Anxious?"

"More like she was just somewhere else, like in a daydream. Some people are always like that, but the last time I saw her, she was like intense and focused. Right here in the moment. This morning, just the opposite. That's what caught my attention. Plus she's a fox and has these silver-blue eyes. Tight little body. An athlete. And these perky little breasts going on, know what I mean? Sort of like one of those Bulgarian gymnasts at the Olympics. Or Lithuanian, something like that."

"Thanks. You did great."

"Is there, you know, like a reward or something?"

"You know, I'm new around here, but I think the Sheriff said something about paying you a big reward if you found out anything useful. And believe me, you did. You should hear from him in about a week."

*   *   *

Toomey had just hung up the phone when another buzz from Tawanda signaled yet another call. "It's someone saying he's returning your call. Should I put it through?"

Toomey had to stop for a moment to think. Who would be calling . . . ? "Put it through," he said with surprising urgency.

It was the call he waited for. After fewer than ten seconds of recalling names and old times, Toomey dove into an explanation of the situation he was encountering. It was brief and thorough, using all the federal law enforcement short hand that would make this short and sweet. Then he popped the question: "Can you help?"

Toomey wanted the assets this man could bring to bear, including a direct and authoritative line to Europe and Interpol's extensive data bases. Toomey already knew that James Philip Finney was on those same data bases, and that the fingerprints of a man known only as Patrick Keough and who was the alleged shooter of the same James Philip Finney was somewhere in the area of Dodge County.

"I'm just finishing an assignment here, Dennis. I'm with the DEA and assigned to Interpol for the moment. If I drop it right now, then everything could crumble. We're talking a major drug trade investigation."

Toomey was stunned. "In Dodge County?"

"Most of the drug activity is closer to the coast. But Dodge County is where it ends up. Think about it. There's open water a few miles away, barren scrub land, places to hide that only an army of all-terrain vehicles could cover, major highways running to Dallas on the west, and up to Atlanta and New York. They can get product to London, Paris and Rome at will. There are major airports down here in every direction and a dozen hidden landing fields in between. It's perfect. The whole deal is set to break in another two days. There'll be forty agents from DEA and five Interpol detectives arriving tomorrow from Orlando. We're talking eight big traders and nineteen little guys handling millions of dollars of coke, crack and heroin every two weeks!"

Toomey knew what these investigations were like and the kinds of peril that an undercover operation could bring to the participants. If all went as planned, the photo ops would be outstanding. There would be "perp walks" galore and the newspapers and electronic press would be there soaking it all up in choreographed fashion.

Toomey decided to press the point, even if he had to guess he was right on Alek Mironev being kidnapped. To his way of thinking, the evidence was there. Besides, he thought, if I'm wrong, what are they going to do? I'm going to retire anyway! "Look, I understand. But we're talking a major international incident here. Who wants to be the guy that says, 'I could have prevented the death of the Russian president's son on American soil?' Not me!" He went on to describe the facts as he knew them, and included the fact that the Tampa office of the FBI was reluctant to give its support. Toomey took that calculated risk that the low reputation of the new Tampa Special Agent in Charge, Martin Weatherbee, was shared in other circles, including Interpol's. To his good fortune, he was right, and that sealed the deal.

'I'll make a call, Dennis, but I can't make a promise. We can keep a lid on the drug thing for a half day before it's ready to break and get our team in here early to do the round up and serve the warrants. If I get the OK from my bosses, what will you need from me?"

Toomey told him.

When he finished the phone call, he called Tawanda into Garrison's office. Tawanda pulled up the vehicle ownership information on her laptop and found that a white Hyundai sedan was registered to Vanya Zakayev. "Issue a BOLO, Tawanda. Can you send it to the surrounding counties as well? She might be in Boca Grande."

"A 'Be-On-The-Lookout' is going to every sheriff's office and police department south of Orlando as we speak. Plus the Highway Patrol. I'm telling them to keep her in view, not stop her. I can change that if you'd like."

"No, that's good. Add this name to your call list." He handed her a name and a phone number. Tawanda looked at it and her eyebrows went up to her hairline. "Really? Him?"

Toomey nodded. He relished the frantic pace, something he hadn't experienced in quite a while. He checked his watch. Almost ten and Garrison could arrive any minute. This little blonde woman is on the move for a reason, he thought. It's time to find out where she's going and why.

THIRTY-FOUR

Emilio was still seething. He'd given Vanya specific instructions to have the boat ready, and instead she shows up at his hotel on Gasparilla Island! In very clear terms, with a barrage of multi-lingual imperatives, he let her know that her attendance was neither invited, appreciated, nor acceptable. He cared little for her hurt feelings, the tears welling up in her eyes or her bowed head. His verbal assault was provoked by pride, ego, classical hubris, not that her sensibilities could absorb such subtlety. He made sure she was in her car and headed back north and to the boat forty minutes ago. Meanwhile, he still had ten more minutes to go in his own boat before he reached the island holding Alek Mironev. In his pocket was an injectable sedative if Mr. Mironev insisted on it, although he felt quite certain that a few hours of discomfort curled up in a barrel was a small price for the captive to pay for his eventual liberation.

He slowed the engine to idle and surveyed the open waters and the waters' edges with binoculars, just in case another boater became curious. It was standard procedure for his journeys here. He would not modify his behavior and take any un-necessary risk this close to the end. He pushed the throttle a bit forward and snaked his way through the mangroves that kept the narrow channel to his landing area hidden from view, ar-rived, and killed the motor. He lashed the boat to a stout branch and walked to the faded clapboard cottage. Over his head, he pulled the ski mask with the cut outs for his eyes.

When he opened the door, he took a few moments to let his eyes adjust; the day was bright, the interior dim. At this point, Alek Mironev was just a dim shadow behind the bars of the cage. "Good morning, Mr. Mironev," he said. His eyes adjusted to the light and he saw a gaunt, bearded young man that the tabloid paparazzi would not ever recognize as the world's most eligible bachelor. "Please stand facing the far side of the enclo-sure if you would."

Alek Mironev was a bit stunned. The usual procedure was for containers of foodstuffs and beverages to be passed through the bars. For a moment too long, Alek Mironev did not move.

"I said move to the far side, Mr. Mironev. I would think you'd be anxious to depart these surroundings and go home."

What did he say? He watched the man in the mask step back outside and wheel in a large blue plastic barrel. Alek had some faded memories of the barrel, but nothing registered clearly.

"Hop to it, Mr. Mironev."

Mironev did as he was told and faced the wall. He heard keys being fumbled and inserted into a lock, then the slow creaking sound of iron on iron as the barred door was opened.

If Mironev was to make a run for it, this was the time. The opportunity was considered by both captor and captive. Mironev was torn: I'm told that I will soon be set free; if I make a run for it and succeed in my escape, where would I find my-self? I have no idea? I have heard no other voices beyond those of the birds and the wind. And what of the snakes? Has my captor lied about the snakes? If so, then what?

Emilio watched the young man's shoulders sag at the precise moment that he dismissed all thoughts of escape. In a calm voice, he said, "I'm going to ask you, Mr. Mironev, to climb into this barrel, after which I'll give you some time to compress yourself into something more compact. If you've done your stretching and bending exercises that I advised, that should be little problem. You get the idea. I won't rush you. If you prefer, I can sedate you, but I'd much prefer that you volunteer. Then I'll secure the top and we'll be off. There are air holes by the way, so you will not suffocate. I'll step back now and give you a moment to climb in. Agreed?"

Mironev turned and faced his captor. The ski mask was black and thick, but Alek could see that the eyes were smiling eyes. This man, this unidentified man who'd been keeping him in solitary confinement, was actually pleased to bring the ordeal to an end. No more pleased than Alek, though, who almost scampered inside the barrel, twisted a bit this way and that, and contorted himself so that his head was just below the rim. He flexed his fingers and tried to wiggle his extremities a bit. Good enough. "We'll leave in just a moment," he said. The cover was placed on top of him and secured with three snapping latches. Then he heard nothing but the low humming of a tune he remembered from somewhere. An opera? He loved to attend the opera when he lived in Bologna. Yes, it was an aria, he was certain. Ah those memories. An evening of opera, a bottle of wine, friends. He clung to those memories and pledged to return one day to Bologna to relive the pleasures.

Alek could feel the barrel tip and heard a slight grunt from the man's exertion as the dolly was wheeled to the door. "Small bump," he heard the man say, and the wheels were over the edge, gently though. The man was considerate enough under the circumstances. Then the sound of the wheels on the soil, fairly smooth going so far. He could only guess how far this leg of the journey was, but he guessed perhaps one hundred yards or more. Then the man's voice again. "I'm going to wheel you on some boards onto a boat. I'll be as gentle as I can."

Alek could feel a slight jolt as the wheels were lifted onto the boards, then a slow go until it reached the boat. He could feel gentle rocking and guessed the boat was in very shallow water, maybe even run onto shore. "Bump coming." The man meant it this time, for the barrel dropped some distance with a loud thud. Alek groaned. "Sorry about that."

Then the sound of the boards being pulled on board, the sound of the motor, echoing in his cramped chamber. Then the fear: What if he's lying? What if he simply pushes me into the sea? Terrors set in and Alek could feel his heart beat in his chest. Death by drowning, the barrel bobbing in the waves, watching the water make its relentless way into the barrel, the gradual settling into the water, then sinking to the bottom, unable to scream, his lungs resisting until the very end when he'd be forced to expel the last volume of air, and inhale the water that would cause his lungs to respond in violent spasms, his brain to scream, his heart to explode with the lack of oxygenated blood. Alek Mironev had never known such fright. The boat climbed to plane and they were making some headway now. He was powerless to do a thing and kept his teeth clenched; would that the man had some sense of decency, he implored. He searched his soul for some small piece of eternal hope, some small prayer lodged in his early years as a churchgoing acolyte. His captor had not disappointed so far, and he wished that to continue. The noise of the engine kept up for perhaps fifteen minutes until he heard a drop in volume and felt the craft settle in the water and progress at a slow pace. If he was going to the bottom of the sea in a barrel, it would happen soon. But no, he felt the boat slow further, the engine set to idle, then a slight bump. They'd reached a wharf or dock. Whatever, they were not on the open water.

The man killed the motor and Alek heard him tying lines

onto cleats or piers. Then the man's voice, much lower this time. "Absolute silence for a bit here, I'm afraid. Not a sound."

The man had been truthful so far and Alek continued to place his trust in him; there'd be no noise from his quarter, no matter what jolts, bounces or drops occurred. The man could count on Alek to uphold his end of the bargain. Then the sound of boards being set along the side.

"We're going up a sort of ramp here." The man's voice was almost a whisper. "Remember. Silence." Alek heard the man straining as the dolly was tilted and moved along the boards, then a small bump onto the dock's surface. He listened. The boards were placed on the dolly now, wedged against the barrel. Rolling across the boards of a dock for some period. Then gravel. Then stopped and set down level. Metal doors opened. Alek heard a latching mechanism, a handle being turned. Vehicle doors opening. Probably a van of some sort. Then the boards being reset. "Up another ramp here." The man's voice was still barely above a whisper. Probably other people in the vicinity. Alek could shout if he wished, but how far would his shouts carry, coming as they would from inside a barrel and from lungs barely able to inflate to half-volume?

In minutes, Alek could sense that the barrel was secured inside the vehicle with ropes or belts and the doors were closed. Another door opened and in a moment the engine roared to life and they were off. "Three hours, Mr. Mironev. Maybe less." The man's voice was at normal levels now. "Relax and think a bit about your impending freedom." Alek did just that. "And thank you, Mr. Mironev. I apologize for the discomfort, but you've been a stellar guest. I do appreciate that." A gentleman, Alek concluded. It could have been much worse.

At the Gulf Breeze Inn in Boca Grande, a man appeared at the front desk and handed the clerk an identification card. The clerk, who'd been working there for several years, had never seen such identification, even in this area where international travel was the rule rather than the exception. He did a double take and studied the man.

Tall, broad-shouldered, shaved head, and dressed in faded jeans and a leather jacket. He didn't give the outward appearance of a law enforcement officer, but his picture did match the photograph. "What can I do for you, sir?"

The man presented him with a description. Any recent guests—male, tall, probably mid-fifties, keeps to himself. He might have been seen in the company of a petite blonde woman. "He might be registered under the name Fortino."

"Of course, sir, many of our guests are here alone and most of them prefer their privacy and their solitude." The clerk closed the guest registration book and folded his hands on top like a priggish school marm.

The man with the curious ID was growing impatient with the clerk. This was the third such hotel on Gasparilla Island he visited this morning, and he was not in the mood for stalling. The first two inns had guest lists that consisted of elderly dowagers and princes of industry who'd long ago passed their mid-fifties.

"Let me emphasize that this is a homicide investigation."

The clerk shrugged his shoulders, opened the book and scanned the guest log, giving the impression that he was giving careful consideration to each name. The man drummed his fingers on the counter while he waited. "No, I think not," the clerk said. "No one staying here matches the description of a tall man of middle age."

The man leaned over the counter and put a large hand on the clerk's shoulder and squeezed hard. Through clenched teeth, he said in a low voice, "Take one more look. *Anyone* in the recent past who matches the description."

The clerk's eyes widened and he fairly whispered a name and room number: "Mr. Fortino, Emilio Fortino, room nine. But he checked out this morning. About two hours ago."

The man released the clerk's shoulders. "Room nine. The key."

The room was yet to be serviced and the man went to work. The room was obviously wiped down, for there were no prints on the door knobs, telephone or any furniture. In itself, this news confirmed the recent presence of the man he was seeking. No casual guest would so thoroughly remove every bit of evidence on his stay. In ten minutes, the broad-shouldered man with the shaved head stood on the veranda of the Gulf Breeze Inn and made a call on his mobile phone. His contact in France answered.

A man meeting the description was somewhere within two hours of this location. A young blonde woman visited the inn earlier and stayed only a few minutes before she left. The subject usually drove a yellow Jeep, but was last seen driving a white van.

Meanwhile, his contact in France told him, his current undercover operation was being terminated at once. A swarm of federal Drug Enforcement and Interpol agents were already descending on south Florida with warrants, indictments and handcuffs at the ready. "You should avoid going back to your area of operations for the moment. It will be quite dangerous for you."

At least, the man thought, even if this effort tracking down some fellow named Fortino comes up empty, there will be a host of other unsavory individuals in the illegal drug trade getting visits soon, and they should be prepared for long stays at their penitentiaries.

Dodge County, later the same morning

Garrison walked into his office late in the morning, his face contorted, his eyes closed, Walter wagging his tail at his side. Tawanda could see the man was in pain.

"You look like hell. I thought you were just going to have a minor blood test or something."

"Spinal tap. I was supposed to stay flat on my back for ninety minutes, but I couldn't just lay there doing nothing. I guess I got up too soon because my head is throbbing to the beat of a marching band and there's a vice squeezing my head at the temples. Toss in the pain caused by what I am certain are steel spikes behind my eyeballs and I have some very good reasons to look like hell. Got any aspirin?"

"Tylenol." She removed a jar from her desk drawer and put three in his open palm. "Take two."

"Two for now, one for later. Where's our friend?"

"In your office. He took over the place and you're on the cleaning crew from now on. He says he can whip your ass in the next election, and I believe him. He does have a lot of news, though. Come on. Keep your eyes closed and I'll walk you in."

Garrison did as he was told and Toomey looked up, phone at his ear, to see Tawanda leading the Sheriff into the office by the hand.

He completed the phone call and said, "That was a friend at the Bureau. Still no sign of this little blond girl. And what happened to you? You look like a crippled veteran coming home from the war and you were on the losing side."

Garrison kept his eyes closed, the dull pain actually lessened as a result. "Fill me in."

Toomey did. The identity of Vanya Zakayev, the sighting at the convenience store, the call from Toomey, the BOLO. "Nothing yet, though. How many small white sedans can there be in Florida?"

Garrison kept his eyes closed tight. "There are fifteen million licensed drivers in this state, and white is probably the most popular vehicle color here. So I'm guessing there are, roughly, only a few million white sedans. But what's your gut tell you?"

"That the game is ending soon."

"I agree. Tawanda? You still here?"

"Haven't moved an inch."

"Tell me. If Special Agent Toomey drives a department vehicle, do we have any liability risk?"

"It's called 'Permissive Use'. We're covered. Why? You want him out on patrol or something?"

"If he drives and I ride, I just want to be OK, insurance and legal-wise."

"I just gave you an expert opinion. Where are you going?"

"I have no idea yet. I'm just thinking. When my eyes are closed, I have trouble driving, and I'm thinking maybe somebody else, like Agent Toomey here, could do some extra duty. Did he have two donuts this morning?"

"One jelly and one chocolate glazed."

"Then he owes us." Garrison removed a set of keys from his jacket pocket and placed them on his desk.

"How did you drive here, anyway?"

"Walter drove."

"Thank goodness. I thought you were driving with your eyes closed."

The intercom burped to life and Tawanda reached over and depressed the button. "What's up Karen?"

"Line 2. Interpol. I think it's the same guy with the French accent that you spoke to before. Says it's important."

"Tawanda pressed the button for line 2 and passed the phone to Garrison. "This is Garrison."

Garrison listened as René Royale from Paris presented him

with a set of facts and positions. The man whose prints were identified on the fishing lure recovered at the scene of the Peace River homicide is suspected of being somewhere in the vicinity of Boca Grande and on the move. "We have just received some intelligence from inside our agency that the suspect was most recently using the name Emilio Fortino. We have an Interpol Special Liaison in your area and he tells us that Mr. Fortino was last seen driving a white van. Our liaison is looking for the man as we speak."

"An Interpol agent is here in Dodge County?"

"I am certain you will learn much more very soon, Sheriff Garrison, but yes, he has been tracking the movements of the suspect." The conversation lasted another minute or two, and Garrison hardly had a chance to put the receiver down when his intercom buzzed again. Tawanda said, "It's your friend Butch Hollis from Lee County."

Garrison picked up the phone. Butch Hollis was a former Dodge County deputy who now worked for the Lee County Sheriff's Office. Lee County covered the southern portion of Gasparilla Island, including Boca Grande.

"Hi Larry, I saw the BOLO from your office this morning. I just thought I'd call and tell you one of our retired deputies just called in to say he saw a white Hyundai a while ago in Boca Grande. He had his scanner on, but he was headed in the opposite direction, so he couldn't catch a full tag number. He caught a couple numbers, though, and it looks like your vehicle. By the time he turned around and tried to find her again, she was long gone. It sure sounds like your girl and she was headed north into Charlotte County. I called them on it, but no one has seen her there, as far as I know."

"Thanks, Butch. What time was that?"

"Maybe forty-five minutes ago."

"Why the delay?"

"Cell phones, Larry. Our guy had to get back to the mainland before he found a place where his signal would work. Sorry."

"Not your fault, Butch. I'm just glad that you've got a retired deputy who pays attention."

After the call, Garrison asked Toomey, "What would you do?"

"Not sure. Probably make sure there are people on the road watching for her between Boca Grande and Sarasota. That's the only other place we know she's been. Maybe she's on her way home."

"Tawanda can call Charlotte County, Sarasota County and Highway Patrol, and maybe we'll get lucky. I'm thinking she was on Boca Grande for a reason. Early ride down there from Sarasota. I'm thinking we should be looking for a tall Hispanic guy wearing a mustache and a floppy hat. Probably driving a white van."

They commiserated for the next ten minutes when the intercom came alive once more. "Sheriff, some fellow named Zeke Peebles is on the phone. Wants to speak with you."

"Zeke Peebles?"

"That's what he said. Says you told him to call if he saw someone."

Garrison shrugged, eyes still closed. "OK. Put him through."

"Sheriff, it's Zeke."

"Right. Who are you, Zeke?"

"You told me to call if I saw that tall guy again."

"What tall guy?"

"The one who can't make change very fast. That tall guy. He was just here."

Garrison's eyes popped open. "Zeke, do you have a tattoo and some dangly things on your nose?"

A long sigh came across the line. "Piercings. They're called piercings."

Garrison asked, "When was he there?"

"He just left about two minutes ago. He just pulled out of the parking lot and turned north toward the Interstate."

"Great, Zeke. What was he driving?"

"White van. A Ford I think."

"Anything else?"

"The *tag* numbers are Vee-Nine-One-One-Eight-Seven-One."

"Zeke, you-da-man!"

"Sheriff?"

"Yes, this is Sheriff Garrison."

"About the reward."

"Reward?"

Toomey cut back in. "Call Tawanda Bradford, Zeke, tomorrow morning at this same number. She has all the reward forms ready and she'll take care of everything for you."

Tawanda and Garrison looked at each other with questioning expressions. Toomey was out of his seat, coat on his arm, keys in his hand. "Coming, Larry?"

Garrison rose, eyes wide open now. "Tawanda, you look after Walter. Agent Toomey and I are going to be on the Interstate. Call out for a BOLO on the van." In seconds, the pair was out of the office and on the road.

"You need to give some directions here, Larry. I'm the new guy, remember?"

"Turn left at the light and switch on the flashers and siren. We've got to catch up with this man."

Garrison reached for his radio and called the department. "Tawanda, did you reach the Bureau?"

"They're on the line right now. I'll get back to you in a minute."

Garrison was tapping the radio, impatient, eager to get more information. Two minutes later, Tawanda was back.

"Here's the deal. They've located the white Hyundai but there's no sign of the girl."

"Where is it?"

"Bradenton, on Third Avenue. They said the engine is still warm so she's somewhere close."

"What's nearby?"

Tawanda had to give that a bit of thought. "The Desoto Bridge, Manatee Hospital. There's a lot right around there. Restaurants, marinas. Palmetto is just north, across the Manatee River."

"The Manatee goes right into the Gulf at that point, right?"

"Right. It's almost at the mouth of the River where it opens up to the Gulf."

"Thanks. What did the Bureau say about our man in a white Ford van on the Interstate? That can't be too hard to find."

""They'll cover I-75 like a blanket."

"Keep me posted. We'll be on I-75 soon and we'll be watching for him, too."

THIRTY-FIVE

Emilio Fortino made his way along the highway at just below the speed limit. He was so close to the end, he could taste the finality and it was sensuous and inviting. Every passing minute, he'd be that much closer to a glass, a fine crystal stem with an enormous bowl, and the swirling garnet of a fine Barolo, one he'd kept aside in his cellar for just such an occasion. He hummed the tune "Il balen" from *Il Trovatore*. Yes, he would arrange an evening at the opera soon. Perhaps a weekend in Milan, in the Magenta District. He liked the quiet hotels and the lively bars and restaurants there. And La Scala! Che bella! The irony of his humming, he mused, was his distracted choice of something from *Il Trovatore*, for he was in a very real sense a wanderer, a traveler, inventive and fond of complexity.

He signaled for the next exit, Ellenton, and turned left at the end. Just ahead was a small office complex with a parking lot. He pulled the van to the rear of the building, removed the false mustache, floppy hat and other paraphernalia from a small satchel he kept on the passenger seat and went to work. He worked deliberately and checked his progress often in the mirror. First the spirit gum, then the mustache pressed into place. Skin-darkening makeup placed strategically. He checked his handiwork and made a few adjustments. Then he slipped on his tennis shoes. If he was going to run across the rocks along the sea wall, he wanted to be sure-footed. When he was satisfied with the result, he put the van in gear. He was just another Hispanic worker delivering a barrel of janitorial supplies. It had worked well and with conviction in the past and it would work one last time.

He pulled back onto the road and headed towards his destination. In minutes, he'd be crossing the spectacular Sunshine Skyway Bridge spanning the mouth of Tampa Bay and in the final act of this drama. He would glance westward, to his left, when he reached the very top of the bridge and perhaps he'd see the wake of the speedboat carrying Vanya and his means of escape. Minutes now. Only minutes.

Garrison twisted left and right, binoculars at hand, looking for any sign of a white van. His headache remained and his eyes throbbed, but he ignored the pain and focused his attention on the task. The flashing lights and siren were off now that they were heading north on I-75, and Garrison didn't want to cause any undue problems on the off-chance that they happened across the sought-after white van. Toomey kept his speed at about eighty, ten miles over the limit, plenty fast for most conditions, but barely keeping up with much of the traffic on I-75.

He took some comfort in the fact that there were many other law enforcement people on this same highway, and the chances favored that one of them would spot the van and call for backup before any move to stop the vehicle was set into motion.

He called Tawanda again. "Nothing yet?"

"Not a thing."

"I figured that he'd be found a lot earlier than this."

"Sheriff, according to the Bureau and Highway Patrol and the Sheriffs of the other counties along Interstate 75, your man will be nailed in minutes. There are too many officers in that space for him to slip through."

Garrison had to agree. I-75 was a limited access highway and if the white van was on it, he'd be found. There were thousands, perhaps tens of thousands, maybe more, white vans in the state, but this one, this one with the tags Vee-Nine-One-One-Eight-Seven-One would be found. No question. Ahead was the interchange for I-275, the main road to St. Petersburg. Garrison did some quick calculating. The white Hyundai was in Bradenton, a city on the southern edge of the Manatee River. The man in the van was experienced with water and the sea. "Take this exit!"

Toomey cut the wheel to the right and roared up the ramp leading to I-275 and heading for St. Petersburg. He didn't ask any questions until they were off the ramp and on the highway.

"What for? I thought Tampa was straight ahead."

"It is. But listen to me for a second. This guy is comfortable with water, right?"

"It was only an educated guess, but we thought so."

"And we know he's on the move and in a van."

"We have Zeke's word on that, Larry, but I'm not sure I'd bet the farm on anyone with pierced nostrils."

"And this Vanya, her car was found in Bradenton, not far from the Manatee River. That river has a dozen marinas right there."

"So you think he's going to do whatever he intends to do near the water?"

"And the lovely Vanya is going to be there for him. In a boat."

"Sounds reasonable."

"It is reasonable. I'm a reasonable guy."

292 / P.D. LaFleur

"So the rest of law enforcement is patrolling I-75 for nothing?"

"No. They're patrolling I-75 because I could be wrong."

Toomey shrugged, as much as he could shrug doing eighty miles an hour in an unfamiliar vehicle.

Garrison pointed. "Look up ahead. It's a white van. A new one."

"Maybe it's just a clean one."

"Maybe. Get up a little closer. I'll see if I can read some numbers from the tags."

Toomey put his foot down and passed three cars, closing within about one hundred yards of a white van traveling in the right lane. He drifted back into the right lane and let up on the gas to match the speed of the van. Garrison leaned forward, peering through the binoculars.

"Vee-nine-one-one . . ."

Toomey completed it for him from memory: "Eight-seven-one."

"See? Like you said, Zeke is da man! Let's just hold this distance. There's a toll booth coming up in another minute or so."

"Do you have an automated toll pass on this thing?"

"Yes, but don't use it. Use another cash lane, or let another vehicle get between us. I want to make sure he stays in front of us." Garrison flipped on the radio and contacted Tawanda with the information. "Let the Bureau know right away. And see if we can't get some people from I-75 moved over here. But not all of them, and tell them Code 2, no lights or sirens. Let's not spook this guy into doing something stupid."

"Right on it. But it could take a few minutes. Be safe and don't do anything stupid."

"Toomey is doing the driving."

"Like I said, be safe."

Rupert Zell was returning from his appointment in Tampa, exhausted and relieved that his exam was over. If the results came in as he expected, he'd be officially a second semester Junior at the University of Southern Florida. He felt confident that he'd done his very best, but anxious that the testing team would see his performance the same way. He'd know in ten days.

He placed a call to his house and spoke to his wife before he climbed into his vehicle, the unmarked red Impala SS that the Sheriff let him drive for his journey today.

Even though he was not expected back at the department for another ninety minutes, he turned on his police radio and checked in with Tawanda. "It's Rupert, Tawanda. How are things back in Dodge County?"

"Where are you, Rupert?" To Rupert, Tawanda sounded even more abrupt than usual.

"I just left USF and I'll be on the Interstate in about three minutes. Why?"

"Just get your happy ass turned around. Get on I-275 south and head towards the Skyway Bridge. Then wait for instructions. Sheriff Garrison and Agent Toomey have somebody in view right now, and it just could get ugly. They're northbound and approaching the Skyway. And keep it Code 2, no noise, no lights."

"I'll head there now."

Rupert needed to reverse direction and head back toward downtown Tampa. He checked the traffic around him. The streets were full of cars, this being the height of Florida's tourist season, but he saw a small opening ahead. With one foot on the brake and the other on the gas, Rupert spun the vehicle 180 degrees with the sound of a loud screech and the smell of burning rubber catching the attention of everyone around him. With his foot to the floor, the car roared ahead. In four minutes he entered the southbound Interstate.

THIRTY-SIX

Vanya coursed through the waves, cutting sharply and smoothly through the water at fifty miles per hour. On another day, she'd enjoy taking this craft for a long voyage, out of sight of land and opened up at full throttle.

On the deck and secured with bungee cords were all the gear she'd been instructed to prepare. The air tanks full and tested. The goggles, the fins, the Sea-Doo underwater propulsion devices. The false documents, credit cards and cash wrapped and sealed in waterproof bags. Everything stowed and ready.

And secure at her side was her Blaser, its clip loaded with .30 caliber metal jacketed ammunition. It had become her best friend in the prior weeks and she would keep it with her until the end. The plan required that she be in position at the shoreline so that Emilio could make his way on board. Then, they would use the power of the speedboat to put some distance between them and the shoreline. They would later abandon the speed boat, leap overboard with their scuba tanks, and use the SeaDoos to reach shore undetected. There, they would dress and be off with new identities and sufficient cash and credit cards to make their separate escapes. She would never see this Blaser again, but promised herself that she would acquire another, and soon. This was, like a scalpel to a surgeon, an essential tool of her new found trade. She could not and would not go forward without one of her own.

Ahead of her was the shore where she'd drop anchor and wait. She moved the throttle back and the boat settled at once into the soft swells, the gentle rise and fall. She let the boat drift and moved the levers into reverse. The boat came nearly to a stop, ten, maybe fifteen feet from shore. She dropped anchor and kept the engines at idle. Large rocks and chunks of coral lined the shore and were draped with mangroves sending their gnarled roots directly into the salt water and into the sand below. On the other side of the mangroves and rocks, here on the north side of the Sunshine Skyway Bridge, was the rest area, the parking lot where in minutes a van would arrive and deposit a blue plastic barrel containing the son of the Russian President. Then her mentor would appear and join her on board. She would move the throttles forward and they would make their way to a point some half-mile from shore where they would don their gear, slide into the water, set the levers on the Sea-Doos to forward and put to sea. Together, they would dive below the surface, out of sight, and head to shore where they would change clothes and leave the area in different directions. Their task would be complete. Emilio would not share his plans with her, but she could almost taste the sharp crisp air of Santa Fe on her tongue.

She kept her eyes on the roadway that led to the parking lot. Emilio would arrive in a white van, and she might be able to see him through the mangroves. That was not a requirement, as he intended to park near the main rest area building, deposit his human cargo, and make his way casually to the shoreline. She was in the exact spot they'd preselected. A man approaching the shore to look at the Gulf waters would gather no attention from any passersby. Then, a quick move to the water and the boat and they would haul anchor and be off. Emilio would don his wetsuit on the way out, and in minutes they would be under-water and on their way.

Vanya wondered where Emilio would go. An Italian by temperament she thought, but he was a man of many secrets, as capable of passing as a stiff-lipped Brit, as a pompous French-man, or a Chicago truck driver. New Mexico, that was her goal. She would do her research and select a home there, somewhere in the mountains.

Emilio's anger earlier in the day caught her far off guard, crushing her high spirits with his insistence on making their moves precisely as scheduled and with no modification what-soever. Perhaps she assumed too much, she thought. But his anger was beyond that which she would expect, his blood ris-ing visibly to his neck and face. When she last saw him, the ire was palpable; she hoped this would have dissipated and that he would be more sanguine, more agreeable. She did want to learn from him, to watch him closely, to even gain a contact or two who might sometime in the future require her services. She might even ask him to refer those occasional contacts in her di-rection as he deemed appropriate. This would be, after all, a business.

Her reverie was broken by the arrival in the lot of a white van. It could be Emilio, she thought. She waited. A minute went by, then two, then three. No Emilio. Perhaps it was not his van. She could barely contain her anxiety and decided that she could at least step to shore and be prepared for Emilio. She sat on the boat's gunnel and prepared to slide into the shallow waters when she stopped and reached for the Blaser. Just in case. Being prepared was better than the alternative. Holding the weapon high above the water with both hands, she took the few steps to shore and crouched down under cover of the boul-ders and greenery.

* * *

Emilio watched for the turnoff as he descended the Skyway Bridge. He signaled and moved right, careful, cautious, the end in sight. The exit ramp to the rest area ran parallel to the highway and reached a stop sign. He turned left at the intersection, went under the highway and reached the parking lot of the rest area. His good fortune continued when he spotted a parking spot almost directly adjacent to the rest area building. He pulled in, shut off the engine and reached for his ever-present cloth. He wiped the steering wheel, door handles, and shift levers. Then he exited the vehicle and stepped out, wiping the door handle on the outside.

In the pocket of his jacket, he felt the weight of his Sig 250. Finding himself required to use the pistol in any fashion was highly unlikely, but, true to his personal mantra, preparation was essential; better to be over-prepared than under-prepared.

He stretched, reaching his arms to the sky and flexing his back muscles. Three hours in a vehicle was not such an ordeal but Emilio was beginning to feel his age. He went to the rear of the van, opened the double doors and slid the boards from the floor of the van to the ground.

He tapped the blue barrel with his knuckles. "We're here, Mr. Mironev. Be silent, at least for the moment. In a few minutes, I will not care if you shout out at maximum volume, but for now, silence is still required."

He reached for the bungee cords that held the barrel in place against the wall of the van and unfastened them. "There could be a few bumps coming up, but nothing serious, I assure you." He slid the dolly under the barrel and tipped his cargo, edging the barrel close to the boards that would be his ramp to the parking lot. "One bump." He forced the dolly over the top edge of the boards and moved the barrel slowly down the length of the boards. "One more."

Alek could feel the bumps, and they were unpleasant. Far

more unpleasant were the cramps that developed in his legs and arms and neck during the journey. He wanted the cover to come off, to reach his arms up, to bend and stretch and bend again.

Emilio slid the boards back into the van and closed the double doors, wiping the surfaces he had touched. He scanned the surroundings. Only a handful of cars, two tractor trailers. It was a quiet time at the rest area. One tip of the barrel and the final leg of the journey had begun. Emilio made his way cautiously to the side of the building and craned his neck around the corner. Two elderly women were exiting the restroom area and a chubby young man was making his way towards the restrooms. One couple was parked at the edge of the lot where a row of picnic tables stood. They sat and ate their lunch. After he deposited the barrel in the building's corridor, he would have to make his way past that lunching couple on his way to the shoreline. He judged the circumstances as suitable and turned the corner, dolly in tow. Thirty feet to the corridor, then twenty and ten. He reached his destination and tipped the dolly erect. He wiped the dolly down, then the barrel. With a quick rap on the barrel, he leaned down and said in a whisper, "Good luck, Mr. Mironev. I'll be making a telephone call shortly and I expect that you will be free within the hour." Then he made his way to the shoreline and the waiting boat.

"What do you think he's doing now?" It was Toomey asking the question. He and Garrison were seated in their vehicle at the far edge of the lot.

"Well, I'm thinking that Alek Mironev is in the barrel, and we hope alive and well. I'm also guessing our man is on his way home. Pull up to that spot over there." Garrison pointed to a spot not far from the couple having lunch. "I'll call Tawanda and make sure everybody knows what's happening here."

"Tell her to call the Coast Guard while she's at it."

From their rear came the sound of an approaching motorcycle. Garrison tried to ignore it but it drove close to his own vehicle. He looked over. There on the seat of his gleaming silver and purple Harley Davidson Soft Tail appeared Virgil Swett. Garrison let out a groan and muttered, "Sonovabitch. This is just what we need."

Swett shut off the engine, dismounted, kicked out the cycle's stand, and walked over to Garrison's SUV, removing his leather gloves as he approached. Garrison wanted to crash through the door, put Swett on his stomach and cuff him.

Toomey, though, reached through the driver's side window and extended a hand. "Virgil Swett, right?"

Swett removed his oversized sunglasses, shook Toomey's hand and nodded. Garrison was speechless. "You know this moron?"

Toomey ignored Garrison and said, "I'm glad I recognized you the other night at the bar."

Virgil Swett nodded and said to Garrison. "Virgil Swett, Interpol."

"The Special Liaison?" Garrison could not believe his eyes.

Virgil said, "We can talk later, Sheriff." He gestured to the white van. "That's the guy you're after, right?"

Garrison tried to clear his head and focus. That this man was not the vulgar blockhead he'd come to know was a puzzle he'd have to consider at another time. For now, Garrison placed his trust in Toomey's judgment. He said to Swett, "We think the kidnap victim is in a barrel near the building. We're going to approach and apprehend this man before he has a chance to escape." The Sheriff motioned for Toomey to put the vehicle in gear.

Swett said, "I'm not armed, but I can make contact with other agencies if you want."

"I think we've got that covered, but thanks. You might do your best to keep civilian vehicles from getting close, though."

Swett nodded. Toomey slowly edged the vehicle forward while Garrison used the radio to contact Tawanda. "Contact the Bureau and the State Troopers. Tell them where we are." Virgil remained at his motorcycle and used his cell phone to call his contact with this update. Toomey brought the vehicle to a stop and both men exited without making a sound. Garrison nodded his head to Toomey and directed him to move the couple away from the picnic bench to another, safer location. Toomey quietly led them to a spot behind the Sheriff's vehicle with instructions to stay low and out of sight.

Behind them, Rupert Zell, who'd been in contact with Tawanda by radio, drove along the edge of the parking area in the red Impala, came to a stop, and surveyed the scene before him. Sheriff Garrison and Special Agent Toomey were well forward and in motion. Nearer to him, and more jarring to his sensibilities, was the figure of Virgil Swett standing next to his motorcycle and talking on his cell phone. The sight was not making sense. Rupert moved his Impala slowly behind the main building and stopped on the far side where he could keep his eye on the Sheriff. Whatever was happening, he wanted to be ready.

Toomey crouched forward, reaching with his right hand to touch the pistol on his hip. He kept it holstered but took comfort that it was there. Unless he could work his way much closer to the target, hitting his target from this distance would be a miracle, but he might get lucky. Garrison looked back at Toomey with a gesture that said, "Take cover and protect yourself." Swett remained standing next his motorcycle, unarmed, while Garrison's right hand continued to rest on his own weapon, a police-issue Glock .40 caliber pistol. If deadly force was going to be necessary, he thought, this Glock would have to do.

Garrison watched the figure of Emilio Fortino eighty yards in front of him, walking slowly in the direction of the shore.

The man looked relaxed, almost nonchalant, just another man taking a break at a rest stop.

Fortino was unaware of the collection of people behind him, and he kept his focus on the rocks and mangroves that lined the waterfront. The boat, his means of escape, with Vanya Zakayev at the helm, he was certain was just yards away and he thought he could even detect the comforting sound of the boat's engines.

Garrison stepped forward and increased the pace of his gait until he was within thirty yards of an ambling Emilio Fortino. Fortino was taking slow, casual steps and making every appearance of a man absently taking in the sights at the shoreline. At one point, he glanced down to his feet and noticed the laces of his tennis shoes were undone. He bent low and began to tie them when he stopped, frozen in place.

Clouds moved slowly across the sky and second hands continued to sweep across clock faces. But in Emilio's world, all motion and all thought stopped.

Garrison slowed his steps and then stopped and waited. Was this a ruse? Why was the man not moving a muscle? Garrison kept his hand on his weapon, took another step forward, and his shoe clicked against a stone and sent it scurrying along the pavement. The noise, barely a rattle, appeared to interrupt Emilio's trance. He stood and turned to his right to determine the cause of the noise.

Garrison unholstered his weapon and stopped, feet spread, his pistol raised and clutched in standard two-hand fashion. "Stop where you are!"

Two hundred yards away and in another corner of the lot, Rupert Zell sat in his vehicle and absorbed the scene that was playing out before him. Alone in his sedan, the only noise was from the traffic passing nearby on the Interstate and the slow tick-tick of the engine fluids as the motor cooled. He willed the arrival of at least some of the dozens of law enforcement vehicles that would be on their way now to this spot. He stepped from the car and kept the Sheriff and Agent Toomey in sight, still wondering why Virgil Swett was in the area. He watched as the Sheriff stopped and raised his weapon. Rupert stepped from his vehicle without a sound, popped the trunk and unlocked a rifle from its rack, double checking its magazine for ammunition. It was an elderly carbine, a Winchester whose manufacture likely predated Rupert's birth, but he was accustomed to the weapon and trained on it at the range. It was, in Garrison's words, a "just in case" weapon, and its use was expected only in the most dire circumstances.

Rupert looked down the scope, a more recent vintage than the rifle to which it was affixed, serviceable but still ancient compared to those available on the market today. He hoped that it had not been jarred or knocked out of alignment since its last use. He closed the trunk slowly and trotted to the edge of the main building to have a better angle on the action and to maintain his cover. Twelve seconds later, he stood at the far edge of the building and scanned the scene through the scope of the weapon.

Directly ahead stood a tall, dark man in a floppy hat. He was facing Sheriff Garrison, his arms at his side. Rupert could see no weapon on the man. Twenty feet behind the man were the boulders and the greenery, beyond and through which Rupert could see the shimmer of the Gulf's surface.

The Sheriff stood fifty or sixty feet from the tall man. He was too distant to distinguish words, but he could see that the Sheriff and the man were speaking. Eighty feet or so behind the Sheriff was a crouching Special Agent Toomey surveying the scene. His weapon, too, was drawn. Something caught Toomey's attention, for with a sharp twist of his head the Special Agent glanced to his right. Rupert raised his rifle and used the scope to try to locate the object of Toomey's sudden attention. Heavy boulders and mangroves lined the shore. Through the thick shade of the greenery, Rupert saw a flash of blond hair, cropped short, and the gleam of a rifle barrel.

Vanya slid forward on the large rock, the rifle positioned at her shoulder and panning slowly across the parking lot. The mangroves were thick and she had only intermittent views of the scene developing before her as the leaves dipped and twisted in the shoreline breeze. She dared not step further forward and risk exposing her position, but moved a few inches to her left and used the barrel of her rifle to move a branch.

Like a tableau that appears with the rise of the stage curtain, the players appeared in full view, center stage framed neatly by the leaves and branches that kept her position obscured. To her right stood Emilio Fortino, hands by his side, palms forward, a slight smile creasing his lips. He spoke to the man in front of him, a man in uniform, hatless, who held a pistol in both hands in front of him. She could see the Sheriff speaking in low, measured tones. Then the Sheriff moved a few steps closer to Emilio and Vanya lost him when a breeze ruffled the leaves. She moved just a few more inches and tried to locate the man once more in her sights.

This will be barely a challenge for her first live firing under pressure, she told herself. One shot to the temple with her beloved Blaser. She was certain she could do it with ease from this distance.

THIRTY-SEVEN

Garrison's voice was steady when he said, "It's over, Mr. Keough, or Mr. Fortino, whatever your name is." He kept his weapon only half raised but the safety was off. One round was chambered and ready for firing.

"Keough? I haven't heard that name in a while. I must say that I never did like it. I understand you have been looking for me, and you are apparently quite persistent."

"I try to be. You understand, then, that I am placing you under arrest for the murder of James Finney."

Emilio never lost his composure. As casually as if he were chatting at a picnic, he said, "Ah, yes, young Mr. Finney. Poor fellow, but not a real loss to the planet if you did your research. I must say I am surprised you found him."

"You do have the right to remain silent, even if you are not so inclined."

"I appreciate that I have the right to a fine American lawyer and all that. But I have to say that I am amazed you put so much of this together." Emilio's eyes did not betray him. With at least curiosity, if not astonishment on the man's face, he continued, "I'd like to find out how that happened. Really. But I am anxious to get to another appointment. You have, shall we say, interrupted me at a crucial moment."

"Alek Mironev. Tell me I will find him in that blue barrel you just dropped off."

Fortino's smile was disarming. "Yes, Mr. Mironev is a somewhat contorted but very alive young fellow. Well nourished and hydrated and none the worse for wear. Not like me. Or you. We are of an age, as we say."

"I won't disagree."

"We have many miles on our collective bodies and our collective souls."

Garrison was not interested in continuing this banter in the open where bystanders could arrive at any moment and find themselves in peril. If a metaphysical discussion was to ensue, he would prefer it in the confines of a secured jail cell. He took two more steps forward and said, "If you would please kneel down now and place your hands, palms down and flat in front of you, I would appreciate that." The Glock was heavy in Garrison's hands and he opened and closed his fingers on the grip to keep the blood flowing.

"That does sound rather crude, but I understand you have your requirements." Emilio maintained eye contact with Garrison all the while as he struggled with his peripheral vision to gather every bit of information about his surroundings. Desperate times call for desperate measures, he knew, and he may have to leap quickly one way or another, then roll and dart to the water's edge. The Sheriff's weapon was held straight in front of him, but he detected some degree of unsteadiness in the man's hands. He just might have some opportunity, however slim.

Emilio maintained a steady heart rhythm and breathing rate as he ran the possibilities through his mind. The options were painfully few but he refused to resign. As in chess, a grand master always finds it better to suffer a draw if a win was not possible; resignation is never an option. He chanced a quick glance to his right. A leap, a drop, a roll and a run, low to the ground. Then a jump into the Gulf and to the boat. He could not see the boat but trusted that that the low rumble from the water's direction was from the boat's idling engines and that Vanya was in position and ready to go. He could do it, he decided and he considered the timing. A blink by the Sheriff, a drop in his arms, a shift in his focus, then Emilio would be off.

Toomey's visual attention was fixed on some undefined, obscure movement to his right, somewhere in the cluster of brush that clung to the rocks. His ears were tuned to the conversation, though, and he appreciated the calm demeanor of the hunter and the prey, each feeling the other out as the endgame was played.

A slight rustle, barely perceptible, revealed only shadows in the scrub and leaves. Someone was there, and it could only be either an accomplice—the blond pixie, most likely—or an innocent, someone who just happened upon the scene, an accident of timing.

From his position at the edge of the building, Rupert could discern flecks of light hair, a forehead, and a rifle barrel. He prayed a soft prayer, including a plea to ensure his accuracy, and squeezed the trigger.

The report bounced in every direction, off the walls of the concrete building, off the expanse of pavement, off the enormous rocks that lined the shore. That shattering sound of the single shot reflected and caromed and echoed until it filled the air from every direction. Toomey heard the whistle of the round, so close was he to the line of fire. He fell at once to the ground and rolled until he reached the scant security of a nearby picnic table.

Garrison turned sharply to his left, then his right, unsure if the round was aimed at him or someone else. Toomey was on the ground. Garrison, who had never suffered a bullet wound, was unsure if it was he who'd been shot. He was only certain that it was not he who fired it, his weapon still cold steel in his hands. Something high powered, a rifle, he thought, not the brief pop and flash of a pistol. He waited for a stab of pain and none arrived.

He turned back to the tall man in the floppy hat who was already on the move, as quick as a hare, darting, curling, then scuttling like a crab across the boulders, the hat flying off as he leaped beyond view. Garrison aimed his pistol and fired. The shot went wide and Garrison squeezed another round, then a third. Then silence. He remained fixed in place and alone. The man he sought had vanished and only a battered straw hat remained.

Garrison trotted to check on Toomey, now huddled beneath the table top and in apparent good health. He holstered his weapon as he ran. "You're OK."

"Over there." Toomey said in a rush and pointing. "In those bushes at the rocks. Someone's there."

Garrison crouched down low and tried to discern movement, any movement, any sign at all. The only sight beyond the expected was a slim metallic barrel poking from the mangrove leaves, still and silent.

"Sheriff!" It was Rupert's voice. "Are you OK?" His voice was raspy, urgent, stronger than a whisper, softer than a shout.

"What?" The confluence of events and faces and sounds rattled and distracted. Seeing Rupert did not fit with his subconscious expectations and the confusion showed on his face. "How?"

"There was someone in the mangroves. That was my rifle you heard." Rupert motioned for the Sheriff to remain behind him. He kept low and stepped forward, his rifle poised, spotting the gleam of the rifle barrel poking through the leaves. He approached in slow measured steps and stopped twenty feet away before he called out. "Come out with your hands up." No response, but somewhere beyond the rocks and the scrub a boat motor was starting up.

Rupert moved to the spot where the rifle barrel remained, motionless, partially exposed, and waited. He knelt down on one knee. No response, no motion. Garrison approached from his rear and slid beside him, pistol at the ready and used his left hand to pull a branch heavy with leaves from the mangrove.

Light silver-blue eyes open, staring sightless at the sky and clad in a wet suit, lay Vanya Zakayev, a single round hole piercing her forehead, clots of bone and brain and tissue splayed behind her head, a spray of red spatter in a crescent over the rocks directly behind her. Rupert stepped forward and looked. He'd never fired his weapon directly at a living human target before and he knelt down on one knee, his brow creased. Garrison said to Rupert, "The safety is off on her rifle. Be careful."

"She had the rifle to her shoulder, Sheriff. She was about to take you out." His tone was apologetic.

Garrison put his hand on the younger man's shoulder. "You did well, Rupert, and I owe you my life." Toomey approached and stood behind them, staring at the sight. They'd all seen death in the course of their work, mangled remains that had minutes before housed vibrant souls. Nevertheless, the sight of such a tiny woman, at once so alive and so ready to charge forward in life, now in an unmoving heap, touched their cores.

Virgil Swett took in the scene from a respectful distance but then trotted forward and climbed atop the boulders to see the speedboat cut a swath through the waves and out to the open waters of the Gulf.

In the distance and closing fast on the speedboat was a US Coast Guard cutter. Toomey joined him on the boulder and Swett said, "They'll catch up with him in just a minute, maybe ninety seconds."

Toomey kept his eyes on the fleeing speedboat and shook his head. "The Coast Guard is going to find an empty boat."

Virgil considered disputing that notion, then stopped. He would have to agree. Behind them in the parking lot a convoy of law enforcement vehicles sped into the parking lot, lights flashing and sirens blaring. Neither Toomey, nor Swett, nor Garrison nor Rupert Zell bothered to turn around.

THIRTY-EIGHT

Washington, DC, one week later

Garrison stood before the full-length mirror in his suite at the L'Enfant Plaza. Looking back at him was a man he didn't recognize, for the image could not possibly be that of Sheriff Lawrence Garrison clad in a tuxedo. The black silk bow tie sat crookedly at the neck and he adjusted it, careful not to undo the knot that had taken the previous fifteen minutes to tie. He spoke to the other gentleman in the room.

"I'm hardly used to this, you know. Where I come from, we don't generally get this dressed up for dinner. I feel like a trussed turkey ready for carving."

"You look magnificent, Sheriff." The speaker was Peter Fournier, the US Secretary of State. "Would you like a spot of Bourbon on the rocks before we leave for dinner?"

Garrison nodded and the Secretary walked to the drinks cabinet and began to create cocktails for the two of them. To Garrison, the Secretary looked like he was born to wear a tux, tall, graceful, and at ease. Fournier noticed the attention from Garrison and said, "Sheriff, I was born in Aroostook County in Maine where we have just as much occasion to get all dressed up as you do in Dodge County. You get used to it."

Garrison accepted the drink and took a swallow. The glass was heavy crystal and the liquid sweet and strong. In truth, he thought, he just might like the chance to get used to life in this circle, the attention, and the plush surroundings. The thought left as quickly as it arrived.

"The Russian Ambassador is anxious to meet you, by the way, and to personally thank you for everything you did."

"I'll try not to disappoint."

"I assure you, you will not."

Secretary Fournier was a former US Senator and enjoyed wide renown for his ability to defuse crucial, tense situations during major world crises. He was at home with nearly every world leader, knew most of their families personally, and was held in the highest regard by everyone who knew him. In spite of the circles in which Secretary Fournier traveled, Garrison felt comfortable in his presence and they sat together in the overstuffed chairs near the window. Rain arrived an hour ago and braids of water trickled down the panes, giving the lights of Washington a soft glow. Several moments passed in silence as the two sipped their drinks. The Secretary spoke.

"The press is not invited to this evening's event for obvious reasons, but you know that Alek Mironev will be there, I'm sure."

"It will be a pleasure to meet him in these circumstances. The last time I saw him, he was stuffed inside a barrel."

"At least he was unharmed. In fact, I think the whole episode might have some beneficial affect on him. He's earned a reputation for irresponsibility and he's been known to embarrass his parents more than once. We'll see whether the changes in him are permanent."

"Maybe his ordeal will help him realize how fragile his life is."

"And how fleeting his fame can be. No one lasts forever in the world of politics, and his father, as powerful as he may be right now, could be just another formerly famous man in short order. When that happens, it's amazing how quickly you find yourself off the 'A list' and the invitations to fancy dinners come to a halt." The Secretary glanced at his wristwatch.

Garrison looked at his wrist and realized he'd taken his watch off earlier. That was just as well, he thought; his utilitarian Timex with its brown cloth band didn't fit with the tuxedo look. The Secretary appeared to be amused by Garrison's move and reached into his pocket. He removed a small package and passed it to Garrison.

"Take it," the Secretary said. "I was going to wait to give this to you later. From a grateful nation." It was a small packet wrapped in white with a ribbon.

Garrison unwrapped it and saw the name on the box and knew what it would be. Nevertheless, when he opened it, the sight caught him off guard and his quick inhale was audible.

"Read the inscription on the back."

Garrison removed the watch, a Movado with a clear black face and a rich leather band, and turned it over. On the reverse were engraved the words, "Thank you, Sheriff Garrison." Beneath were the date and the initials of the President of the United States."

"Put it on. It will look great with the tux."

A knock on the door of the suite brought Secretary Fournier to his feet. "I'll get this." The door opened, and Dennis Toomey stood at the entry, fully dressed in his own tuxedo. He stepped into the room, a broad grin on his face.

"Special Agent Dennis Michael Toomey, I'm not sure that Sheriff Garrison expects you, but welcome." The Secretary shook hands with Toomey. This was certainly not the first meeting of the two.

Garrison walked forward and shook Toomey's hand as well. "Why didn't you tell me?"

Secretary Fournier interjected, "I hope you don't mind, Sheriff. Dennis and I go back a few years. But let's talk about this later. We ought to get moving. There's a limo waiting for us downstairs."

The evening officially began with a private reception at the embassy of the Russian Federation with a few invited guests. Alek Mironev grasped Garrison's hand and shook it with vigor and gratitude. It was Mironev who took Garrison by the elbow and introduced him to the guests, including the Russian Ambassador. After a toast of champagne, the Russian Ambassador answered a tug at his sleeve from an aide. Garrison was certain that an important call would require his attention. But the Ambassador just nodded and smiled. "Yes. Right away. I'm sure this weather delayed her arrival." At once, the aide retreated to the doorway and opened it, greeting Raisa Mironev, wife of the Russian President and the mother of Alek. Alek greeted her with a kiss and took her by the arm to meet Garrison. She gave the Sheriff a warm hug and said, "I am so proud to meet you, Sheriff Garrison. I have heard so much about you. I'm sorry I missed the appetizers. This weather slowed down my arrival." Garrison's did his best to keep his jaw from hitting the floor.

Dinner was a dream that Garrison could barely remember. Raisa Mironev sat on his left and Alek on his right. By the end of the evening, they were all on a first name basis, and Raisa Mironev invited Garrison to visit Moscow. Alek insisted that Garrison accept. He would be Garrison's personal guide.

After dinner and warm goodbyes, Toomey and Garrison retired to the hotel for a glass of port in the Sheriff's suite. Toomey raised his glass in salute. "To my good friend and a real hero, here's to you." They touched glasses and sipped.

"What a night, Dennis. I guess I've got to make plans to visit Moscow."

"Can you ever get back to wearing that Sheriff's hat when you get home?"

Garrison removed his tie and unfastened the collar button of his starched formal shirt. "With pleasure." He took a long sip and turned to Toomey with a question. "So you and Secretary Fournier go back a ways?"

"You know I'm divorced." Garrison nodded; Toomey mentioned an ex-wife somewhere in a conversation.

"Her name was Angela Fournier."

"And Angela is . . . ?"

"Peter's first cousin." Garrison thought about that for a moment.

"So what's next? I mean, before Moscow."

"Tomorrow I get a VIP tour of Washington that Secretary Fournier arranged. I go home the next day. Then it's back to work with Walter."

"Who's watching him while you're here?"

"Tawanda, so he'll be spoiled rotten by the time I get back."

Toomey understood. He'd seen how attached she was to Walter and how he sought her out for special ear scratches and dog treats.

Garrison said, "Virgil Swett sent me a nice note, by the way. Not a lot of detail, but he did apologize for the role he had to play when he was undercover. No one has seen him since he rode off from the parking lot on his motorcycle."

"He's probably on another case in some other part of the world already. That's the way they operate."

"I suppose."

Toomey looked over at the side table next to the sofa. On it was a small silver frame with a quotation written in fancy script and in a foreign language that Toomey took to be Spanish. He asked Garrison, "Is that yours?"

"Of course, you idiot. It's the one you sent a couple days ago. I took it with me because it means so much to me."

Toomey's face revealed that he knew nothing about this.

"You didn't send it?"

"Was there a postmark?"

"Nothing." Garrison looked at it with a new sense of curiosity. "You don't know what this says, then?"

"No clue. I have enough trouble with English."

"It's the eighth béatitude. *Bienaventurados los pacificadores: porque ellos serán llamados hijos de Dios.* It means 'Blessed are the peace makers, for they shall be called children of God.'"

"Christ's Sermon On the Mount. Matthew, Chapter 5."

"You're religious?"

"After twelve years of catholic school and seven years as an altar boy, I know the drill."

Garrison held the gift close and wondered. "Maybe I should have dusted it for prints."

"You think it's from him?"

Garrison kept his eyes on the gift, somehow made more precious to him. "I do."

Toomey looked at the gift in his friend's hands and asked, "He's probably on another assignment too."

"I don't think so, Dennis. It's just my hunch, but I don't think the man would have had regrets if I did shoot him when I had the chance. It's something I saw in his eyes."

"Is that why you let him go?"

"Let him go?" Garrison was stunned that Toomey would even suggest that.

Toomey said nothing but let the concept turn over in Garrison's mind before he said, "It's not important." He started to take off his bow tie and undo the stiff collar of his tuxedo shirt. "And by the way, Sheriff Garrison, you are indeed a betting man. You just don't know it."

Garrison pursed his lips and considered that assessment. He hated being transparent but accepted the comments from his friend. He turned to Toomey and asked, "How about you? Where do you go from here?"

"I'm turning my retirement papers into the Bureau, but you probably figured I was already on my way out. What you don't know is that Tawanda found me an apartment about five miles away from your office in Dodge County."

Garrison's eyebrows arched. "Tawanda found you a place?"

"Am I blushing?"

"A little."

"She says I could maybe spend time with Rupert Zell, sort of give him some help on investigation techniques, that sort of thing. If you don't mind me hanging around."

There was a silence that extended for several seconds while the two assessed each other. Garrison said, "I noticed how jealous you get when Tawanda rubs Walter's ears."

Toomey reached over from his seat and clinked glasses once more with Garrison.

THIRTY-NINE

Camposanto, Province of Modena, Italy

Four thousand five hundred miles away, in a hillside villa overlooking rolling hills of olive trees, Emilio Fortino poured a small glass of Amarone, the rich, sweet wine from fermented raisins. He savored the aroma before letting a few drops reach his lips and tongue.

The fireplace was barely a glow now, and he'd set the book he'd been reading on the table beside him. The recording he'd listened to, Beethoven's *Fidelio*, had been over for several minutes. His bones ached and he was looking forward to a prolonged period of rest and relaxation. No climbing trees to sample the fruit, no hefting of oil barrels. Not for a while at least.

Grigori Malko, the poor unfortunate who found himself thrust against his better judgment into the middle of the Chechen scheme, was certainly through forever. Emilio tossed the newspaper into the fire and watched the corners of the pages curl and blacken. Today's edition of the International Herald Tribune included the report that Grigori Malko was killed in an automobile accident near Moscow. "A trusted and promising member of Russian bureaucracy," the paper wrote. No accident, he thought.

Another Chechen dying for the cause.

He sipped the Amarone once more and enjoyed the warmth. Rain was expected tomorrow, but he could already feel the forecast in his joints. He leaned back in his chair and closed his eyes. In his imagination, he conjured an image of a living and breathing Vanya Zakayev. In his mind, she was smiling, holding her rifle to which she'd become welded, proud and strong, ready to take on the world. Her eyes, so filled with hope, however misguided, filled him with memories of his own youth. He'd once been that young, eager, talented, anxious to put himself to the test, lusting for the excitement, the challenge and the rewards that his profession, performed well, would provide.

His reverie was broken by a subtle knock on the door.

"What is it?"

It was Donato, his housekeeper. He stuck his head through the doorway. "Just checking, signore. I am going to bed and I wanted to make sure you were OK."

"Fine, Donato. Thank you. Good night. . . . "

"Welcome home, signore."

Also by P.D. LaFleur

Mill Town
ISBN 978-0-9792597-1-5

The decades-old murder of a young woman in a small town remains unsolved. When her brother reignites the investigation, old suspicions resurface and tear at the fabric that holds the community together. This is a spot-on portrayal of life in a small town.

Mill Town was awarded a Gold Medal for Fiction at the 2009 Independent Publishers Book Awards and the Gold Medal for Fiction at the Florida Publishers Association 2009 President's Book Awards.

Vengeance Betrayed
ISBN 978-0-9792597-0-8

Geoffrey Ramsden is a powerful member of British Parliament who has very personal reasons for scheming to disrupt any talks of conciliation in Northern Ireland. When the troubled American wife of a diplomat stumbles across elements of his scheme, she turns to someone she trusts, and mayhem erupts on both sides of the Atlantic.

In the Company of Strangers
ISBN 978-1-4196089-1-9

Matthew Keyes, through a telescope on the observation deck of a Boston skyscraper, has just witnessed a horrible crime. When the police investigation turns up no evidence, Keyes pursues the case on his own.

Novels by P.D. LaFleur are available at fine bookstores and on-line retailers.

Author website: pdlafleur.com
Author email: author@pdlafleur.com